PARALLAX VIEW

ALLAN LEVERONE

Special thanks to Elderlemon Design for the outstanding cover art, and to
JD Smith Design for the print edition formatting.

1

May 20, 1987
2:25 a.m.
Nikolayev South Shipyard, Ukraine

Tracie Tanner carefully eased open another drawer in the dented, World War II-era metal filing cabinet wedged behind the general manager's desk at Shipyard Number 444.
Where's that damned file?
She'd been searching for nearly half an hour already with no luck, unable to decipher the Soviets' Byzantine filing system. Her eyes burned from the strain of reading reports typed in Cyrillic on substandard Russian-made typewriters, and she could sense time ticking away—surveillance reports indicated the guards' patrol patterns included a walk-through of this very office every forty-five minutes or so.

The darkened office smelled sour, its cement block construction retaining the unpleasant fishy stench of the Black Sea combined with old sweat. She clenched a small penlight between her teeth to free up both hands for the search, and she worked methodically, flipping through file after file under the most likely tab headings.

Tracie, a CIA clandestine ops specialist, had been assigned to remove the guidance system software specs for the Soviet aircraft carrier *Buka*, scheduled for commission later this year, and replace them with bogus specifications. Construction had been completed

1

on *Buka* years earlier, but bugs in the ship's sophisticated software had delayed commissioning ever since.

Four years ago, in a successful nighttime operation, another CIA clandestine ops specialist had broken into this same office and replaced the proper specs with useless, CIA-generated data. Now the goal was to repeat the scenario and delay launch of the *Buka* for several more months, if possible.

Tracie worked quickly but thoroughly. Next to the office door the Soviet bureaucrat in charge had placed a large aquarium filled with exotic fish, and the steady drone of the water filter motor began to lull her into drowsiness. She blinked hard, closed the filing cabinet drawer, and opened another. She had worked her way through nearly two-thirds of the file cabinet and found nothing.

And then, there it was.

The first folder in the new drawer.

It was blue, filled with several dozen sheets of numbers, diagrams and specifications. Tracie lifted out the folder and compared some of the sheets inside it to corresponding sheets of paper in the dummy file she'd brought with her. They appeared identical. The differences in the specifications were so minute it would take a team of engineers months to decipher the problem, and that was after they had discovered there *was* a problem.

She smiled in the darkness and removed the original specs, sliding the forged documents into the file folder in their place. She rolled the drawer closed, slowly and quietly, and then stood, relieved to be finished. She placed the original software specs into a small briefcase and snapped it shut.

Padded quietly across the office.

And dropped her flashlight. It slipped out of her hand and clattered to the floor, rolling to a stop against the closed door.

Dammit.

Tracie froze, waiting to hear a shouted challenge or footsteps pounding down the hallway.

Nothing.

She waited fifteen seconds. Twenty. Thirty. Then she breathed a sigh of relief and picked up the flashlight. *Be more careful, dummy.*

She eased the door open and stepped into the hallway.

And walked straight into a Soviet security guard's Makarov

semiautomatic pistol.

Tracie stepped backward instinctively, calculating the odds of reaching her Beretta 9mm inside the shoulder holster under her jacket. Result: not good.

The guard said, "Stay right where you are," in Russian, and Tracie moved back another three steps, hoping he would follow her into the office. He did.

She stepped back and he moved forward.

Stepped back again and he followed, still holding the gun on her.

She backed into the manager's desk, studying the guard. He was barely more than a kid, maybe eighteen or nineteen, and he wore a threadbare Red Army uniform that had probably been handed down from other soldiers two or three times, maybe more.

His hands were shaking, just a little, and he said, "You're coming with me."

I don't think so, Tracie thought, but raised her hands to chest level in submission.

"All right," she answered in Russian, hoping her slight English accent would be undetectable. "This is a simple misunderstanding. I can explain."

"Not my problem," the guard said. "You will explain to my superiors." He gestured with his head toward the door.

"Go," he told her, "and do not try anything stupid." The Makarov stuttered in his hands and Tracie hoped he wouldn't shoot her by accident.

The guard stepped aside to allow Tracie to pass him into the hallway. He brushed up against the table holding the aquarium, and as she moved past him she pushed hard, a blur of motion in the semi-darkness, and smashed his hands straight down the side wall of the fish tank, gun and all.

The glass shattered and the guard gasped, the sound almost but not quite a scream. He pulled the trigger reflexively and the gun fired, the slug ricocheting wildly and barely missing Tracie. A wave of water and fish flooded out of the tank, soaking Tracie and the guard.

Even in the dim light, she could see the razor-sharp glass had ripped a gash in the guard's forearm. Had she been sliced, too? No time to worry about that now.

The guard stumbled forward and Tracie ripped the gun out of his hands, slamming it against his temple in one motion. He sank to his knees, stunned. She hit him again and he dropped to the floor. He didn't move. She prodded him with her foot and he lay still.

He was out cold.

But now she had another problem. The shipyard was patrolled at night by a two-man security team, and if the other guard were anywhere near he would certainly have heard the gunfire. He could be on her in seconds. Tracie unlatched the briefcase and dropped the unconscious guard's Makarov inside, then snapped it shut and eased out the door again, Beretta drawn, alert for the second security man.

He was nowhere in sight.

She made her way out of the building and through the shipyard, moving between concrete and aluminum structures like a wraith. At the edge of shipyard property, she turned toward the Black Sea shoreline and an inflatable boat that would take her to a U.S. Navy submarine stationed nearby.

She disappeared into the inky Ukrainian night.

2

May 28, 1987
11:15 p.m.
The Kremlin, Moscow, USSR
Mikhail Gorbachev's residence

Mikhail Gorbachev trudged into his den. He was exhausted and felt like a man carrying the weight of the world on his shoulders. Raisa had gone to bed hours ago, but sleep would prove elusive for Mikhail tonight. He eased onto his plush leather office chair, selected a sheet of custom stationery, and got to work.

This might be the most important letter he would ever write, and it was imperative he compose it here, at home. Working in his office, filled as it was with cameras and other monitoring equipment, would risk his words being seen by the wrong set of eyes.

KGB eyes.

So he began writing, taking his time despite the fact he had put in a full day already and had another long day planned for tomorrow. He paused every few seconds to rub his chin and think. It was critical every word be phrased to convey the proper sense of urgency. Mikhail knew full well the letter's recipient would be suspicious, if not outright dismissive, of the veracity of his words and the motives behind them. And that was assuming the letter even reached its intended destination.

Mikhail knew he was probably under surveillance here, too, but working at night in his home office was not an unusual occurrence and should not elicit undue suspicion. More importantly, the quality of the surveillance cameras here was likely a step below those placed inside his executive office. It was a risk, but a calculated one, and worth taking.

He had long-since become accustomed to being watched. Clandestine KGB surveillance was ingrained in the consciousness of Soviet society, accepted as just as much a part of the late-twentieth century Russian experience as exquisite vodka and blisteringly cold winters.

Still, he hunched over his work, shielding the letter to the maximum extent possible with his body. The KGB might not be able to read the specifics of what he was writing, but after several recent heated policy disagreements they could probably guess the subject.

And that made this communiqué one of the most dangerous pieces of paper in the world.

Once he finished crafting the letter, the next step would be to enlist a trustworthy courier to make delivery. That would be a tricky and dangerous proposition, and where his plan could easily fall apart. A contact well versed in espionage techniques would be the obvious choice, and as Soviet Secretary General, Gorbachev could take his pick of the skilled KGB operatives in their considerable arsenal.

But there was a problem. This assignment would require personal loyalty, and a career spy would have no reason to remain loyal to Mikhail Gorbachev. In theory, Russia's espionage services existed to support the Communist party, of which he was titular head.

The reality, however, was much different. KGB agency chiefs enjoyed tremendous autonomy and were accustomed to wielding power for their own benefit. Mikhail knew if he entrusted this mission to the KGB, the document would not be out of his hands thirty minutes before it would be undergoing intensive scrutiny, with potentially dire consequences.

For him as well as others.

But Mikhail Gorbachev had not risen to power through the cutthroat ranks of the Soviet political system by being timid—or by being stupid. He wielded power and influence too, plenty of it, and his inner circle was filled with men fiercely protective of him. Not only because he was their friend and confidant, but also because their livelihoods depended upon his maintaining power. Were he to be overthrown, the new Russian leader would bring in new lieutenants, disposing of the old power brokers in whatever manner they saw fit.

Including making the most knowledgeable—and thus most dangerous—of them disappear.

Gorbachev knew the courier would have to be a man inside his inner circle, but it could not be someone so close to the general secretary that he was indispensable, because the odds of the man completing the mission successfully and also returning to Moscow alive were slim.

Practically nil, he thought grimly.

The Soviet leader took a break from composing his letter and flipped it face down, then he stretched out in his chair. His eyes were tired, burning from the exhaustion of a full day followed by the stress of tonight's illicit work. Tomorrow he would have to carry on as though he'd gotten a good night's sleep. It would not be easy, but then nothing was easy in a world where Mother Russia's hold over the rest of the Soviet republics was slipping steadily away.

The world was shrinking, and people who at one time were easily controlled via intimidation were beginning to demand freedoms unthinkable just a decade ago under Russian rule. No one inside the Kremlin wanted to admit it, but the burden of repressing the citizens of so many nations, all yearning for freedom and self-determination, was stretching the Soviet Union to the breaking point.

Things had to change, and they had to change *soon,* but most inside the ruling body of the USSR refused to see it. They buried their heads in the sand and pretended the year was still 1962.

Mikhail Gorbachev knew better. The Soviet Union was headed for disaster. It was inevitable, and would tear his country apart. Some inside the KGB had set a plan in motion that would cause a massive shift in global conditions, allowing them to consolidate power, and he could not allow that to happen. The plan was too extreme. It would trigger World War Three.

So he would do what must be done. But to challenge the KGB hard-liners openly would be foolhardy and likely considered treasonous. He would disappear without a trace in the middle of the night, just as millions of his countrymen had disappeared under Josef Stalin. The KGB could make it happen, his status as Communist Party general secretary notwithstanding, and no one would question a thing. A new leader would be installed and the system would lurch along toward its own demise.

This was why he worked in exhausted solitude at his desk while the rest of Moscow slumbered. This was why he risked everything. For his beloved country.

He yawned and rubbed his eyes. He whittled down the list of potential couriers in his mind. He chewed on the decision endlessly until he decided on the perfect candidate.

Aleksander Petrovka's official title was Undersecretary for Presidential Affairs. Aleksander would do as instructed, particularly if properly motivated. He was fairly intelligent for a party apparatchik, maybe even bright enough to pull off what Mikhail required of him.

Tomorrow they would talk, and Mikhail would put his own plan in motion, the one that would, with any luck, negate the KGB's. He would dispatch Petrovka to East Berlin on the first available plane. The KGB would know something was up but would be unable to stop him, provided Mikhail acted quickly and decisively.

He nodded, alone in his office. Having selected a courier, Mikhail felt a great weight lifting from his shoulders. The plan would either work or it would not, but solidifying things, even if only in his mind, made Mikhail feel better, like he was accomplishing something of great significance.

He straightened in his chair and got back to work.

3

May 29, 1987
10:10 a.m.
The Kremlin

Aleksander Petrovka was suspicious and nervous; Mikhail could see that the moment the man entered his office.

Petrovka worked in the Kremlin as a member of Mikhail Gorbachev's personal staff, but his status within the general secretary's inner circle was not so lofty that he'd ever had occasion to take a private meeting with his boss.

"Aleksander," Mikhail said, rising and extending his hand. It was critical he put his underling at ease.

Petrovka shook his hand uncertainly. "You wished to see me, sir?"

"I did," Mikhail said, smiling. "Come, let us stroll the grounds." He knew this development would arouse further concern in Petrovka, but it could not be helped. His office was certainly under surveillance, with listening devices as well as cameras, so broaching a subject as sensitive as Mikhail's here would get them both arrested for treason before the hour was up.

The men remained silent until they had exited the building. Mikhail could feel Aleksander's discomfort; it was rolling off him in waves. As they strolled through flower gardens just beginning to bloom in the dank Moscow climate, the secretary spoke in a near-whisper to avoid detection by ubiquitous KGB listening devices.

"You are being entrusted with a great honor," he began. "A patriotic duty. You are being given the opportunity to perform a service to your country far beyond anything you might previously have imagined possible."

Aleksander remained silent and Mikhail removed an innocent-looking envelope from his suit coat. He held it up for Aleksander's inspection but kept it close to his body, protecting it as much as possible from view of surveillance cameras.

"You are to leave immediately. We will provide you with a change of clothes for your overnight stay in the GDR. You will be driven straight from here to Tushino Airfield and fly via private plane to East Berlin, where you will turn this envelope over to an operative at the location revealed to you just prior to landing. Please note this envelope has been sealed in wax with my personal insignia, and its contents are classified Top Secret, not for your eyes or anyone else's except its intended recipient. The consequences of opening it would be severe and immediate. Do you understand?"

Aleksander nodded slowly. Mikhail could see he understood. Severe consequences in Russia meant only one thing.

"How will I recognize the envelope's recipient?" Aleksander asked.

"I am told he suffered facial disfigurement in an automobile accident years ago. A long scar on his right cheek. But you needn't worry, I have passed your description along and your contact will be watching for you. He will address you as 'Dolph' and you will respond, 'Hello, Henrik.'"

The secretary continued. "After delivering this envelope to your contact, your mission will be complete. You may enjoy the rest of your evening in East Berlin and then fly home tomorrow. Simple, yes?"

Mikhail knew Aleksander wanted to question him. Hell, he could see the man wanted to refuse the assignment. But he also knew he would do as asked. His place was not to question. He was a bureaucrat and had been given an assignment by the most powerful man in the USSR. What else could he do?

Aleksander reached out reluctantly and took the envelope. He held it between two fingers, nose wrinkled as if smelling something offensive.

"Remember," Mikhail said. "No one is to open this letter."

"What if…" Aleksander's voice trailed off.

"What?" Mikhail asked, annoyed. The lack of sleep was catching up to him and he still had a busy day ahead.

"Well, what if I am challenged, you know, by the authorities?"

Mikhail reached into his pocket and removed a pen and a small pad of paper. He jotted something down and handed it to Aleksander.

"The authorities would have no reason to challenge you, but if you encounter any difficulties, this is my private residential telephone number. Very few people have it. Anyone wishing to question you can call me, any time, day or night, and I will be happy to explain the situation."

It was clear to Mikhail that Aleksander was not pleased, but that did not matter. He placed the envelope in the interior breast pocket of his suit coat and the men began walking toward the building. Mikhail knew he had just passed the point of no return. He hoped Aleksander Petrovka was up to the challenge.

*   *   *

May 29, 1987
10:30 a.m.
The Kremlin
KGB monitoring station

Viktor Kovalenko squinted, his eyes glued to a tiny black-and-white monitor. The screen was crammed into a metal rack mounted on the wall next to his desk alongside eleven similar monitors. Each transmitted a different view of the Kremlin's exterior.

The image was small, but he could see enough to know something unusual was happening. General Secretary Gorbachev was speaking with one of his assistants, something he did regularly throughout the day. But normally the men would be surrounded by aides and secretaries and assorted party apparatchiks. This meeting was being conducted one-on-one, almost an unheard-of scenario with a low-level bureaucrat like Aleksander Petrovka.

The men were engrossed in an intense conversation, Gorbachev doing most of the talking, Petrovka's body language suggesting he would rather be almost anywhere else in the world. Gorbachev removed something from his pocket and after stressing a point, finger waggling, handed the object to Petrovka.

Kovalenko glanced at his watch and jotted the time down on a pad of paper, along with a notation regarding Gorbachev's odd behavior. He watched the small Russian-made Ekran television monitor closely as he lit a cigarette and took a deep drag.

Tried to determine the significance of what he was seeing. Decided to play it safe.

He picked up a telephone handset and dialed a number from memory.

The call was answered on the first ring, as Kovalenko had known it would be. It always was.

He laid out the details on the phone for the KGB watch commander: the virtually unprecedented change to General Secretary Gorbachev's routine. The seeming reluctance with which Aleksander Petrovka received Gorbachev's words. The secretive passing of an object—perhaps an envelope, perhaps not—between the two men.

Despite his familiarity with Gorbachev—he had been assigned to this post for over three years—Kovalenko could not guess what the general secretary might be up to. Something was definitely amiss, though.

Colonel Kopalev listened without comment for five minutes or more as Kovalenko reported his observations.

Finally, when Kovalenko had finished, the colonel said, "Continue observing Secretary Gorbachev. When he leaves his office for the day, I want it thoroughly but discreetly searched. Have your men look for anything unusual and then report back to me with your findings."

Kovalenko grimaced. "Respectfully, Colonel, the object was passed to Petrovka. I very much doubt any evidence will remain in Secretary Gorbachev's office by the end of the day. There's probably none in there now. If I may suggest following Petrovka—"

"Thank you for your assessment, Major. Of course we will follow Comrade Petrovka. But it changes nothing as far as you are concerned. You have your orders. I will expect to hear from you immediately if your search turns up any useable information."

"Yes sir," Kovalenko replied, and the connection was abruptly broken at the other end. His boss had just slammed down the receiver.

He replaced the handset in its cradle and lifted his middle finger at it, fully aware that *he* might be under surveillance as well, that his insolence was probably being observed, but he was annoyed enough not to care.

He lit another cigarette and resumed observing the activity in and around the Kremlin.

4

May 29, 1987
10:20 p.m.
Berlin, German Democratic Republic

The vodka burned in a familiar and not unpleasant way as it rolled down Aleksander Petrovka's throat. He gulped down his first glass in a matter of seconds and realized he should have ordered two at once from the heavy-set barmaid when she had made her first pass by his table.

He shrugged. She would return soon. Any good barmaid could recognize the heaviest drinkers in a crowd instantly. Her livelihood depended upon it.

Aleksander knew it was important to keep his head clear and his wits about him during the upcoming rendezvous. This was only his second trip into the GDR, and every face appeared hostile, suspicious of the Russian interloper. But the prospect of getting through the next hour—indeed, the rest of his life—without the fuzzy reassurance provided by a liberal dose of vodka was unthinkable. The enormity of this mission was not lost on Aleksander, nor was its potential to destroy his life, and for the thousandth time since being summoned by Gorbachev he questioned his commitment to the general secretary.

Nobody defied the KGB and got away with it.

And Aleksander knew that by carrying out the instructions Gorbachev had given him, he was defying the KGB. There was simply no other way to look at it. The very circumstances of their meeting this morning were enough to convince him of that fact. No office. No aides. Just he and the most powerful man in the Soviet Union.

Aleksander forced his thoughts back to the present and the raucous East German club. He maintained a continuous watch on the crowded discotheque, eyes darting, alert for potential threats. The notion that the Undersecretary for Presidential Affairs, the very definition of an anonymous apparatchik, would recognize a threat even if it appeared before him and announced itself, was laughable. Aleksander knew this, yet he could not stop himself.

In his obsessive concern for security, Aleksander almost missed the blocky figure of the barmaid approaching his table. She asked him a question, which was lost in the din of the club and the uncertainty of a foreign language, and Aleksander nodded, handing her his empty glass. He assumed she must have asked if he wanted another drink, which he most certainly did. What else could it be?

The barmaid took his glass and clomped away. Standing behind her, entirely hidden by her bulk until she stepped around him, was a smallish, unassuming-looking man, dressed casually, with a receding head of buzz-cut sandy hair and a pale face dominated by black horn-rimmed glasses.

And a jagged scar running diagonally down his right cheek.

In his hand he clutched a glass of clear liquid, presumably vodka.

The man nodded at Aleksander and then sat across the small table without waiting to be invited. "It has been a long time, Dolph," he said with a tight-lipped smile.

Aleksander stared at the man, nerves tightening. He was supposed to respond. Call the man by a code name. What was it? He had been rehearsing it just a moment ago and now it was gone.

The man's eyes narrowed and sweat broke out on Aleksander's forehead. He felt as though he might suffer a heart attack.

Then he remembered.

"Henrik!" he burst out. "It is wonderful to see you, Henrik."

The stranger relaxed and leaned across the table, waiting to speak until Aleksander had taken the hint and leaned forward as well.

Then, speaking as softly as possible in the noisy club, he said, "Do you have the item?" His Russian was flawless.

The barmaid returned with his drink and Aleksander remained silent while she dropped the glass onto the table, vodka slopping over the side. As her hefty form plowed back through the crowd toward the bar—Aleksander could not help picturing a gigantic Tupolev airplane steaming down the runway for takeoff—he returned his attention to his new friend. The man sat drumming his fingers.

Aleksander nodded. "Da. I have it."

He reached into his breast pocket before realizing how suspicious it would look for him to withdraw the item here in the tavern and pass it across the table to his contact. Although no one seemed to be paying any attention to them, Aleksander knew *someone* would remember once the KGB started questioning people. The KGB could be very persuasive.

Suddenly terrified, Aleksander froze, hand on the envelope sticking partway out of his pocket. What should he do? How could he avoid becoming the object of everyone's attention and still complete the mission Gorbachev had entrusted to him?

The Soviet leader was not someone to be trifled with. In his own way he was as imposing and intimidating as the faceless killers of the KGB. One didn't rise to the position of general secretary of the Communist Party without possessing an iron will and a cold ruthlessness.

The contact saved him. He smiled reassuringly, rising and leaning over the table, clapping Aleksander on the shoulder with one hand and deftly plucking the envelope from Aleksander's pocket with the other. The envelope disappeared in an impressive sleight of hand, one worthy of a professional pickpocket.

"You're doing fine," the man said, again in Russian, as he leaned back in his chair. He had clearly been briefed he would be dealing with a novice.

Then he continued, speaking quietly. "Here is what we're going to do," he said. "We'll share a drink and light conversation, just a couple of old friends catching up. Then I will get up and leave the club. You will wait a few minutes and then follow."

The contact leaned back and began laughing uproariously, as if Aleksander had just said the funniest thing he'd ever heard.

Aleksander stared, surprised by the man's sudden outburst, before realizing he was supposed to join in. So he did, feeling silly. He took a big pull on his vodka, emptying the glass. The fuzzy reassurance he'd been waiting for began to tingle through him and Aleksander welcomed it with enthusiasm.

He waved the barmaid over to their table—she hadn't gotten any better looking, even after two tall vodkas—and ordered another round for himself and his new friend. After all, it was what the man had just said he was supposed to do, right?

The shroud of fear and uncertainty that had been hanging over Aleksander since his meeting with the general secretary began to lift. For the first time Aleksander began to believe things might actually turn out all right. He was almost finished with this frightening business, and then he could return to Moscow and get on with his life, safe and secure in bureaucratic anonymity.

His contact made small talk for a few minutes, and Aleksander returned the conversation with inanities of his own. They laughed now and then, just two men reconnecting after time apart. They could be friends, brother, coworkers.

Still no one appeared to be watching. Aleksander's concern continued to melt away. He knew it was probably due to the affects of the alcohol but he didn't care. The sense of relief was too pleasant.

At last, Aleksander's contact pushed his chair back on the dirty floor and stood. Aleksander stood too and the man with the scar reached across the small table, shaking his hand and drawing him close at the same time.

"Remember," he whispered in Aleksander's ear. "Go nowhere for the next few minutes. Have another drink. Relax. Allow time for me to slip away. Then you should disappear. Good luck."

Then he laughed again, smiling and nodding at Aleksander. He turned on his heel and melted into the crowd.

5

Klaus Hahn slipped the envelope into his breast pocket and picked his way through the crowd. American disco music blasted through tinny speakers in the background, and the temperature had skyrocketed inside the densely packed tavern. He was sweating profusely, and not just from nervousness.

A veteran of more than a decade of service to the American CIA, Klaus looked forward to the day when his beloved Germany would be reunited. No more East and West, with the ugly concrete and barbed-wire barriers splitting the country arbitrarily and needlessly, in some cases literally tearing families apart, half living on the side of freedom and opportunity and half on the side of repression and paranoia. Klaus Hahn's goal was to help end the fear and forced servitude on the eastern side of that wall.

Klaus had not hesitated on that day years ago when co-opted by his CIA handler, a man known to him only by his alias, "Mr. Wilson." He had made no secret of his willingness to work in the name of freedom, and when approached by Mr. Wilson had enthusiastically accepted the opportunity to contribute, even in some small way, toward a free and unified Germany.

The majority of the tasks Klaus had handled over the years were relatively small and risk-free. Most often his assignments had simply involved funneling names and addresses of hard line Communist sympathizers to Mr. Wilson, as well as names and contact information of other freedom-seeking individuals like himself.

Tonight was different, though. Mr. Wilson had approached

Klaus with the offer of something much more substantial. Something big. So big, in fact, that Mr. Wilson had said this would be the last job Klaus would ever do for the CIA. Klaus would be toxic after this.

"Toxic." That was the exact phrasing Mr. Wilson had used. If the job was completed successfully, Klaus could expect an uncomfortable night of questioning by local authorities and, quite likely, the Stasi, the German Democratic Republic's feared secret police.

If unsuccessful, well, Mr. Wilson had not spelled out any details under that scenario, but elaboration had not been necessary.

"Stick to your story when you're questioned," Mr. Wilson had told him. "Do not deviate from it. You stopped off at the club for a few drinks after work. You ran into an old friend from school, quite by accident. You do not even remember his name. You shared a drink and discussed sports, women, whatever. Then you left. They will not believe you, but there will be nothing they can do about it. After several hours of intense questioning, they will reluctantly release you. But you will be watched, and we can never meet again. Your work for us will be finished."

Klaus had agreed. He was not afraid of a night of questioning, by the police *or* by the Stasi. He was disappointed his work toward the cause of a reunified homeland was going to end, but he had no choice but to accept when Mr. Wilson stressed the importance of the assignment.

He wiped his brow with his sleeve, weaving through the crowded tavern, moving steadily toward the door. Halfway across the floor he turned sideways to allow a pretty young redhead to pass by. It was his contact, and she was dressed provocatively, in skintight black leather pants and a silk blouse that did little to hide her considerable assets.

She caught his eye and flashed a smile before rubbing against him out of necessity—the crush of thirsty bar patrons crowded them from all sides.

They squeezed past each other. Klaus felt a brief tug and then the envelope was gone and so was the girl. He continued toward the door as Mr. Wilson had instructed him to do. He had been told not to look back but he couldn't help it—he took a quick peek behind as he exited the front door. The beautiful young girl was nowhere to be seen.

Klaus strolled into the cool Berlin night, glad to be free of the claustrophobia-inducing, sweat-soaked, sexually charged atmosphere, not to mention the annoyingly loud music. He turned left and began walking toward his car, moving faster now.

Before he had made it five steps, a hand gripped his elbow. Attached to the hand was a tall, skeletal man dressed in a dark suit. An unbuttoned overcoat flapped in the chilly breeze.

The man said, "Where is it?"

Klaus answered, "Where is what?"

"Don't play stupid. Where is the envelope?"

Klaus wrenched his arm free and turned, staring directly into the man's eyes. The street lighting was dim and shadows running from the man's hook nose across his face gave him the appearance of a vulture.

"I don't know what you're talking about," he said.

"You're coming with me," the man said, and Klaus knew his night of questioning had begun.

6

Tracie Tanner lifted the envelope effortlessly from her East German contact and slid it down the front of her blouse. The heat generated by all the bodies crammed together inside the tavern was stifling, and Tracie thought the envelope might have to be peeled away from her skin with a chisel when she finally made it to safety. She felt naked without her weapon, a Beretta 92SB, but her skimpy attire left no room for it.

Tracie had nursed her glass of soda water and loitered on the other side of the room, watching out of the corner of her eye as her contact received the envelope from an extremely nervous Russian bureaucrat. She watched while rebuffing a succession of young East German men doing their best to capture her attention.

The moment her contact—she had never met him, had been told only that he was an East German citizen committed to reunification of his country—shook his companion's hand and turned toward the door, Tracie offered a dazzling smile to the young German currently chatting her up and gave him a little wave. "Nice meeting you."

The kid blinked in surprise, jaw hanging open, his disappointment obvious. Tracie turned and strode across the room to intercept her contact.

The exchange went off without a hitch, and the moment Tracie had secured the envelope she turned and began working her way through the dense crowd toward the rear of the club. The bass track thumped and the people shimmied as Tracie headed for the swinging door behind the bar leading to the back exit.

She breezed around the open end of the bar, where three bartenders struggled to keep pace with their drink orders. As she barged through, the one closest to her raised his eyebrows.

"Hey! You're not allowed back here." His voice was gruff and insistent.

Tracie smiled brightly and blew him a kiss and continued on. She pushed through the swinging wooden doors as if she owned the place and moved straight toward the service entrance in back. To her right, dozens of beer kegs gleamed dully in the washed-out lighting. To her left, far off in the distance at the end of a narrow corridor, she could see people hard at work in a small kitchen. The smell of stale beer and spoiled meat hung in the air, heavy and thick.

Aside from those kitchen workers, Tracie was alone in the storage area, at least for the moment. She had thought the bartenders would be too busy to follow her and she was right. She breathed a sigh of relief, wondering how in the hell it had failed to occur to the KGB to cover this potential escape route. Apparently they considered the possibility of a switch remote, given that they were dealing with a frightened Russian bureaucrat.

She kicked it into high gear now and broke into a trot. As she neared the rear exit, a stern voice from behind her growled, "Stop right there."

Tracie cursed under her breath as she gauged the distance to the door, calculating the odds of surviving a headlong dash for freedom. It was just too far. The Russian secret police were not accustomed to being ignored, and neither were the Stasi, and Tracie knew the operative behind her would be expecting full and immediate compliance, regardless of which organization he represented.

No choice. She stopped and turned slowly, holding her arms out at her sides and away from her body, spreading her fingers to show she was unarmed. She hoped her blouse hid the envelope resting against the sweat-soaked skin of her belly. If not, she would probably not survive beyond the next few seconds.

The man who had stopped her wore the forest-green camouflage summer field uniform of the NVA, East Germany's National People's Army. Tracie took in the uniform and breathed a sigh of relief. The KGB had indeed thought to cover the back entrance, but had used a People's Army lieutenant to do so, rather than a KGB or Stasi operative.

She might still get out of this.

"What's your hurry?" the man said, his weapon trained on Tracie. She said nothing and he took a couple of aggressive steps toward her. She willed him to take a couple more.

A loopy grin spread across her face and Tracie wobbled forward a step, then back. She allowed her eyes to glaze over.

"What'rr you doing in the ladies room?" she said, intentionally slurring her words. "You shou'nt be in here." Then she giggled, hoping she wasn't overdoing it.

The tension in the lieutenant's posture relaxed slightly and the look of suspicion creasing his face eased a bit. Tracie thought she saw him stifle a grin. The gun, however, remained pointed at her midsection. If he fired now, the slug would probably punch a hole right through the envelope.

The soldier took another couple of steps forward, this time moving with more swagger and less aggression, lowering his gun and sealing his fate. He was almost close enough.

As he took another step, Tracie stumbled to one knee. He was eighteen inches in front of her. Any closer and he might conceivably be *too* close. It was time to act.

She shot to her feet, propelling her body forward, grabbing her captor's gun with her right hand. The man took a step back in surprise and Tracie yanked hard, jerking his body toward hers as he squeezed the trigger reflexively. The sound of the gunfire was loud and Tracie hoped the thumping bass beat out in the club had covered most of it. The people working in the kitchen down the hall would have heard, but she wasn't worried about them.

The soldier clubbed her on the side with his left hand as she used his momentum against him, flicking her head forward, the movement tight and compact. Her forehead impacted the man's nose and she could hear the bones shatter even above the damned disco music and the ringing in her ears from the gunshot.

He crumpled immediately, blood streaming over his mouth, which he had opened in a scream of pain. It gushed out, spilled down his face, and splattered onto the dirty floor. It looked like a miniature Niagara Falls. Tracie grabbed the soldier's weapon and yanked it away from him. His finger jammed in the trigger guard and Tracie felt it break.

The man staggered, splattering blood onto her leather pants and boots. He was practically out on his feet. She pivoted her hand to the side, like a hitchhiker trolling for a ride, and then reversed direction and slammed the butt of the pistol against his temple.

His eyes rolled up into his head and he dropped straight down. She flashed back to her encounter with the security guard in the Ukraine less than ten days ago. *All my dates end badly.*

She hoped she hadn't killed the man but couldn't afford to take the time to find out. By now the KGB agents monitoring the front of the club would have discovered the man they followed was empty-handed, and it wouldn't take long before they realized they had been victimized by the oldest trick in the book, the bait and switch. Within minutes, maybe less, this place would be blanketed, locked down, and if Tracie were still here when that happened she would never get out alive.

A chorus of screams and pounding footfalls told her the soldier's gunshot had been heard. She dropped to one knee and turned, raising the man's bloody gun. An elderly man and woman—they each had to be seventy years old if they were a day—burst out of the hallway and into the storage area. They were undoubtedly the pair she had seen working in the kitchen, although they had been too far away to identify for sure.

"One more step and you die," she said in German, pointing the gun in their direction, hoping her voice hadn't carried into the bar.

The pair skidded to a stop, the old woman banging into the old man in front, sending him careening helplessly toward Tracie. He fell to the floor and scrabbled backward, almost knocking the old woman over in the process. It looked like a Three Stooges routine, and under other circumstances might have been funny.

Right now, though, the only thing on Tracie's mind was escape. She had already been inside the building far too long.

She rose to her feet and said, "Go back to the kitchen and stay there for at least ten minutes. If you move before ten minutes has passed, I'll come back and kill you both. Do you understand?"

The pair nodded at the same time, then turned and hurried

back down the narrow hallway. They moved quickly but did not scream or yell into the front of the club for help, as Tracie had been afraid they might. She waited until they had reentered the kitchen and then sprinted for the door.

She burst into the night, the oppressive heat of the club vanishing in an instant. The service entrance opened into a narrow, trash-littered alley. A row of frost-covered garbage cans had been lined up next to the doorway and the rank stench of spoiled food hung in the air like smog over L.A. The alley was deserted.

She slowed to a fast walk along the crumbling pavement, moving south, knowing their East German collaborator had been instructed to turn north after leaving the club—not that he would have gotten far before being intercepted by the KGB or the Stasi. The alley opened onto a quiet street one block south of the bar. A pedestrian glanced at her suspiciously but kept walking. If he noticed the blood staining her leather pants he kept it to himself.

Your lucky night, pal, Tracie thought grimly.

She turned a corner and walked a hundred yards. Parked at the curb was a battered Volkswagen, twenty years old if it was a day. Tracie pulled the door open and eased into the driver's seat. She sank into the worn fabric and rested her head against the steering wheel, breathing deeply, adrenaline still coursing through her body.

After a moment she started the car. She flicked on the headlights and drove slowly away.

7

May 29, 1987
11:25 p.m.
Berlin, GDR

Aleksander savored the relief he felt following the departure of his contact. He took a deep pull on his vodka and smiled. It wasn't up to Russian standards, but it was better than he had expected to find in Germany.

He wondered how long he should wait before departing. His contact had said "a few minutes," and Aleksander wanted nothing more than to leave this club behind and get on with his life.

He tried not to think about the envelope but couldn't help doing so. General Secretary Gorbachev had indicated it would eventually be delivered to the *Americans*, of all people, which was strange, but Aleksander didn't claim to know anything about international diplomacy. Didn't want to, either. If Comrade Gorbachev wanted the Americans to have the envelope, and was willing to go to such great lengths to conceal its contents from the KGB, who was Aleksander to question the decision?

He shrugged. It was no longer his problem to deal with. The damned envelope was out of his possession and good riddance to it. He had done what was asked of him, had performed admirably, he hoped, in service to his country and the Communist Party, and could finally relax.

He looked at his watch and decided enough time had passed for his contact to disappear into the night.

Aleksander finished his vodka—was that his third or fourth glass? Fifth?—and slammed it down on the tiny table before struggling to his feet, swaying unsteadily. The German vodka may have been a mediocre substitute for the real thing, but it still packed a satisfying wallop. He placed some of that phony-looking GDR money under his glass and staggered through the crowd, unnoticed and unimpeded, just another Friday night drinker on his way home to face the wrath of his frau.

Aleksander pushed through the door into the cool German night. The stars glittered overhead and a light breeze caressed his flushed face. He felt light-headed, more than he should after just a few glasses of vodka, but decided it was due to lack of sleep and the tremendous strain he had been operating under.

But none of that mattered now. He had done his duty and was in the clear.

He turned right and staggered unsteadily along the dimly lit sidewalk, occasionally sidestepping an onrushing pedestrian or couple walking arm-in-arm. Tomorrow he would take a cab to the airport and fly home to Moscow and the reassuring monotony of his invisible bureaucratic life.

Tonight, though, he walked unhurriedly, enjoying the fantasy he had constructed in his alcohol-fuzzed mind. He was a superspy, a man counted on by all of Mother Russia and indeed, all of the USSR, to keep the empire safe. He felled all enemies of the state and was treated like royalty by the Supreme Soviet. He was James Bond, only on the proper side of the equation.

It was an enjoyable fantasy, and Aleksander was lost in it when two men overtook him from behind. They were on him before he knew what was happening, and when they reached him, each one grabbed an elbow in a vice-like grip and propelled him forward.

"Do not say a word," the man on his right side whispered fiercely into his ear in Russian, and Aleksander did not say a word.

He risked a quick glance to his right and then his left. The two men were dressed identically—black overcoats, black slacks, black shoes, even black Homburgs covering their heads. They escorted him directly past the entrance to his hotel, walking him roughly half a kilometer along the main road, still busy with pedestrians at this relatively early hour.

None of them paid any attention to him or to the men dressed in black. Aleksander's heart was racing but he tried not to panic. One call to Secretary Gorbachev's office and this misunderstanding would be cleared up.

The strange threesome continued, moving so far down the sidewalk that they left the flickering World War Two-era streetlights behind. They turned a corner into a secluded alleyway, walking Aleksander to an East German-made Trabant automobile parked in the shadows. The car was ancient, tiny.

They shoved him wordlessly into the back seat. One of the men leaned over and lifted a foul-smelling cloth from a well-sealed plastic bag in his pocket and pressed it to Aleksander's face.

Aleksander willed himself not to panic and tried not to breathe.

Eventually he did both, in that order, and everything went black.

8

Aleksander regained consciousness slowly. He was seated on a hard chair, probably in a basement or storage room of some sort. It was cold and dark and damp and smelled of rotting vegetables and something vaguely sinister. Copper, maybe? Aleksander wasn't sure.

He could hear voices muttering somewhere nearby. Two people, it seemed. He was afraid to open his eyes to check.

His hands and arms ached. He tried moving them but they'd been secured tightly to the chair, arms pulled behind his back, wrists shackled together. Tried his feet next. Same result. Each ankle had been affixed to a chair leg with something heavy and solid, probably a length of chain.

Aleksander felt queasy and weak. He knew he had been drugged into unconsciousness inside the tiny East German automobile and wondered how long he'd been out. Was he even still in the German Democratic Republic? Was he back in Russia? Somewhere else?

He concentrated on the voices, trying to pick up enough of the conversation to determine what language they were speaking and how many people were inside the room with him.

No luck. The voices were too muffled.

He risked opening his eyes, just a sliver, and moved his head

29

very slowly to look around. In the dirty yellow light of a single bulb he could see a pair of shadowy figures huddled together in a corner of the room. The image blurred and doubled, then cleared. The lingering effects of whatever drugs he had been given, Aleksander guessed.

The men were sitting around a rickety table drinking something hot out of mugs—Aleksander could see steam rising into the air even from here—and his stomach clenched and rumbled.

He wondered how long it had been since he'd eaten. He wondered whether he would ever eat again. The terror of his predicament struck him like a wrecking ball and Aleksander puked all over the floor, the vomit burning his gullet on the way out. *Cheap German vodka.*

Aleksander sobbed once before stopping himself. His eyes widened in mounting panic as the men pushed their chairs back and began walking across the room.

The men stopped directly in front of him. One was tall and thin, skeletal. The other was completely bald. Aleksander looked up in fear, feeling like he might be sick again. He hoped when the vomit erupted from him it wouldn't splatter all over his captors.

"Welcome back to the land of the living, Comrade," the bald man said in Russian. It meant little, since his East German contact had spoken Russian, too. "Time is of the essence, so let us skip the preliminaries and get right down to business, shall we?"

Aleksander's terror was nearly overwhelming. His stomach rolled and yawed. He was afraid to speak for fear of vomiting again.

But as terrifying as his situation was, he knew he still possessed the ultimate trump card—provided he had been kidnapped by Soviets. If these two weren't citizens of the USSR, he didn't know what he was going to do.

"Where is it?" the bald man said. So far skeleton-man had not spoken.

Aleksander had no choice but to speak now. He hoped he wouldn't puke on the men, but they were standing perilously close.

He swallowed hard. "Where is what?" he croaked. He hadn't realized how thirsty he was until just now.

"Do not play games with us. Doing so will only cause you needless pain," the bald man said, and skeleton-man drew back his foot and kicked Aleksander in the shin, hard, with his steel-toed boot. The pain exploded, racing up and down Aleksander's leg like an electrical current.

He screamed in agony and fell forward, desperate to cover up, to protect his injured shin, but could barely move with his wrists shackled to the chair behind his back. He hadn't heard anything crack but couldn't believe the bone hadn't shattered.

"*Where is it?*" the bald man repeated, his voice slashing like a knife.

"I don't know," Aleksander gasped. "I passed it along just as I was instructed to do. Where the other man went with it after he left the club I have no idea."

"You know him," the man said. It was not a question. "You have done business with him in the past."

"No. Never. I swear. I've never seen him before."

"You were laughing and joking like old friends, Comrade Petrovka. Do not insult our intelligence."

"I was just doing what I was told to do by my contact, to blend in, that is all. I haven't been to East Germany since I was a teen, I swear. You can check my travel records if you don't believe me."

"Oh, we will, don't worry about that. Next question, and this is important, so try to pay attention: what was the item you delivered?"

"I do not know."

"I don't believe you, traitor."

"Traitor?" Aleksander looked up at his tormentors, sweat dripping into his eyes. His shin throbbed with every pounding beat of his heart. He knew now was the time to play his trump card. It might be his only chance.

"No," he said. "I am not a traitor. I was doing exactly as ordered by General Secretary Gorbachev. I am a member of his staff and am here on official state business."

"Official state business?" the man said, his voice mocking and cruel. He turned to his partner. "Did you hear that, Vasily? He is here on official state business, representing Secretary Gorbachev himself."

The man turned his attention back to Aleksander. "Well, I have news for you, Comrade Aleksander Petrovka of Ivanteyevka.

Mikhail Gorbachev is just as much a traitor to his homeland as you are. We care nothing for Mikhail Gorbachev's orders. If Gorbachev's reckless stupidity is not checked, he will be the downfall of the Soviet Empire, and Vasily and I are just two of many who refuse to allow that to happen.

"Betraying your country under the orders of a fellow traitor is no excuse, Comrade Petrovka. So I ask you again, and for the last time: what was the item you delivered to your contact?"

Terror flooded through Aleksander's body. The terror overwhelmed the pain so his throbbing shin ceased to exist. The terror overwhelmed his queasy stomach so he no longer felt he was about to puke. The terror was everything.

These men *were* Russians, but it did not matter. They were Russians, but the word of Mikhail Gorbachev meant nothing to them. They were accusing him of treason, but *they* were traitors. The irony struck him like another kick to the shin.

Aleksander realized he was breathing heavily, forcing air in and out through his mouth like a panting dog. He was hyperventilating but could not stop himself.

This was bad.

This was worse than bad.

This was a nightmare come to life.

"WHAT WAS THE ITEM YOU DELIVERED TO YOUR CONTACT?" the bald man screamed in Aleksander's face. Spittle sprayed from the man's mouth as if from a fire hose. A fat gob of saliva splattered the side of Aleksander's nose and dripped slowly into his mouth.

Aleksander sobbed. "I don't know! Secretary Gorbachev gave me a sealed envelope. Inside was some kind of document, I do not know what. He forbade me to look at it."

His tormentor stepped back and looked at his comrade. He seemed genuinely shocked. "You risked your life to deliver a document and...you *don't even know what it was?*"

Aleksander hung his head and shook it miserably. He would never see Tatiana or his children again. He would never see the sun rise over the Moscow skyline. He was going to die here in this dirty, dark torture chamber at the hands of two people he had never seen, two people who believed him a traitor to his country. And there was nothing he could do about it.

A wrenching sob shook his body and pain flared in his shin. "The envelope was sealed. I could not have opened it even if I wanted to."

His two captors shared a laugh as though he had said something funny.

Then his interrogator switched gears. "Your contact. He was a German, was he not?"

"Yes, that is what Secretary Gorbachev told me, and I don't know why he would lie about it."

The two men grunted and his interrogator spit on the floor. "Yes, why would he lie?" the bald man said. "He is destroying his ancestral homeland, the land Russians have spilled blood to protect for generations, but surely he would not *lie*.

"Now, getting back to the document the traitor Gorbachev asked you to pass along to the German, What was it?"

"I already told you, I do not know."

The man waved a hand like he was brushing a fly away from his face. "Do not take me for a fool, please, Comrade. There is no one alive who would not look inside the envelope the first chance he got. *What was it?*"

Aleksander raised his head and looked at the man beseechingly but said nothing. What could he say that he had not already tried? It was clear another denial would be ignored.

And then, out of nowhere, inspiration. His contact! "If you were watching me, you must have been watching my contact, too," he said, speaking quickly, enthusiastically. "If you can find him, you can take the envelope from him and see for yourselves what it contains."

"Thank you for your very helpful advice," his tormentor replied with exaggerated politeness. "Your German collaborator claims to know nothing as well, and he passed the envelope off before we were able to intercept him."

The man shook his head in disgust and spit again on the floor. "We are getting nowhere and time is passing quickly."

He smiled at Aleksander, his lips a thin bloodless slash. "I would like to say I am sorry for what is to come next, but alas, I cannot. I have little patience for traitors, but would gladly have ended you quickly had you only given me the information I require. Now, I am afraid you are in for a rather unpleasant little while. I can't be more specific because, you see, I don't know how long it will take you to die. One can never predict these things, but the elapsed time will probably seem much longer to you than it actually is."

The other man walked away and began dragging equipment across the concrete floor, placing it next to Aleksander's chair. He didn't seem sorry, either.

He whistled a tuneless ditty as he expertly clamped a set of booster cables to a series of automobile batteries stacked atop a wooden pallet on wheels. A cable ran from the batteries to a small box fitted with dials, switches and a couple of grimy meters.

To Aleksander the box resembled the transformer from the small electric train set he and Tatiana had given their son, Aleksander Junior, for his fourth birthday last year. It had taken months to save up enough money to buy the toy, but the look on his son's face when he opened the gift had been worth every bit of sacrifice.

Tears spilled down Aleksander's cheek at the memory and mixed with the spittle drying on his face.

The quiet man continued working and whistling. Two cables extended from one side of the transformer-like box, snaking across the floor and terminating at Aleksander's shackled feet. At the end of each cable was a shiny copper connector, spring-loaded and fitted with sharp teeth.

A feeling of dread wormed its way through Aleksander's gut and he no longer suspected he was going to throw up again. He knew it.

The quiet man unbuckled Aleksander's belt and pulled it free of his trousers. He unsnapped Aleksander's pants and unzipped the fly and motioned impatiently for him to lift his ass off the seat.

Numbly, Aleksander did as he was instructed, and the man yanked his trousers and underwear down to his ankles.

And Aleksander puked, barfing up the acidy-tasting remnants of the East German vodka, not caring this time that it splattered all over the quiet man. He began babbling, begging for his life, begging for mercy. Begging.

The quiet man continued, unaffected. He attached the copper ends of the two cables to Aleksander's bare scrotum, tugging lightly on each one to ensure it was fastened securely. Then he walked behind Aleksander's chair, returning seconds later with a bucket of foul-looking water. He splashed some on Aleksander and the cables.

He looked at Aleksander, his eyes hard and remorseless. "Goodbye, Comrade," he said. They were the first and last words Aleksander ever heard him say.

Then he walked to the small table on wheels upon which the transformer-like box was placed, and he flipped a switch.

Then he turned a dial.

Then Aleksander's situation changed for the worse.

It took a long time for him to die.

9

May 30, 1987
12:15 a.m.
Ramstein Air Base, West Germany

"Hello?"

"Is this Mitchell?"

"Who wants to know?"

"Kopalev."

"Yes, it's Mitchell."

"You are alone, yes? You can speak freely?"

"Yes."

"Good. Because we have a job for you."

"Go ahead."

"An item has been taken out of Russia through the GDR and is being flown to America from your air base."

"So? Stuff flies out of here to the States all the time."

"Not 'stuff' like this. It is critical this item not reach its intended destination. You will ensure that it does not."

"What is the item?"

"An envelope addressed to your President Reagan. We believe the envelope contains a handwritten letter from Mikhail Gorbachev betraying his country."

"I'm supposed to intercept a letter? In one small envelope? I don't know anything abut mail delivery. It's not possible."

"It *is* possible, Major. And it will be done. We have been paying you good money for many years and you have provided little return on our investment. Now it is time for you to earn those tens of thousands of American dollars we have deposited into your bank account."

"But...how?"

"The item is far too valuable to be left unguarded. It will be placed on the first available military flight leaving Ramstein for the U.S. and will be carried personally by a member of your CIA. We believe that representative will be a young woman, red-haired and beautiful."

"A beautiful, red-haired CIA spook?"

"That is correct. We have two witnesses who saw such a young woman execute one of our men in cold blood. We are certain she is in possession of the item. The airplane she boards for the United States is the airplane the envelope will be on. You are to ensure that airplane never reaches its destination."

"Crash a U.S. Air Force jet? Are you out of your mind? Why can't I just steal the letter and deliver it to you through a contact?"

"You propose stealing a Top Secret document from a CIA professional? It would never happen. You would be dead before you got within three feet of her."

"But if I can?"

"You do not understand. This item could conceivably change the entire balance of world power. It is imperative it be destroyed. We cannot risk you being caught trying to steal it. You will crash the airplane and thus destroy the letter. Those are your orders. They will be followed. Period."

"I already told you, it's impossible. It can't be done."

"You will find a way, Major."

"You're a fucking crackpot. Forget it. I'm out. Find someone else to do your dirty work."

"Major, you will never guess the report I received today."

"Report? What are you talking about?"

"One of our operatives followed Roberta as she drove little Sarah to dance class this afternoon. He tells me, Major, that your daughter is getting quite beautiful. Growing like a weed, as you Americans like to say."

"He what? Roberta and Sarah? Listen here, you psychotic bastard, you leave my family out of this, do you understand?"

"The roads, Major, they are so dangerous in your country. Automobile accidents are a daily occurrence, often fiery crashes where the victims, sometimes mothers with their young children in the back seat, they crash their cars and burn to death in the aftermath. They may survive the initial accident but then literally cook to death inside the burning vehicle. So sad, Major. So painful for the victims. So avoidable."

Silence.

"Are you still with me, Major? Are you paying attention?"

"I'm here, you sick son of a bitch."

"Good. You will ensure the airplane carrying the item of which we spoke never reaches your country. If you do not, well, let us just say I hope you have many photographs of your beautiful little family to keep their memory alive."

"I—"

"Do not think about alerting the authorities, either. We *will* get to your wife and child if you do not follow your instructions to the letter. Please believe that."

Silence.

"Do you believe that, Major?"

"Yes, God help me. I believe that."

"Then get started planning. You have a lot of work to do and very little time. The item is either already on base or will be soon. It won't be long before the plane carrying it will be lifting off, likely with the CIA operative as the sole passenger."

"Damn you."

"Oh, and Major? One more thing."

"What?"

"Good luck. And goodbye."

10

May 30, 1987
2:35 p.m.
Ramstein Air Base, West Germany

The back of the envelope was sweat-stained to an off brown from being plastered to Tracie's skin in the stifling heat of the East German dance club. The front, where was scrawled, "President Ronald Reagan," by Mikhail Gorbachev, if her handler was to be believed—and Tracie believed him—remained undisturbed.

After fighting her way out of the dance club, Tracie had snuck out of East Berlin uneventfully—it was never a problem if you had the right contacts—and driven as fast as she dared back to Ramstein Air Base in West Germany in a waiting CIA-supplied car.

By the time she arrived at Ramstein it was approaching six a.m. She napped, exhausted, in an empty apartment maintained just outside the base by the CIA. After just a few short hours of sleep she was awakened by telephone and advised that her flight to Andrews Air Force Base in Maryland would depart at eleven p.m.

Tracie showered and dressed, reveling in the luxury of a little time to herself and the added bonus of an unlimited hot water supply. In many of the locations she had worked as a CIA field operative there had been no water at all, much less hot water.

During her shower, Tracie placed Gorbachev's envelope atop the ceramic toilet tank cover, less than four feet from where she stood soaping and rinsing. Her assignment had been to retrieve the letter, spirit it out of East Germany, and then accompany it to Washington, never allowing it out of her sight until its delivery to the president, and that was what she intended to do.

She had slept with one hand curled around the letter, cradling it like a tiny baby. She slept fitfully, but then she always slept fitfully, awakened by the slightest hint of a sound, a disruption in the room's air currents, a barely perceptible noise outside her window. Her supersensitive sense of perception, even while asleep, had kept her alive in some of the most dangerous locations on the globe.

Tracie had performed missions in Asian and Middle Eastern countries where being female meant you had no rights, possessed no intrinsic value other than what the men around you were willing to bestow upon you. You could disappear without warning at any time and for any reason, and no one would ever question why.

The United States government would be no help, either, as her missions were almost always off the books and so highly sensitive that if she were captured, rather than fighting or negotiating for her release, the government would deny her very presence in country, all the way up the official channels.

This was the life of a CIA Directorate of Operations agent. It was Tracie Tanner's life, and a career she had never once regretted pursuing. It was a solitary, often lonely life, but as the daughter of a four-star U.S. Army general and a career State Department diplomat, Tracie had been groomed for it right from the start.

After graduating Brown University in Providence, Rhode Island, with a degree in linguistics, Tracie had been recruited into the ranks of the Central Intelligence Agency. She had trained for three grueling years, initially at The Farm and then in the field, under a crusty old badass veteran of a quarter-century of covert operations whose real name she still did not know.

Then she began working solo missions under her mentor and direct CIA supervisor, Winston Andrews. Despite her inability to share even the broadest of details about her career with her parents, she knew they were proud of her decision to devote her life to the cause of freedom and service to her country.

But right now, all Tracie cared about was the steaming hot water blasting out of the shower in the small apartment. She washed the sweat and grime of the mission off every inch of her body, then rinsed off and started again, scrubbing until she felt completely refreshed, regenerated and ready to begin the second half—the easy half—of her assignment. She would accompany Gorbachev's letter to the White House, bypassing all official and diplomatic channels before hand-delivering it to its recipient, President Ronald Reagan.

The mission would then end with an official debrief at Langley. Tracie hoped she might be fortunate enough to wrangle a few days off afterward to visit her folks in suburban D.C., but knew that was probably a pipe dream. Too many things were happening in too many hot spots around the globe for the agency to allow one of their most valuable assets to hang out like a normal twenty-seven year old single woman.

In any event, the rest of the trip should be a cakewalk. Tracie calculated the length of the flight and the time difference between West Germany and Washington, D.C. Eight hours in the air, more or less, and a six-hour time difference meant they would touch down at Andrews around 2:00 a.m. local time.

The 11:00 p.m. departure time was not exactly a typical flight schedule, but then Tracie had long ago adjusted to the unusual hours the job of a CIA spook entailed. After being advised of the critical nature of the mission, the Air Force would have needed time to prep an airplane and get a flight crew together.

Then the flight would depart. The time was irrelevant to that schedule.

Tracie stepped directly under the shower nozzle, rinsing shampoo from her luxurious mane of red hair, enjoying the warmth of the water, always keeping one eye on the innocent-looking envelope propped against the wall on the toilet tank.

Finally, reluctantly, she twisted the faucets, sighing as the blast of water slowed to a trickle and then disappeared entirely. She stepped from the shower, dried off and dressed, and then quickly blow-dried her hair.

With the extravagance of the hot shower out of the way, she wandered the apartment, the time passing slowly as she waited to leave Europe behind.

*   *   *

May 30, 1987
10:10 p.m.
Ramstein Air Base

Tracie woke with a start and checked her watch. She had drifted off to sleep stretched out on a small couch while watching a soccer match on the apartment's black and white television, and now feared she may have slept through her flight.

Ten-ten. *Shit.* She'd have to hurry but would probably make it. If she timed it right, she might even manage coffee. Dinner she could take or leave, but the thought of departing Ramstein for a long flight to the States without an invigorating jolt of caffeine was unacceptable.

She threw her clothing into a small canvas bag—traveling light was second nature to Tracie Tanner after seven years of CIA service—and slid Mikhail Gorbachev's letter into the interior breast pocket of her light jacket. Then she rushed out of the apartment, jumped into her car, and drove onto the base.

She dumped the CIA car outside a small commissary adjacent to the airfield, hid the keys under the front seat, and hustled inside. She passed a pair of young airmen who made no attempt to hide their admiration of her running figure.

She ignored them. They didn't have coffee. Besides, she had long since gotten accustomed to men staring at her. Also ogling her, leering at her and propositioning her.

Tracie checked her watch. Twenty-five minutes until her scheduled departure. She choked down her coffee. It was scalding hot and almost undrinkably strong, just the way she liked it. Then she grabbed her bag, checked for her precious cargo—the letter was still there—and then double-timed to the airfield. Someone would retrieve the car later.

Tracie had been instructed to check in at Hangar Three, and now she slowed to a walk about a hundred feet from the door, crossing the tarmac at precisely 10:55 p.m.

Outside the hangar, a gigantic green U.S. Air Force B-52 tow-ered above her, the eight engine high-wing jet appearing almost impossibly large. It had to be close to two hundred feet from wingtip to wingtip, and the fuselage soared high above like some kind of fabricated metal dinosaur. The notion of the huge hunk of metal getting airborne, much less staying that way and flying all the way to the United States seemed outlandish, some kind of magic trick or optical illusion.

Tracie had logged endless hours aboard dozens of different air-craft, from medevac helicopters to Boeing 747s during her tenure as a CIA covert ops specialist, but had never been aboard a B-52. The sheer enormity of the aircraft was staggering.

From where she stood, it looked like every other airplane she'd ever flown aboard could fit inside this behemoth. The wings thrust-ing outward from the top of the fuselage seemed to go on forever, swept back and hanging down slightly, as if the weight of the eight jet engines hanging in clusters of two was simply more than they could bear. The fuselage itself stretched off into the distance; to Tracie's eye it appeared nearly as long as the wingspan's width.

She froze in place, marveling at the engineering miracle perched atop its tiny-looking wheels. She could feel her jaw hanging open and closed it, embarrassed. She felt like a country bumpkin on her first visit to the big city.

Standing directly in front of—and far below—the nose of the huge aircraft was an officer, probably late-thirties, handsome in a grizzled, seen-it-all way. He had obviously been awaiting her arrival, and he smiled at her reaction to the B-52.

"May I see your ID, ma'am?" he asked.

Tracie handed it over, shaking her head in mute admiration of the aircraft.

The officer said, "We get that a lot from people who've never been up close to a BUFF before. It's pretty impressive, isn't it?"

"That's an understatement," Tracie answered.

The officer handed Tracie's ID back and said, "I'm Major Stan Wilczynski, and I'll be Pilot in Command for tonight's flight. I'll introduce you to the rest of the crew shortly."

She returned the major's smile. "I'll bite," she said. "What's BUFF?"

Other than you, she wanted to add, wondering how long it had been since she had enjoyed any male companionship outside of official duty status and realizing she couldn't remember. She kept her remark to herself, though, noting the major's wedding ring.

He chuckled. "BUFF's our nickname for the B-52. Stands for 'Big Ugly Fat Fuckers.' And they are all of that, but these babies have served with distinction for a quarter-century, with plenty more years to come. Some say the new B-1 will make the BUFF obsolete, but I'll believe that when I see it."

Tracie nodded, noting the reverence in the pilot's voice as he talked about the plane. "How long have you flown the B-52, Major?"

"It's Stan to my friends, Miss Tanner. And I've been involved with these Big Ugly Fuckers almost since my first day in the Air Force. Sometimes it feels like I've spent my whole life inside one of these beasts. Can't imagine a better way to serve my country, to be honest."

Tracie grinned. The man's enthusiasm was infectious, and went a long way toward breaking down her caution, a trait she came by naturally and one that had served her well over the course of her seven-year CIA career. But there was no need for it now; she was clearly among friends.

"Anyway," Wilczynski continued, "I've bored you long enough. I just can't help bragging when the subject is my baby."

He gestured affectionately toward the aircraft's nose. "Whaddaya say we climb aboard and get ready to leave this continent behind?" The major turned and indicated a metal ladder hanging from an open hatch in the bottom of the aircraft.

"I'm not bored at all," Tracie answered, starting up the ladder. "I love hearing a professional discuss his passion."

Major Wilczynski paused. "You know, I've never really thought about it in those terms before, but you're right, I do have a passion for these old birds."

He started up the ladder behind Tracie and they disappeared into the B-52.

11

May 30, 1987
10:50 p.m.
Ramstein Air Base

A maze of equipment ran the otherwise empty length of the air-craft's interior, wires and cables seemingly placed in random loca-tions, performing tasks Tracie could not imagine. The flight deck featured two seats placed side by side, each with a yoke where the steering wheel would be in a car. Avionics clogged the area below the windshield and the console between the two seats, gauges and dials and switches and levers that somehow allowed the flight crew to manage the almost mystical task of lifting the B-52 into the air and keeping it there.

She gazed into the empty cockpit, marveling at the engineer-ing prowess involved in the production of such a complex aircraft. Tracie felt as though she would rattle around the vast interior of the aircraft like an elderly widow inside an otherwise deserted mansion, regardless of how many passengers were aboard. The BUFF made her feel tiny and insignificant.

She turned left, away from the flight deck and toward the rear of the aircraft, and ran straight into Major Wilczynski. His body was solid and muscled, the physique of a man who welcomed physical labor.

She stumbled and he grabbed her arm, and she chuckled. "Sorry about that," she said, not really sorry at all, again reminded how long it had been since she'd spent any time with a man not involved in some way in the espionage game.

Any personal time.

"Not a problem," Wilczynski answered. "I apologize for sneaking up on you. I just wanted to take a moment to introduce you to the rest of the team."

He nodded to a pair of airmen who had climbed up the ladder and now stood next to them. "This isn't my standard flight crew. We're mixing and matching personnel thanks to other commitments and the unscheduled nature of the trip. Not that we mind, of course. If there's one thing an airman loves to do, it's fly.

"Anyway, our copilot for today's mission is Major Tom Mitchell. Tom needs to get stateside as quickly as you do, thanks unfortunately to a family emergency, but I can tell you he's a solid flyer."

A pasty-faced officer, doughy and lumpy, stuck his hand out without a word and Tracie shook it. Mitchell's skin felt hot and sweaty and he seemed preoccupied to Tracie, who in her work as a CIA field operative was accustomed to sizing up strangers immediately. Often the success of a mission—not to mention whether or not she would continue breathing—came down to her ability to effectively gauge who could be trusted and who could not.

And this man set off alarm bells.

Mitchell's eyes shifted continuously, like they were following invisible ping pong balls bouncing back and forth across an invisible table. He barely met her eyes before sliding his gaze restlessly over her left shoulder. He shuffled his feet and rocked side to side like he would rather be anyplace else in the world but here.

"It's nice to meet you," Tracie said, attempting to prolong the handshake for a moment and failing, as he withdrew his moist grip from hers almost immediately.

Major Mitchell said nothing. He smiled reluctantly, the gesture making him look more ill than welcoming, and then turned and walked away. He brushed past Tracie and Major Wilczynski and disappeared onto the flight deck. Wilczynski watched Mitchell go, his eyebrows raised in mild surprise.

He shook his head and returned his attention to Tracie. "And this young man," he indicated an officer standing next to the spot Mitchell had just vacated, "is Captain Nathan Berenger. Nathan is a long-time member of my crew, having served as our navigator for almost five years. I can guarantee that with Nathan on the job, we won't have to worry about getting lost on our way back to Andrews."

Captain Berenger offered his hand, as Mitchell had done before him. In contrast to the copilot, however, Tracie felt a welcoming vibe emanating from the navigator that was almost as strong as Wilczynski's.

She took his hand and a smile creased his face. "Try to ignore Tom," he said softly. "I don't know what's bugging him—he's been pretty preoccupied lately. Family troubles or something, I guess. But Major Wilczynski and I will take good care of you."

He raised his voice to a normal level. "It's a pleasure to meet you, and if you need anything, you let me know."

Berenger's grip felt as strong and competent as Mitchell's had weak and indecisive. Tracie returned the captain's handshake—and his smile—enthusiastically. Something was off about Major Mitchell, that was for sure, but these two crewmembers struck her as competent to a T. Besides, she was standing in the middle of a U.S. air base, aboard an Air Force jet, surrounded by a professional military flight crew. What could possibly go wrong?

"Now, if you'll excuse me," Berenger said, "I've got to get busy doing all the real work so this guy," he nodded at Major Wiczynski, "can play aviator and soak up all the glory on today's flight." He winked at Tracie and clambered down a metal stairway to the navigator's position below the flight deck.

"Berenger's the best," Wilczynski told her. "On a typical combat mission we would feature at least two more crew members, a bombardier and an electronic warfare officer. Since this is a noncombat mission, it's been determined that these positions can remain unfilled for tonight. The rest of my guys are enjoying a little R and R."

"I'm sorry to add to your workload and take you away from your own R and R," Tracie said. "I certainly didn't need *this* much transportation." She opened her arms, indicating the gigantic interior of the B-52.

Wilczynski laughed. "No apology is necessary, believe me. In fact, I should be thanking you. I need to maintain currency in this behemoth, so instead of commanding a boring training mission next week, I get to fly across the pond and make a quick trip home.

"Besides," he added conspiratorially. "Like I said before, if there's one thing we all love to do, it's drink."

The comment took Tracie by surprise and she laughed.

"But since we can't be doing that, the next-best thing for us is flying. We love it, and believe me when I say this is not work for us."

He lowered his voice as Captain Berenger had done. "Even for Major Sourpuss in there," he said with a grin.

"Now that the introductions are over," he said, "feel free to check out the rest of the aircraft. Try not to get lost back there, though. I'll let you know when it's time to buckle in for departure."

12

May 30, 1987
10:30 p.m. EST
Somewhere over the North Atlantic

The B-52 floated across the sky nearly five miles above the vast, empty expanse of the Atlantic Ocean. The air was smooth, with only the occasional light bump of turbulence—like a city bus driving over a pothole—and the roar of the eight jet engines had been muted in level flight to a steady thrumming that was felt more than heard inside the cabin.

At the controls, Tom Mitchell felt as though his stomach might launch its contents all over the instruments at any moment. The gentle rocking of a large aircraft in flight had never affected him in this way before. But then he had never been about to murder four people—including himself—before, either.

He could barely think straight. He was a traitor, although no one would ever discover that devastating fact. Crashing the BUFF into the Atlantic after killing everyone on board would eliminate any evidence of foul play, satisfying the Russians and sparing his family. There was no radar coverage hundreds of miles off the United States coast, so by the time air traffic control realized the B-52 was missing, most of the aircraft and associated crash debris would already be beneath the water's surface, well on its way to the ocean floor.

Add to that the fact that the area to be searched would be

massive, thousands of square miles of uninterrupted watery desolation, and Tom Mitchell knew the odds of his treachery being discovered were astronomically long.

So that was the plan. Crash the airplane into the ocean.

The problem was that Tom was having trouble executing the plan, not to mention everyone on board the aircraft. It wasn't that he was afraid of dying, not exactly. Anyone making a career out of military service eventually found a way to make peace with the possibility of sudden violent death. Not to do so was to risk a mental breakdown. Tom had long ago accepted that concept.

Murdering three innocent people, though, had never been part of those calculations. There was a world of difference between being blown out of the sky by an enemy missile during a bombing run and placing his service weapon inside his mouth and pulling the trigger after first shooting everyone else aboard an airplane. So he delayed the inevitable, stomach jumping and rolling while he desperately searched for another way out.

Working with the KGB had been simple at first. A Godsend. He had raked in some serious cash—an extra two grand a month was a lot of money for a United States Air Force officer—in return for passing along what often seemed like relatively harmless intel: aircraft specs or division personnel rosters or armament information.

Tom wasn't stupid; he had known he was crossing a line from which he could never return when he relayed that first bit of information to the Russians, but keeping a German mistress was damned expensive.

Besides, serving in the USAF was boring as hell. Acting as a go-between—he refused to consider himself a spy, although late at night, unable to sleep, tossing and turning and staring at the ceiling, he had to acknowledge that was exactly what he was— brought a bit of excitement into his life.

Last night's phone call had hammered home with crystal clarity the horrible mistake he'd made. He had been tempted to tell Boris Badanov with the thick Russian accent to go to hell. He'd done exactly that, in fact. The KGB could come and take him out if they wanted. He'd probably never see it coming and death would at least be a way out of the corner into which he'd painted himself.

But the threat to his family had changed everything. Tom hadn't even realized the Russians knew he was married until last night. He realized now how foolishly blind he had been—of *course* the KGB would learn all they could about their new asset, of *course* they would keep that information close to the vest, pulling it out only when needed—but Roberta and Sarah were thousands of miles away, safe and anonymous in Herndon, Virginia, well out of range of the KGB.

Or so he had thought.

How wrong he'd been.

Kopalev knew way too much about his family, tossing the information out casually, like it was no big deal. Tom's blood had frozen in his veins last night with Kopalev's threat to snuff out the lives of his wife and child, and in the most agonizing manner possible.

He thought hard, his eyes alternating between the B-52's instruments and the endless blaze of impossibly bright stars outside the windscreen. Maybe he could question the CIA agent currently dozing in the rear of the aircraft. No one had confirmed she was CIA, but then, no one had needed to. It was obvious. A civilian woman, appearing at Ramstein out of nowhere carrying Top Secret paperwork with instructions from the highest levels of government for a priority lift across the pond?

CIA.

And of course Kopalev had name-dropped the CIA connection quite effectively.

As a CIA spook, the woman might be able to use her connections to protect Tom's family. But she certainly would ask the obvious question of *why* the family of an Air Force nobody was in need of protection from the KGB, a question he could not answer. He would be forced to kill her anyway.

Tom shook his head and cursed under his breath. He knew Wilczynski was watching him curiously. He didn't care. He was fucked. He was well and truly fucked.

As an Air Force pilot, Tom Mitchell was intimately familiar with the concept of parallax view, which stated that the angle at which objects are viewed will determine how they appear to the viewer. Parallax view was one reason why a good pilot learned early in his career to rely on his instruments while flying, even on a clear, bright, sunny day.

Eyes could be fooled. Instruments could not.

The concept of parallax view applied to other situations as well. Look at a scenario from one angle and it can appear completely different than when viewed from another. But Tom realized this situation was the exception. No parallax view in the world could change one simple fact: he was going to have to do as the KGB had ordered, or sentence his own wife and child to death.

And that he could not do.

So the decision was easy, even if executing that decision was not. And Tom knew he was running out of time. Soon the giant B-52 would be approaching land, flying over U.S. soil down the east coast to Andrews Air Force Base, and while he could still carry out the murders, crashing the jet onto the U.S. mainland would never satisfy the KGB. There would be no way to guarantee the item they wanted destroyed had actually *been* destroyed, and his family would remain at risk.

So he had to do it soon.

The clock was ticking.

13

May 30, 1987
11:15 p.m.
Atlantic Ocean, 150 miles off the coast of Maine

Tracie tried with little success to catch a few Zs in the minimally upholstered seat. It was bolted to the side wall of the B-52, which had probably flown hundreds, if not thousands, of missions. The seatback was rickety and the vinyl upholstery worn and cracked.

The ride was free, though, and complaining would accomplish nothing, so Tracie stretched out as well as she could and dozed, unable to manage a deep sleep. Something was bothering her.

The sense of unease she had felt upon meeting Major Tom Mitchell back at Ramstein had only intensified after departure. Several times during the first couple of hours of the flight, Mitchell had stepped back from the flight deck and observed her as she pretended to sleep, her eyes barely open under her thick eyelashes. In each instance he had approached stealthily and stood off to the side in an attempt to remain unobserved.

He was sizing her up, that much was obvious. The question was why?

After the first instance Tracie had debated opening her eyes and confronting him directly, but her instincts told her that would be a mistake, and she had learned years ago not to question those instincts. They were the subconscious mind's way of protecting its owner when the conscious mind could not quite wrap itself around a problem.

Paying attention to a nagging feeling had saved her life on more than one occasion, and Tracie was no more likely to ignore her instincts than she was to jump out of this B-52 with no parachute.

Mitchell hadn't appeared at all over the last couple of hours, though, which meant either his curiosity had been satisfied, or he was flying this leg of the trip and couldn't leave the flight deck. She guessed it was the latter—his ongoing nervousness and desperation were clear to her. The man was clearly operating under some serious stress.

She opened her eyes a slit, observing her surroundings without revealing her wakefulness. All was quiet in the cargo area. Mitchell was still nowhere to be seen.

Tracie stretched and wondered how close the big aircraft was to the North American shoreline. She had flown from the U.S. to Europe and vice-versa many times and had developed an innate sense of the trip's timing. They had to be getting close.

She was considering unbuckling her lap restraint and wandering up to the cockpit when a sharp popping noise erupted from the front of the aircraft. Then another. It sounded like exploding firecrackers.

Except they weren't firecrackers.

Someone was shooting on the flight deck.

A voice shouted in surprise and alarm. The B-52 yawed violently to the left and began a steep dive. Tracie felt her body pull against the seat restraints and she fumbled with the buckle. Her fingers scrabbled for the metal release and missed.

She tried again and managed to lift the buckle but the straps would not budge.

She was trapped. Her heart was racing and she felt a rising sense of panic. She had just seconds to get to the front of the airplane or likely become a victim. She yanked on the seat belt release again as the sound of the jet engines screamed in her ears, the airplane still in a diving left turn.

Then she realized why she could not escape her seat. The tension of her body pulling against the restraint would not allow the mechanism to unlock. She reached for a handhold built into the side of the plane and pulled hard, grabbing the metal seatbelt release with her other hand and yanking upward.

It gave. She was free.

She tumbled into the aisle, sliding into the fuselage and smashing her shoulder against an aluminum duct, denting the ductwork and sending a sharp pain zinging through her neck. Then the airplane leveled off and she fell to the floor.

Tracie slipped her Beretta out of her shoulder rig and sprinted toward the cockpit as a third shot ripped through the aircraft.

The scene on the flight deck was chaotic and gruesome. Navigator Nathan Berenger lay on the floor, partially blocking the narrow entrance to the cockpit. Most of his skull had been blown off, his head barely recognizable as human. Blood had splattered everywhere, as had bits of bone matter and human tissue.

Tracie's half-second glance at Berenger told her all she needed to know. The navigator was dead or soon would be, beyond help for certain.

At the controls, Major Stan Wilczynski was struggling with Tom Mitchell. Wilczynski had been shot at least once and was bleeding heavily from a wound in his shoulder, but he fought grimly for control of Mitchell's gun. He had somehow managed to level off the diving B-52 while locked in a life-and-death battle with his fellow crewmember and was now screaming obscenities at him.

Tracie dropped to one knee and sighted down the barrel of the Beretta.

"Drop it!" she screamed, knowing Mitchell would never do so but hoping to at least distract the crazed officer. She didn't dare shoot because the angle was wrong—there was every possibility the slug would strike Wilczynski and she would end up killing the man she was trying to save.

Mitchell glanced up in wild-eyed surprise at Tracie and Wilczynski took advantage of the opening, pounding a fist into the side of Mitchell's face. Tracie heard bones crack and wondered as she waited for Mitchell to fall whether the broken bones were in Wilczynski's hand or Mitchell's face. Or both.

But Mitchell didn't fall, and he didn't drop the gun. He hung on, grappling with Wilczynski, the men jockeying for the upper hand. The B-52 again began yawing to the left as one of the fighting men jostled the yoke.

"Dammit," she muttered under her breath, itching to put Mitchell down but still without a clear shot.

Then the situation went from desperate to out of control. Mitchell released his grip on Wilczynksi, taking another fist to the face but slugging Wilczynski in his wounded shoulder with the butt of his gun.

Wilczynksi's eyes rolled up in his head and he slumped back, but before Tracie could squeeze off a shot, Mitchell pulled the trigger. The bullet caught Stan Wilczynski in the side of the head and knocked him sideways, blood misting.

Tracie didn't hesitate. She fired, and Mitchell slumped against the instrument panel like a rag doll. She fired again and the second shot hit home as well. She fired a third time and Mitchell crumpled to the floor.

She kept her gun trained on him, breathing heavily, certain Mitchell was dead.

It appeared everyone else was dead inside one of the most complex aircraft ever manufactured.

And Tracie didn't know how to fly.

14

May 30, 1987
11:22 p.m.
Atlantic Ocean, 100 miles off the coast of Maine

Stan Wilczynski had a headache. A bad one. It wasn't like waking up after having a few too many cold ones at the OC, and it wasn't like the dull throb at the back of the skull he was prone to getting when overtired. It was more like someone had taken a ballpeen hammer to the side of his head.

He groaned and tried to roll over. Maybe if he could sleep a little longer the damned headache would go away. But he couldn't turn onto his side. He was stuck. Must have gotten twisted up in the sheets.

He opened his eyes reluctantly and the pain intensified, a battering ram blasting through his head, building and building until he was afraid his skull would explode.

He blinked hard and his blurry vision doubled and tripled, and it occurred to him with sudden, terrifying clarity that he was dying. He closed his eyes again, willing the pain to go away. It lessened slightly.

Thank God for small favors.

Then he realized someone was talking to him. It was a woman's voice but it was not a voice he recognized. The voice was tense, worried, speaking to him calmly but insistently. Even with the pain ripping through his head, Stan could sense the intensity

behind the words. He kept his eyes closed and concentrated hard.
"Stay with me," the voice was saying. "You can do it. Stay with me and breathe."

And Stan remembered.

He wasn't in bed at all. He was in the cockpit of a B-52. He had been flying that female CIA agent back to Andrews Air Force Base from West Germany when Tom Mitchell had gone stark, raving mad, murdering poor Nate Berenger and then shooting Stan. He remembered struggling with Mitchell for his weapon. He couldn't remember how the struggle had ended, although it seemed suddenly clear he'd lost it.

Their passenger must have subdued Mitchell and was now trying to save his life. He didn't want to open his eyes, having no desire to re-experience the agony associated with doing so a moment ago, but he knew he had to. He screwed up his courage, praying for strength. Then he blinked his eyes open, doing his best to ignore the accompanying flash of pain.

The CIA agent—he tried to recall her name and couldn't—knelt over him, holding her blood-soaked jacket to his head. Stan knew the blood was his and tried to ignore it. He felt light-headed, weak and disoriented. He focused on his rescuer and her stunning red hair, and after a moment three blurry CIA agents became two and then, somewhat miraculously, one.

She was still talking to him, calm and encouraging, but her ashen face gave away her concern. "Welcome back to the land of the living," she said tightly.

"Great to be here," he mumbled. "But I don't know how long I'll be able to stay."

He felt woozy and his stomach pitched and rolled. "How bad is it?"

"I'm not going to lie to you," she said. "It's bad. I'm not even sure how you're conscious right now. Mitchell's second shot struck you in the head."

"Who's flying the plane?" he asked, struggling to remain conscious.

"No one. I managed to straighten the wings and return us more or less to a straight flight path, but we're slowly descending." Her voice sounded thin and reedy and she was clearly fighting panic.

"Have you radioed for help?"

"Not yet. I've been a little preoccupied."

"Oh. Right. Sorry about that." Stan nodded and instantly regretted doing so. The pain in his head returned full-force. The battering ram had taken a break and a sledgehammer took its place.

He closed his eyes and concentrated on settling his upset stomach. He knew if he tossed his cookies, the pain would explode and he would probably lose consciousness again. And if that happened, he doubted he would ever reawaken.

Stan forced himself to focus. The lure of sleep was almost overwhelming. He wanted nothing more than to let go and leave this nightmare behind. But it was obvious the CIA agent wasn't a pilot and would never be able to land the B-52 herself. It was impressive that she had managed to straighten the wings—the BUFF must have been in the slightest of rolls—but after that she had clearly run out of ideas.

He opened his eyes. The pain rolled back in like a massive tsunami but stopped just short of unmanageable.

"Let's get this big tin can on the ground, shall we?" His vision blurred and then cleared. More or less.

She sighed, her relief palpable. "Absolutely. What do I do first?"

"You get the hell out of my way and let me fly."

15

May 30, 1987
11:27 p.m.
Atlantic Ocean, 70 miles off the coast of Maine

The badly injured pilot was out of his seat, crumpled on the floor, and Tracie knew sliding him upright would be a risky proposition. He had already lost a lot of blood by the time she reached him, and she had been forced to pick one of his two bullet wounds to apply pressure to. The choice had been easy—the head trumped every other body part in terms of importance—but blood continued to ooze sluggishly from his shoulder wound whenever he moved.

She would have to let go of the jacket she was pressing against Wilczynski's skull in order to lift him. He was not a huge man, but she was much smaller, and although she had no doubt she could lift him, she knew she could never manage it one-handed.

The same thought seemed to occur to Wilczynski and he said, "Wait. We have a first-aid kit aboard the aircraft. I think you should bandage my head wound before we do anything else."

Tracie felt the steady descent of the B-52 and her panic began rising again, threatening to overwhelm her. "How much time do we have before we hit the water?"

"It depends on how much altitude we've lost. You'll have to check the altimeter."

She craned her head but couldn't read the instruments from her position, crouched over Wilczynski's seat. "You're going to have to maintain pressure on the jacket yourself for a second. Can you do that?"

"Yes," Wilczynski answered, although Tracie questioned the accuracy of his response. He was clearly trying to avoid any movement of his head and he looked pale and weak.

"Okay. I'll go as quickly as I can." She waited until the injured pilot had lifted his hands, then removed hers and helped him position his in what she hoped was the best location. The amount of blood soaking the jacket was frightening.

When he indicated he was ready, she stood and scanned the instruments, amazed at the sheer number of gauges, dials and switches.

Finally she found the altimeter. "Twenty-three thousand, five hundred feet," she said.

"And how long has the plane been flying itself?"

Tracie thought hard. It seemed like forever, but in reality was probably not long at all. "Ninety seconds," she guessed.

"Okay," he answered and then was silent for a moment. "We have maybe five minutes before we go down."

Shit. At the rate the color continued to drain out of Wilczynski's face, Tracie wondered if he would last another five minutes.

"Where's the first aid kit?" she asked, hyper-conscious of the seconds ticking away.

He pointed to a metal box clipped to the fuselage behind what had been Mitchell's seat, then quickly returned the hand to his head. Tracie leaned over the dead bodies of Mitchell and Berenger, unclipped the kit, and then returned to Wilczynski's side. She opened the box and rummaged inside, removing a roll of gauze.

She gently removed Wilczynski's hands and pulled the jacket away from the head wound. Blood surged out of a ragged, splintered hole where the side of his skull used to be. For the second time since discovering Wilczynski alive, she wondered how in the hell he was still breathing.

And how long it would be before he stopped.

She anchored one end of the gauze on the back of his head with her left hand and began unrolling it, wrapping it expertly around and around with her right, moving as quickly as she dared. She finished wrapping Wilczynski's head and secured the bandage, then examined her handiwork quickly, anxious to move the pilot. The portion of the gauze located directly over his injury had already begun darkening, changing from a pristine white to a frightening maroon, but the patch job looked secure enough, at least for now.

She nodded and forced a smile. "There. Good as new."

Wilczynski smiled and the effect was ghastly. A thick smear of blood coated the side of his face and his teeth had been stained a blackish-red from all the blood he had swallowed.

"I appreciate the lie." He closed his eyes and Tracie knew he was steeling himself for the pain to come.

After a moment he opened his eyes again. "Let's take our seats and get this thing on the ground."

Tracie nodded and knelt over his prone body, straddling his legs. She slipped her hands under his armpits. His flight suit was sticky with blood. She eased the pilot's body up and forward, until she had gotten him into a sitting position on the floor, legs straight out in front of him, next to his seat. He had maintained a grim silence through all the jostling, despite the pain he must be feeling.

This is one tough bastard, she thought. *But things are about to get a lot worse.* She looked him in the eye and could see he knew.

"Are you ready?" she asked quietly.

He nodded.

She hooked her arms under his armpits at the elbow, locking the two of them in an awkward embrace. Then she struggled to a kneeling position and began rising, her legs screaming in protest as they took the brunt of the two hundred pound man's dead weight.

When she had lifted his body to where his butt was level with the flight seat, Tracie took a half-step left and then dropped the pilot as gently as she could into the seat.

He groaned and his eyes rolled up into his head and he began sliding back toward Tracie. She used her small body to brace his larger one in the seat and then buckled him into his harness.

Wilczynski's eyes were closed and his pallor had turned a sickly grey. A thin sheen of sweat coated his features, mixing with the drying blood and forming a hideous Halloween mask. His head slumped against his chest.

Tracie feared he was dead. She placed two fingers lightly against his neck, just under his right ear, and felt for the carotid artery. The pulse was steady but faint. Wilczynski was still alive.

For now.

Stay with me, please. I can't fly this thing on my own.

Tracie wondered how fast they were descending. She pictured the Atlantic Ocean, vast and empty, sliding beneath the aircraft, waiting to swallow them whole if they didn't begin climbing soon. The darkness outside the windscreen was immense, the blackness unbroken. There was no way to tell how close they were to the water; it could be twenty feet or twenty thousand.

She fought against the panic. Lifted her head and glanced at the altimeter. Two thousand feet. And dropping.

She closed her eyes. *Take a deep breath. Steady yourself. Do what you have to do.* That meant trying to reawaken Major Wilczynski. He had been lucid prior to losing consciousness. If she could rouse him, maybe he could fly the B-52.

She hoped.

Another look at the altimeter. Twelve hundred feet. Descending.

She bent and slapped Wilczynski's face lightly, more of a light open-palmed tap than an actual slap. Two taps to the right cheek and then two to the left. Right, left, one more on each side.

Wilczynski stirred and muttered but his eyes remained closed.

Nine hundred feet.

She tried again, this time increasing the force of the blow and speaking loudly. "Stan, wake up! Stan, we're dropping into the ocean. You need to wake up and fly this plane!"

More mumbling and his eyes fluttered, but they were vacant and unfocused.

Five hundred feet.

Last try. She grabbed his good shoulder and shook him, not wanting to risk worsening his head injury but not knowing what else to do. "Stan, listen to me, we're going to crash if you don't wake up right now! Stan!"

This time his eyes fluttered and remained open for a couple of seconds. "That's it," she encouraged. "Stay with me, Stan."

Then his eyes rolled up into his head again and he was gone.

Two hundred feet.

It was too late. They were going to drop right onto the surface of the Atlantic Ocean, where the giant B-52 would be ripped to shreds by the resistance of the water.

Tracie cursed and leapt into the right seat, the one most recently occupied by Tom Mitchell. She scanned the instruments desperately, trying to remember what she had seen pilots do in the past. Increase power with the throttles. Raise the nose of the aircraft with the yoke. Do something with the flaps—she couldn't remember what. Raise them? Lower them? *Goddammit!*

Fifty feet.

Tracie reached for the throttle with a shaking hand. She would shove the throttle forward and raise the B-52's nose and hope for the best. She would not go down without a fight.

She placed her hand on the lever and was surprised to feel not the cold metal of the throttle but the warmth of another human hand. She turned in surprise and saw Stan Wilczynski staring back at her, his face drawn and grey, his lips trembling from the exertion of staying conscious, but his eyes clear and lucid.

"Get your hands off my airplane," he said.

16

May 30, 1987
11:32 p.m.
Atlantic Ocean, 35 miles off the coast of Maine

Wilczynski added power and placed the aircraft in a shallow climb, moving slowly and deliberately.

Tracie guessed he was mentally reviewing a checklist, although she doubted his Air Force training had included flying a B-52 with part of his skull blown off and the rest of the crew lying dead at his feet. His face was ashen and his lips were white. She wondered how long it would take for him to pass out again; it seemed inevitable.

"Fifty feet," he said thickly. "That's what I call cutting it close."

"Too close for comfort," Tracie agreed, her hands shaking.

"I need you to call air traffic control and let them know we're in trouble." Wilczynski lifted the radio mike off a metal stand and handed it to her.

"Who will I be talking to?"

"Everybody." The pilot tuned the radio to VHF frequency 121.5. "This is the emergency frequency. Every ATC facility monitors it. Everyone within range of our transmission will hear it. In a few seconds we'll have more help than we know what to do with. Just make a Mayday transmission. Identify us to the controllers as Bulldog 14."

Wilczynski closed his eyes and slumped in his seat and Tracie feared he had lost consciousness again, but a moment later he reopened them and began adjusting power settings.

Tracie keyed the mike. "Mayday, mayday. This is Bulldog 14 with an emergency situation."

The response was immediate. The radio crackled to life. "Bulldog 14, this is Boston Center, we've been looking for you. You missed checking in at a compulsory reporting point. What's the nature of your emergency?"

Tracie looked at Major Wilczynski. "What do I tell them?"

"Tell them the rest of the crew is incapacitated and we need a vector direct to Bangor International Airport. It was a SAC base in World War II and it's the closest airport with a runway long enough to land this beast on."

Tracie relayed the message and the controller said, "Roger that, Bulldog 14. Radar contact seven-zero miles northeast of the Bangor Airport. Cleared to Bangor via radar vectors. Fly heading two-five-zero, climb and maintain one-six thousand. Bangor altimeter two-nine-eight-seven."

"You get all that?" she asked Wilczynski. He nodded.

"Roger," she said into the mike.

"What assistance will you need when you land?" the controller asked, and Wilczynski said, "Tell them we'll need ambulances and the crash crew standing by. We'll need everything they've got."

Tracie relayed the message and as the B-52 gained altitude, climbing steadily and reassuringly, she said, "Bangor? As in Maine? Isn't that city tiny?"

"The city is small, yes, but the airport is huge. It's the former Dow Air Force Base, and although they only have one runway now, it's mammoth. Eleven thousand feet, with a one thousand foot overrun at each end. That's almost two-and-a-half miles of pavement for us to land on, and the way I feel right now, we'll probably need every last inch of it."

Tracie fingered the letter to President Reagan. She had removed it from her jacket and placed it in the back pocket of her trousers before using the jacket to stanch the blood flowing from Wilczynski's head wound. The envelope was flecked with spatters of blood but otherwise appeared undamaged.

The aircraft—and thus the letter—seemed to be out of danger, at least for the moment, but Tracie knew the odds of Major Mitchell's sudden deadly rampage being unrelated to the secret communiqué from Soviet leader Mikhail Gorbachev were astronomical. Those kinds of coincidences just didn't happen.

"Uh, isn't there a military base we could divert to? Wouldn't that be more secure?" She recognized the lack of logic inherent in the question. After all, *this* flight had originated from a United States military base and had been manned entirely by U.S. military personnel, and they had still nearly ended up in the Atlantic Ocean after a bloodbath inside the plane. If the attack was the result of someone trying to prevent delivery of that communiqué, that someone's influence was obviously far reaching. And deadly.

Tracie knew all that, and she knew landing at a military base might not make any difference. She didn't care. It had to be safer than landing unprotected at a civilian airport.

Her question became moot, though, with Wilczynski's answer. "Well, there is Loring Air Force Base in northern Maine. It's a SAC base and it's got plenty of runway. Problem is it's in the wrong direction if you're trying to get to Andrews, and it's farther away from our current position than Bangor. And that's why I don't want to divert there: I don't know how much longer I can stay conscious. The way I feel right now, our best bet is to get this Big Ugly Fat Fucker on the ground ASAP."

Tracie knew the flight commander was right. She had no way of ascertaining the extent of his injuries, but having seen the gaping head wound, with the splintered skull bones and massive blood loss, she realized his actions were nothing short of heroic.

"Bangor it is, then," she said.

* * *

May 30, 1987
11:49 p.m.
Bangor, Maine

Runway 17 at Bangor International Airport stretched out in front of the B-52 like a ribbon, visible to Tracie on this moonlit night even from more than twenty miles away. The weather was clear, but controllers at Bangor Tower had lit the airport up like a Christmas tree. The approach lights glowed and the sequenced flashers stabbed through the night, an insistent finger of light pointing toward the approach end of the runway.

In the few minutes since Major Wilczynski had regained control of the aircraft, the flight had proceeded smoothly but his condition seemed to deteriorate steadily. Blood continued to soak the bandage wrapped around his head and now it seeped through the gauze and ran slowly down the side of his face, disappearing under the collar of his jumpsuit. He had stopped talking and seemed to be focusing all his energy on landing the plane.

He moaned softly and his head bobbed onto his chest before bouncing back up sluggishly. He wavered in his seat.

"Hang in there, Stan," Tracie said. She squeezed his hand and he nodded weakly.

The B-52 turned onto a long final approach, wobbling unsteadily as Wilczynski struggle to maintain control. He had asked for at least a fifteen mile straight-in, explaining to Tracie that although the goal was to get on the ground as quickly as possible, in his current condition he didn't trust his ability to get the aircraft stabilized if they turned any closer than that.

Through the windscreen she could see flashing emergency lights lining the runway on the side closest the control tower. At least one rescue vehicle had been placed at each taxiway intersection. Tracie assumed it was to provide for the quickest response no matter where along the two-mile-long stretch of pavement they landed.

Or where they crashed.

The wings rocked and the aircraft shuddered, the runway sliding from left to right and then back again as Tracie watched anxiously. Wilczynski was struggling to keep the B-52 lined up with the runway centerline. He shook his head and cursed and grabbed for the microphone.

"Wind check," he demanded, and the controller's response was almost instantaneous.

"Wind two-zero-zero at eight, cleared to land."

The B-52 dipped suddenly, the left wing dropping like an elevator until pointed almost directly at the ground.

"Goddammit," Wilczynski muttered and added power, wrestling with the yoke and somehow straightening the big aircraft out again.

Against all odds they were still lined up with the runway, but Tracie knew now they were too high. The thirteen-thousand-foot-long expanse of pavement stretched out in front of them, promising safety, but it seemed far below. It looked to Tracie like they would have to drop almost straight down to avoid overshooting the runway, and she wondered whether the injured pilot had enough left to make a second try if they ended up too high and had to go around.

He seemed to have the same thought. "We gotta get this thing down, *now*," he said, and pushed forward on the yoke, pulling back on the power and the same time and forcing the bird's nose toward the ground.

The engines quieted and Tracie could hear the wind screaming around the airframe. She realized she was holding her breath and her hands gripped the sides of her seat so tightly she wondered how her fingers remained unbroken.

The ground rushed up at the B-52, rising impossibly fast. The lights of the tiny city of Bangor and its sister city, Brewer, shone in the distance, straddling the Penobscot River southeast of the airport. Centuries-old evergreens, tightly packed and massive, filled the windscreen, growing larger and larger until Tracie was sure the plane would fly straight into the forest.

At what seemed like the last possible moment, Wilczynski eased back on the yoke, lowering the landing gear and the flaps, and the plane leveled and slowed like someone had stood on a set of brakes.

The runway reappeared again in the windscreen as if by magic.

Tracie marveled at the skill of the B-52's only living crew member, badly injured, maybe fatally injured, but still handling the gigantic craft like the professional he was.

The trees flashed past under the wings as the B-52 descended steadily. They were maybe three miles from the approach end when Wilczynski turned to Tracie and smiled. His lips were white and so was his face, and blood flowed steadily down his left cheek as if the gauze bandage had never been applied. He looked like death warmed over but incredibly he was smiling.

"I've got it slowed as much as I dare. We're going to make it," he said, and then without warning his eyes rolled up into his head and he slumped forward. His safety harness kept him in his seat but the force of his movement pushed the yoke forward and the B-52 dropped like a rock.

Tracie grabbed for the yoke instinctively and missed, and the plane descended smoothly into the forest.

The wings sheared off the tops of trees. The interior rocked and bucked and the only sound Tracie could hear over her own screams was sheet metal shrieking as the wings tore completely clear of the fuselage.

The cabin bounced hard, ricocheting off a treetop and coming down onto another and then what was left of the plane rolled and tumbled and dropped to the forest floor.

And something struck Tracie in the head and the world went black.

17

May 30, 1987
11:49 p.m.
Bangor, Maine

Shane Rowley's Volkswagen Beetle bounced along the deserted country road toward Bangor International Airport. Bob Seger's amplified voice filled the car's interior, drowning out the eggbeater sound of the engine as it strained to keep up with Shane's lead foot.

Seger was rhapsodizing about getting lucky in "Night Moves." It was one of Shane's favorite songs, and singing along with the lyrics almost made Shane forget, if only for a few minutes, the paralyzing fear and bitter disappointment he had felt this afternoon.

It had been a long day at Northern Maine Medical Center, yet another in an endless string of appointments with specialists to determine the cause of the debilitating headaches he had been experiencing over the last few months.

Today had been the worst.

"A brain tumor," the current specialist had said after examining X-rays and Cat scans and the results of a series of tests. "I'm very sorry, but there's nothing we can do. The tumor is advanced and growing rapidly. We can make you comfortable as the end draws near," the man had said, and Shane barely heard him. He felt outside himself, like he was watching a bad TV movie about his life.

Shane had feared the worst almost since the nasty headaches had begun. "How long do I have?" he asked numbly.

The specialist, an older, officious-looking man, said, "Hard to tell," as if he were analyzing a theoretical concept instead of the impending end of another human being's life. "Anywhere from a few weeks to a couple of months. Probably no longer than that."

And Shane had thanked the man. He still didn't know why, it just seemed like the thing to do. Then he had stumbled out of the office and gone home, driving all the way on autopilot, unable to remember a thing about the trip when he nosed into the parking spot outside his apartment.

He had so much to think about but he needed to sleep. As an air traffic controller at Bangor International Airport he was accustomed to working shifts at all hours of the night and day, and tonight he was scheduled to work midnight to eight in what he knew would be one of his final shifts ever. Once the FAA flight surgeon learned of his diagnosis, Shane would be medically disqualified from working traffic, and that would be the beginning of the end. He knew he should have informed his superiors already of his medical issues, but had not been able to bring himself to do so.

One more shift, he had told himself, *for old time's sake.* Then he had tumbled into bed for a few hours of fitful sleep. In the morning, at the end of his overnight shift, he would advise Air Traffic Manager Marty Hall of the tumor. After that he would turn in his headset and go home to die.

Shane crested a hill, the Beetle's engine wailing. He was lost in Seger's voice, trying not to think about the cancer growing in his head, when a gigantic airplane whooshed over the car.

"Holy shit!" He ducked instinctively. The plane's strobes filled the interior of the car with pulsing light and Shane wrestled the steering wheel, fighting to keep the Beetle on the road as the huge aircraft roared seemingly inches above the treetops.

Shane's heart thumped madly. The plane—it was too dark to identify the aircraft type but the thing was enormous—rocked left and right, barely under control, and Shane knew instantly it would never make the airport. He knew it would never make another hundred feet unless it climbed immediately, and he was right. The hulking jet no sooner cleared his car than it veered right and descended straight into the forest.

Shane slammed on the brakes. The Beetle screeched to a halt

in a spray of gravel and dust. The airplane had disappeared from sight, but moments later a deafening crash shook the ground, then a muffled *boom* rolled through the night.

The guys working up in the control tower would even now be alerting the airport rescue vehicles to the accident. Shane knew that like he knew the back of his hand. He even knew who was working up there—it was the crew he was on his way to relieve on the midnight shift.

But although the crash scene was probably no more than two or three miles from the airport, finding the downed aircraft in the dense forest would be no easy task. Rescuers would likely be forced to locate the crash site by helicopter, a process that would take a considerable amount of time.

Shane knew there were probably no survivors, but in the unlikely event anyone *had* survived, they would need help immediately. Help no one else was around to give.

He shut down the Beetle and rummaged around in the glove box for a flashlight. He flicked it on and grimaced at the weak yellow beam. He tried to recall the last time he'd replaced the batteries in the damned thing and couldn't remember ever having done so.

Shane leaped out of the car and plunged into the nearly pitch-black woods. The moon was full and the skies clear and there was a fair amount of ambient light out in the open, but by the time he had traveled ten feet into the dense forest it was as if the moon had gone into hiding. He reluctantly flicked on the light, wondering how long it would take for the batteries to die, and began picking his way deeper into the woods.

The going was slow and Shane had no idea whether he was even traveling in the right direction. Getting lost in the woods would be easy to do, especially at night. If he wasn't careful he could find himself wandering in a big circle and missing the crash site entirely, or walking off in the wrong direction and not being able to find his way back to the road. He worked his way around boulders and over downed trees, moving slowly toward where he guessed the plane had gone down.

Ten minutes later, sweat covering his body despite the chilly nighttime Maine temperatures, a hint of a glow suffused the darkness and Shane knew he was getting close. Then he heard the sound of fire crackling and smelled the oily stench of burning fuel and something else, thick and metallic. He picked up his pace and burst into a small clearing created by the crash.

The wrecked fuselage lay in a heap, charred metal twisted almost beyond recognition. The nose of the aircraft was canted to one side, half-buried in the forest floor. Long slabs of sheet metal, probably parts of the wings, littered the wreckage, some hanging from neighboring trees, some slashed into the forest like knife blades.

A fire had begun burning in the middle of the fuselage and was rapidly spreading along the airframe in both directions, sending noxious black smoke skyward. The heat from the blaze was unrelenting.

Shane shaded his eyes with a hand and peered into the artificial brightness. After the near-complete blackness of the forest, the sudden intense light was unnerving.

He scanned the length of the wreckage quickly. If any passengers had been sitting in the middle portion of the plane they were now dead, consumed by fire in the unlikely event they had survived the impact.

The tail section had not yet begun to burn, but accessing that area would be impossible due to the intense heat of the fire. He had emerged from the woods directly in front of the nose, and reaching the rear of the aircraft would take too long at the rate the fire was progressing. Any survivors back there faced a hideous death. Shane hoped that if anyone had been seated in the rear they had died instantly in the crash.

An image rose in his mind of people choking and suffocating on that thick black smoke before being burned alive, and he forced it away, focusing his attention on the front of the aircraft. The flames had not quite reached it, although they would soon. The windshield was gone, with jagged shards of glass thrusting out of the frame haphazardly.

He moved forward, sidestepping razor-sharp pieces of torn sheet metal, some tiny and others a big as his VW Beetle. Wreckage littered the landscape. It was hard to believe all of it had come from the massive hulk now threatening to burn out of control in front of him. The closer he came to the plane, the more the heat began to overwhelm him. He shrugged out of his jacket and held it between the flames and his face in an effort to gain a bit of relief from the searing temperatures.

At last he reached the twisted metal of the cabin. The fire's crackling had become more pronounced, roaring and wheezing like a living being as it raced along the airframe. Shane knew he was running out of time. The heat was becoming unbearable and soon the flames would engulf the entire aircraft.

As he scrambled up an unidentifiable piece of equipment torn clear of the fuselage he could feel the heat radiating through the soles of his sneakers. He wrapped his jacked around his right arm and hand, hoping it would provide protection against the shards of glass and ripped sheep metal. He grabbed the windshield frame for support and hoisted himself up, then peered through the smashed windshield into the scene of death and destruction.

Bodies littered the cockpit, none of the moving. Two men wearing United States Air Force flight suits had been tossed around the interior of the craft during the crash. Their bodies were smashed and broken. One of the men was missing most of an arm, the bloody stump extruding from his uniform. The other had been wedged into a tiny opening along the side of the cockpit, bent awkwardly backward, his spine clearly broken.

Two other victims—one man and one woman—remained strapped into their seats. The man also wore a flight suit. His head was wrapped in a bloody gauze bandage, as if he had been attempting to fly the plane while badly injured.

The woman, however, did not wear a flight suit. She was dressed in civilian clothing, a pair of jeans and a button-down blouse. Her eyes were closed and her head lolled on her shoulder. Blood oozed out of a deep gash on her left leg.

They were all dead. They had to be. The crewmembers lying in the cabin, bent and broken like dolls after a child's tantrum, were clearly beyond hope. And the other two must have been killed in the crash.

Fire licked at the small open doorway to the rear of the flight deck, the guttural roar of the blaze sounding to Shane like the shriek of some inhuman monster. Poisonous black smoke roiled at the top of the wreckage. It was accumulating fast and the heat radiating through the broken windshield was suffocating.

Shane shook his head. Was there any point in crawling into the plane and risking being trapped inside with the other victims? The damage was so extensive survival seemed unlikely in the extreme.

In just the few seconds he had been checking out the interior of the cabin, the flames had engulfed the doorway and threatened to consume the cockpit. It was time to escape before he perished, too.

As her prepared to drop to the ground the woman moved. She lifted her head off her shoulder and moaned, eyes still closed.

This changed everything.

Without thinking—he knew if he hesitated at all he would never be able to do it—Shane shoved with his feet and hooked his arms at the elbows over the metal windshield frame. He pulled himself up and scrambled through the smashed-out windshield into hell.

He tumbled through the opening, landing face down atop the body of the crewmember with the missing arm. The man's body slumped sideways from the impact and Shane could see that half his skull was missing.

He pushed off, sickened by the sight. Something had gone horribly wrong inside this airplane, something much more than a simple mechanical problem. Maybe the damage to this man's skull had been caused by the crash. Maybe. But that strange injury, together with the bloody gauze bandage around the pilot's head and the presence of a civilian woman where one of the crewmembers should be, set alarm bells ringing in Shane's head.

But none of that mattered, at least not at the moment. The inferno was advancing, gaining momentum, racing toward Shane and the crash victims like a rampaging demon. The intensity of the heat was excruciating. The flames greedily consumed the oxygen, making it nearly impossible to breathe.

He ducked his head, kept his body as low as possible to avoid breathing toxic fumes. He turned toward the pair of victims still strapped into their seats. He already knew the woman was alive, so he quickly reached across her body and pressed his fingers under the man's ear, feeling for a pulse.

There was none.

He tried again, his fingers smearing sticky, half-dried blood around the man's neck. Still nothing.

Time was running out. He could feel his hair beginning to singe and his skin felt as though it might burst into flames at any moment. And the fire was still coming, passing over the body of the man who had become wedged into the wreckage.

Shane knew the inferno was being fed by oxygen entering through the smashed windshield. The very damage that had made it possible for him to access the cabin was now turning a foolhardy rescue attempt into a suicide mission.

He stood and thrust his head through the broken windshield, breathing deeply of the fresh northern Maine late-spring air. He took several deep gulps of it, finally holding his breath and turning back inside the fetid, foul, superheated air of the wreckage. He bent and fumbled with the buckle on the woman's safety harness, wrenching at it with his fingers until eventually releasing the belts.

He reached around her waist, grateful for her small size, and pulled her from her seat. He lifted her over his shoulder into an awkward fireman's carry and struggled to his feet, hoping he wouldn't accidentally force her head into the deadly black smoke and kill her while trying to save her. The distance from the seat to the smashed windshield was only a couple of feet, but debris covered the flight deck, which was already tilted at an angle. Maintaining solid footing was impossible.

Shane stumbled and dropped to his knees. The woman's body slipped off his shoulder and he caught her. He felt weak and disoriented. The heat was relentless and he tried to ignore it as he shambled forward again. He thrust the woman's head and upper body out the smashed windshield, her lower half still trapped inside.

Behind Shane, the seat the woman had occupied burst into flames. He knew the male crewmember's seat would follow suit any second now, and his clothing would likely ignite next.

He pushed against the wreckage with his feet, his legs feeling rubbery and insubstantial. He reached for the window frame and pulled his body through, wheezing and coughing, choking down fresh air, amazed to still be alive.

There wasn't room to turn his body in the window frame like he had done on the way into the plane; the female victim's body took up too much room. So Shane wriggled through the opening and dropped headfirst out of the plane. He twisted as he fell, trying to drop onto a shoulder, hoping he wouldn't slice his head open on the wreckage. He landed with a crash that jarred his body but left him uninjured.

The night was crystal clear, and as he breathed deeply he felt as though his lungs had been scoured with steel wool from sucking in superheated air. Coughing and hacking, he stood and reached back into the doomed aircraft, grabbing the woman by the legs and trying to lift her clear of the window frame. The left leg of her jeans was soaked with blood and he lost his grip.

He wiped his hand, smearing blood over his clothing, and tried again. This time he grasped her belt loops and used them to pull her upward. He was at an awkward angle, making lifting her difficult. He looked inside the cabin, shocked at what he saw. Flames engulfed the wreckage, tongues of orange racing toward the unconscious woman's legs.

He was out of time. Giving up on lifting her clear, Shane locked his arms under her armpits and dragged her body through the opening. He worried her already injured leg would be sliced open further by shards of glass and metal but could not afford to waste any more time.

Her body pulled through inch by inch, the resistance substantial, as if the aircraft was releasing its final victim only with extreme reluctance. Her knees cleared the opening with a ripping sound that Shane could hear clearly even over the roar of the fire.

Then she was free. They tumbled backward, away from the wrecked plane, landing in a heap on the forest floor. Shane rolled the woman's body gently off his, then crouched next to her and hefted her once more onto his shoulder. He struggled to his feet and began moving as quickly as he could manage away from the aircraft and toward the road.

He had lost his flashlight in the confusion and pictured himself stumbling around blindly, lost in the near-complete darkness, the woman dying because he might be within ten feet of his car and never know it.

At the edge of the clearing, Shane stopped and took one last look at the devastation of the crash scene. It was a sight he knew he would never forget.

Then he turned and plunged into the darkness.

18

May 31, 1987
12:02 a.m.
Bangor, Maine

Shane was panting like a dog when he finally reached the road. His legs burned and his back throbbed and the dead weight of the unconscious woman felt like a thousand pounds, rather than the one hundred or so it probably was.

He stumbled through the thick brush, grateful to have found his way out of the wilderness. The road was brightly lit by the full moon, in stark contrast to the impenetrable blackness under the canopy of trees. Shane peered in both directions, looking for his car. There were still no rescue vehicles in sight, although he could hear sirens off in the distance. Whether they were heading in this direction, he couldn't tell.

Far to the north, Shane spotted an indistinct lump in the shadows at the side of the road and decided it was probably his car. He had taken great pains to walk as straight a path as possible on the way out of the woods and had still missed the Bug by at least an eighth of a mile. He sank to one knee, gulping air, trying to catch his breath while still holding the crash victim.

He wondered how much damage he was doing to the young woman by carrying her. Moving her at all was a calculated risk—if she had suffered a broken neck or back, he could be causing irreparable damage—but leaving her at the crash scene and waiting for rescue vehicles that might arrive too late was out of the question. If her injuries didn't kill her, the northern Maine chill might. Even this close to June, on a clear night like tonight the temperature could easily dip below freezing.

Shane staggered to his feet. He half-walked, half-trotted to his car, reaching it after what felt like half an hour but was probably no more than five minutes. He yanked the passenger door open and lowered the young woman onto the seat as gently as he could. Blood dribbled out of the gash in her leg, but the flow seemed to have slowed.

He lowered the seatback as far as it would go and reached into the rear of the vehicle, feeling around until he found the heavy winter coat he kept for emergencies. He secured the still-unconscious woman with the safety belt and then propped her injured leg on the coat. He slammed the door closed and sprinted around the front of the car before dropping into the driver's seat and firing up the engine.

He wheeled onto the empty road, then glanced at his injured passenger and blinked in surprise. She had awakened and was staring at him. Her eyes were open and she watched him intently, but she had not moved.

"It's okay," he said softly, not wanting to frighten her. "You were in a plane crash and I'm taking you to the hospital." He cranked the temperature knob to the right, knowing the result would barely qualify as lukewarm.

Her eyes fluttered and Shane thought she was about to lose consciousness again but she didn't.

"Major Wilczynski," she said weakly.

Shane shook his head. "You were the only survivor. Everyone else in the cockpit was dead. I'm sorry."

She lay back on the seat, eyes closed, and then bolted upright in a panic, groaning and holding her head the moment she did. She steadied herself and reached into the back pocket of her bloody jeans and withdrew a tattered envelope.

"Thank God," she muttered, collapsing back onto the seat.

In the distance Shane could hear the scream of sirens growing steadily louder. The rescue vehicles were beginning to hone in on the crash site. Shane wondered whether he should turn around and wait for them. Maybe handing this woman off to an ambulance crew would be wiser than driving her to the hospital himself.

But they were less than five minutes away from Bangor proper, less than ten minutes from the hospital, and as someone who had grown up in this remote area, Shane knew well how vast the wilderness really was. The rescue crews could be well within earshot and still not find the site for twenty or thirty minutes. Or more.

He flipped on the Bug's dome light and glanced repeatedly at the injured woman as he drove. Blood continued to leak from her thigh. Her jeans were covered in it, some half-dried and crusted, the rest still glistening wetly in the dim light. Her skin color was a shocking white, not surprising considering her blood loss. He decided he was doing the right thing.

Flipping off the light, he said, "Don't worry, we'll be at the hospital in just a couple of minutes."

She mumbled something in return and he missed it. "What?"

"I said no hospitals."

Shane shook his head. He must have heard her wrong. "You have to go to the hospital. You look like death warmed over."

"You really know how to sweet-talk a girl."

"Sorry about that, but you definitely need medical attention."

"*No,*" she repeated emphatically. "I said no hospitals." The strength of her voice and the intensity of her response surprised him, and he raised his eyebrows.

"What are you talking about? You were in an *airplane crash.* Of course you're going to the hospital. Where else would I bring you?"

"Anywhere," she said. Her voice had returned to its previous weak volume, barely more than a strong whisper. "This hick town have a bus station?"

"Of course."

"Then you can drop me there."

Maybe this young woman's problem wasn't a head injury. Maybe she was just batshit crazy.

"You think any bus driver's going to let you board? Your leg is awash in your own blood and you look like you just lost a gunfight. Besides, if you try to stand up on your own right now, you're going to drop like a felled tree. I'm sorry," he said, "but you're going straight to the hospital."

The young woman leaned forward, reaching down to her right

ankle and fumbling around. What she was looking for, he had no idea. The longer he rode with her, the more Shane was inclined to believe she really was crazy. He glanced forward onto the deserted road and when he looked back, he found himself staring straight down the barrel of a handgun.

"No hospitals," she said.

* * *

May 31, 1987
12:10 a.m.
Bangor, Maine

Tracie concentrated on not puking. Her head pounded relentlessly and unless she focused hard her vision insisted on wavering, sometimes disappearing entirely. She knew she had suffered a concussion—hopefully it was *only* a concussion—and the gash in her leg throbbed with every beat of her heart.

She needed stitches.

She needed sleep.

She wasn't going to get either.

She forced herself to hold the gun steady on her rescuer. "No hospitals," she said, and to his credit the guy didn't even blink.

"O-kay," he said. "Then where to?"

"You're right about one thing. I can't take a bus looking like this."

"Tell me something I don't know," he said drily.

"But they'll be watching the bus terminal before long," she muttered, thinking out loud, struggling to concentrate through the haze of pain and confusion. "They probably don't have any operatives in this tiny nowhere town—"

"Thanks, on behalf of all Bangor residents."

"—but they will very soon and then I'll be trapped. *Dammit,*" she said, punching the seat in frustration.

"What kind of trouble are you in?" her rescuer asked. "And

what were you doing in a military plane out of uniform? You're not in the military, are you?"

Tracie gazed at the young man, thinking. He had reacted much differently to having a gun stuck in his face than she had expected him to—much differently than most civilians would—and she liked that. And he *had* risked his life by climbing inside a burning B-52 in the middle of nowhere to haul her ass out of the fire. Literally.

She had been semi-conscious in the aftermath of the crash and thought she was hallucinating when his body tumbled through the smashed windscreen, dropping like an angel from heaven as the fire worked its way through the cabin.

And he seemed genuinely concerned about her condition. She decided to take a chance. What choice did she have?

"You're right," she said. "I'm not in the military. My father is a state department bigwig and he's dying. I was on an emergency flight home because he has only days to live and I want to say goodbye." She teared up, mentally congratulating herself on the acting job, even after a plane crash and with injuries.

"Bullshit," he said, and that was when she saw the sign approaching rapidly on the right: NORTHERN MAINE MEDICAL CENTER.

"I told you, no hospitals," she said sharply, leaning forward to jam the barrel of the Beretta under his chin, ignoring the accompanying pain.

"We're not going to the hospital," he said in annoyance, "although I think you're making a mistake. You've lost a lot of blood, that gash in your leg needs to be examined, and it seems pretty clear you've suffered a concussion, at the very least. But what the hell, I'm not your guardian. You want to be a damned fool, that's none of my business."

The Volkswagen bypassed the hospital's entrance and continued along the lightly traveled road.

"So, where *are* we going then?"

"My apartment's not far from here. I'll patch you up the best I can and you can crash there for a few hours while you figure out what you want to do next. Your story is complete bullshit, but I'm not going to just drop you off in the middle of this 'tiny nowhere town,' as you call it, injured and alone. I wasn't raised that way. Maybe you won't go to the hospital, but I can't just leave you, either."

Tracie said nothing. She was stunned. This guy was a total stranger, he had risked his life pulling her from a burning airplane, and by way of thanks she had threatened him with deadly violence. Now he was driving her to his home. And to top it off, he was cute as hell.

"Think you could get that gun out of my face?" he said into the shocked silence, and she lowered the Beretta to her lap. She was really starting to like this guy.

"What's your name?" he asked.

"Name? Why do you care about my name?" She was instantly suspicious.

"Jesus," he answered in exasperation. "I'm just making conversation. It's what people do. For example: I'm Shane Rowley, it's nice to meet you."

Tracie stared at him, thinking, and then chuckled despite the pain. She must be getting paranoid. There was no possible way anyone on either side of the geopolitical fence—USSR or United States—could have known that B-52 was going to crash-land while trying to divert to Bangor, Maine. Thus, there was no possible way this guy could be anything other than what he claimed to be: a Good Samaritan who had been driving past, seen the plane go down, and pulled her out of the burning wreckage.

She sighed and smiled. "My name's Tracie," she said softly, realizing with some surprise that she hadn't introduced herself to a civilian stranger using her real name in well over half a decade.

"See, that wasn't so hard. We're making progress." He hung a left at a red brick bank building that was maybe five stories high—what passed for a skyscraper here in Nowhereville, USA—urged the Beetle up a hill, banged a couple more turns, and drove into an apartment complex overlooking a good-sized river. Small pools of sickly yellow light dotted the parking lot from poles spaced too far apart to do much good.

Her rescuer guided the Bug into a spot directly under one of the poles.

Tracie said, "No, not here."

"What are you talking about? My apartment is right in front of us."

"Not under the light," she said. "Park in one of the dark spots."

He looked at her like she was crazy—he seemed to be doing that a lot—and she said, "Please. Humor me."

He shook his head, shifted the car into reverse, and backed directly into another spot roughly midway between two of the light poles lining the rear of the lot.

"Better?" he asked.

Tracie nodded. "Better." She unsnapped her seat belt and opened her door, placing her right foot on the pavement.

"Wait," the young man said and she ignored him. She grabbed the roof for support and swung herself out of the car. Instantly a wave of dizziness and nausea rolled through her.

"This might have been a mistake," she said.

Her savior said something in return but she couldn't make it out. A buzzing sound started up in the distance, like maybe someone had chosen the middle of the night to fire up a chainsaw. The buzzing got louder and Tracie realized it was coming from inside her head. Black spots bloomed in her vision, making the weak light in the parking lot seem even weaker.

She was vaguely aware of the driver rushing around the front of the Volkswagen. She let go of the car and took one shuffling step toward the apartment complex and then another, and then the pavement rushed up to meet her and the world went black.

Again.

19

May 31, 1987
12:25 a.m.
Bangor, Maine

The woman collapsed into his arms and Shane shuffled backward, trying to keep his feet. She wasn't very big, maybe five-two and all of a hundred pounds soaking wet, but her momentum had been moving forward as she staggered away from his car. It was like catching a hundred pound bag of potatoes someone had tossed at you.

Although, he thought, *a bag of potatoes probably never felt this good.*

He glanced around the lot. Empty. That made sense considering the time, but if a neighbor happened to glance out a window, couldn't sleep or whatever, the Bangor Police would be all over this apartment complex within minutes. A man, half carrying a woman, unconscious and covered in blood, into his apartment in the middle of the night. Christ, he'd look like Jack the Ripper.

But then, maybe a visit from the cops wouldn't be such a bad thing. Shane had never had a gun pointed at him before and decided he didn't like it very much. This beautiful crash victim was obviously hip-deep in some serious shit, and who was to say she wasn't one of the bad guys?

Shane didn't think so, though. He liked to think he possessed a pretty reliable bullshit detector—he'd seen right through the dying father yarn the injured woman had tried to spin—and his instincts told him the girl was trustworthy, at least to the extent she didn't want to cause him harm.

And in any event, she was completely helpless now. He couldn't very well just dump her on the side of the road. So, resigned to risking possible arrest, he hoisted her onto his shoulder one more time and walked as quickly as he could to his apartment.

He dug his key out of his pocket and stabbed for the lock. He staggered through the front door, kicked it closed, and crossed the living room to his old couch. He lowered his guest onto it as gently as he could.

She groaned and muttered but her eyes remained closed.

Then he backtracked, locked and dead-bolted the door, and then sank to the floor, out of breath and exhausted. Shane looked at his watch. Twelve thirty a.m.

Shit. He had to call work. He should have been there half an hour ago. Between climbing into burning wreckage, saving a pretty—if very strange—young woman from certain death, and staring down a gun barrel, he had completely forgotten about work.

He trudged across the living room and checked on the girl on the way to the telephone. She was right where he'd left her, still out cold, pale and unmoving.

Again Shane thought about the hospital and wondered briefly about personal liability should the woman die on his couch. It didn't seem likely, but still, she had been through a lot, had lost a lot of blood, and who really knew how badly she had been injured in that crash?

He decided he would make his call and then tend to her.

Shane dialed quickly. He knew the tower supervisor, who normally would have gone home at midnight, would still be in the facility making notifications and coordinating with rescue personnel about the aircraft accident, and he was right. The line rang seven times, eight, and then was answered on the ninth ring by supervisor Chuck McNally.

"Bangor Tower," McNally barked into the phone, gruff and intimidating. Shane realized the line had probably been ringing off the hook since the accident and felt a stab of sympathy for the supervisor, normally the most kind-hearted of men but right now probably at the end of his rope.

"Chuck, this is Shane. I'm sorry about not calling sooner, but—"

"Shane, where the hell are you? We've had a crash just off the airport. Things are fucking insane, man. Tonight was definitely not the night to blow off work without even a call." Shane listened to McNally rant and broke in when the man slowed down to take a breath.

"That's why I'm calling, boss. I know about the accident. It happened right next to me as I was driving to work. The damn airplane fell out of the sky and almost landed on my car. I climbed inside the wreckage, man. I pulled a victim out alive."

The line fell silent as McNally processed the information. "You saw the crash?"

"I didn't actually see it happen because of the trees, but I sure as hell heard it. I stopped the car and hiked out to the crash site to see if I could help anyone, and damned if there wasn't a young woman trapped in the cabin. Anyway, I'm really sorry, but there's no way I can come in to work tonight, I'm exhausted and banged up and even burned a little bit."

"You were inside the wrecked airplane?"

"Yeah. It was a frigging nightmare."

"Holy shit. I can imagine. Anyway, under the circumstances, sick leave is approved, obviously. I'll be in the tower until morning, anyway. But listen, an NTSB accident investigation team is already on the way. They'll be here tomorrow along with representatives of the Air Force, since it was their airplane. Given what you told me, they're going to want to interview you, so call the facility first thing in the morning and plan on coming in here sometime during the day to talk to the investigators."

"Will do, Chuck, and thanks."

"No problem. What's the victim's condition? Have the doctors told you anything?"

"There are no doctors. She's passed out on my couch even as we speak."

"Your couch? What are you talking about? She's at your apartment?"

"Yeah, she refused to go to the hospital." Shane said nothing about the young woman waving a gun around.

"But you said she's passed out. Why didn't you take her straight to a doctor?"

"She was conscious in my car and she insisted. She didn't pass out until we got back to my place."

"Christ, Shane, don't be an idiot. Get that girl to the hospital, like, right now."

"Yeah, I guess I should," Shane answered, knowing it was the smart thing to do but knowing also he was not about to do it. "Anyway, thanks again, Chuck, and good luck. I know you're busy."

"It's just paperwork bullshit at this point. I'll be fine. Get that girl to a hospital."

"See ya." Shane hung up the phone and glanced around the kitchen's open entryway into the living room and saw Tracie watching him from the couch. She looked even paler than before, but he figured regaining consciousness had to be a good sign.

He flashed a smile. "How are you feeling?" he asked.

"Never mind that," she said shortly. "Who the hell were you talking to just now?"

"My supervisor, if it's any of your business," he said, angered by her tone and, he had to admit, a little hurt by her attitude. After all he'd done for her, who was she to snap at him for no reason?

"Your supervisor? Who do you work for? Why do you need to talk to your supervisor in the middle of the night?"

"Again," he said, "not that it's any of your business, but I'm an air traffic controller at Bangor Airport and I'm supposed to be at work right now. I thought my supervisor might consider it rude of me not to let him know why I didn't show up, especially tonight. They're kind of busy. It seems there was an airplane crash. I'm lucky I still have a job."

She was silent. Shane could see her thinking. "Did you tell him about me?" she asked.

"Of course. You're the whole reason I'm here and not there. It wouldn't have made sense for me to say I stopped and watched the burning wreckage of a crashed military jet before blowing off work and returning home."

She blew out an angry breath and shook her head. "You could have said you checked inside the plane and didn't find anyone alive. Dammit!"

Shane spread his hands in frustration. "Why would I do that? What would be the point?"

He turned toward the kitchen, anger building, and then spun back around to face the injured woman. "Who the hell are you? Why were you on that plane? Where were you coming from? What were you doing that's so freaking top secret you can't even see a doctor after a goddamned plane crash?"

Again she was silent and Shane could see her weighing her options for a response.

Finally she sighed. "Never mind," she said. "Forget it. I don't mean to seem ungrateful after all you've done for me, but I simply can't talk about it. I'm sorry."

She closed her eyes and leaned back on Shane's two Syracuse University throw pillows his proud mother had knitted when he was accepted into their journalism program after high school. He'd graduated with a degree he never used, opting instead to apply for a job with the FAA after the disastrous PATCO strike in 1981, when President Reagan fired the illegally striking air traffic controllers en mass. His mother, angry and hurt, had never asked for the pillows back.

Shane walked across the room and perched on the arm of the couch at her feet, unsure of what to say. Tracie's face was still bone white, shiny from a thin coating of sweat. Her eyes looked glassy.

"Sorry I'm dripping blood onto your couch," she said, her voice weak, and suddenly she looked very young and vulnerable.

Shane waved a hand airily. "This old thing? Don't worry about it. I picked it up for twenty bucks at the Salvation Army. I should apologize to you for subjecting you to all those potential germs."

She attempted a smile.

"Speaking of germs..." he continued.

"I know. I need to clean this wound."

"I'll help you. I have a decent first aid kit in the bathroom."

She narrowed her eyes and Shane raised his hands in surrender. "My intentions are honorable, I swear," he said. "Come on, I'll help you to the bathroom. I think I still have a pair of gym shorts from high school that are too small for me. You might be able to wear them without them sliding right off. I'll toss them in and you can put them on, and then we'll clean your leg in the bathtub."

Tracie nodded and rose to a half-sitting position, gritting her teeth against the pain. Shane pulled her arm around his neck, then stood slowly and the pair began stumbling awkwardly across the living room. When they reached the bathroom, he kicked the toilet seat cover down and eased her into a sitting position on it.

"If you want to get those bloody pants off, I'll be right back with the shorts."

She nodded tiredly.

He pulled the door close as he was leaving and heard her say "Thank you" as he was walking away.

*   *   *

The wound was deep, but to Shane's eye looked clean. He went to work on it, washing it as gently as he could with warm, soapy water and then disinfecting it with hydrogen peroxide. Her burns appeared minimal and Shane knew she'd been extremely lucky. Tracie was mostly silent, stoic, occasionally grunting or gasping through gritted teeth, but she never complained and even helped steady her leg with both hands.

After patting the wound dry with a clean towel, Shane pulled a new, sealed Ace bandage out of his medicine chest. He opened the package and began wrapping the stretchy gauze around her leg as tightly as he dared, closing the sides of the puncture wound together and sealing it.

The bleeding had stopped, more or less, and when he finished he examined his handiwork and said, "Well, you should still be in the emergency room for stitches, but it looks like you might live to see another day."

"I was afraid of that," she answered jokingly. "Now if this invisible guy will stop hitting me in the head with a baseball bat I'll be good to go."

"Concussion?" Shane asked.

She nodded. "Probably. I know I'm supposed to be woken up every hour or something, but screw that. If I can manage a few hours of solid sleep, I'm sure I'll be as good as new. If you don't mind helping me back to your couch, I'll sleep a while and then I'll be out of your hair in the morning, I promise."

"No worries," Shane said, helping her to her feet. "Except you're not going to use the couch. You're sleeping in my bed."

She raised an eyebrow. "Assuming an awful lot there, cowboy, aren't ya?"

He laughed. "Don't worry, you'll be alone. I'll take the couch."

"I'm not going to take your bed and make you—"

"I know, I know, you're tough as nails. A real badass. We've already established that. You could sleep on a bed of nails if you had to. Just do this one little thing for me, okay? My mom would never forgive me if she found out I made an injured woman sleep on the couch. You'd actually be doing me a favor," he said with a smile.

She sputtered and shook her head, but allowed herself to be led into the apartment's only bedroom. He helped her under the covers and turned out the light.

"Goodnight," he said, but she was already asleep.

20

May 31, 1987
8:40 a.m. local time
Moscow, Russia, USSR

"We have a problem." The man on the other end of the telephone line spoke in a hushed voice, but concern was plainly evident in his tone.

"Of course we do," Vasiliy Kopalev said. "There is always a problem." As head of the KGB's American Operations Branch, Vasiliy spent most of his time dealing with one emergency or another from one of his small cadre of operatives stationed throughout the United States. He lit his cigarette and inhaled deeply, savoring the bite of the tar and the smooth flavor of the smuggled Lucky Strikes. *The Americans may be a threat to Mother Russia, but they make one damned fine cigarette.*

"Maybe so," the voice continued, "but this problem is bigger than most."

"Get on with it, then. Are you going to make me guess?"

"The airplane carrying Gorbachev's letter has crashed, and—"

"That was the plan, remember?"

"No, you do not understand. The plane did not disappear over the ocean. It crash-landed near an airport here in the U.S. In Bangor, Maine."

"What?"

"That is not the worst of it."

94

"Of course not," Kopalev muttered. Suddenly his Lucky Strike tasted bitter. He sucked down a deep drag anyway—he was going to need it.

"Tell me," he sighed, exhaling cigarette smoke.

"All of the crewmembers are dead, except the woman."

"Except the woman."

"That's right. The CIA operative has vanished. Virtually the entire B-52 was destroyed in a massive fire following the accident, so it is of course possible the letter burned up in the blaze, but given the fact the agent has disappeared, it would seem likely the letter survived and disappeared with her."

"Yes, it would seem likely," Vasiliy agreed. He was silent for a moment, thinking. "We cannot be certain what is contained in that letter, but I have a pretty good idea."

The man on the other end of the line waited patiently. Vasiliy knew he didn't care what was in the letter. It was not his job to care what was in the letter. His job was to carry out Vasiliy's instructions, thus his words were irrelevant until they contained those instructions.

"You are stationed in Boston, correct?"

"Da."

"And you have two comrades also stationed in Boston, correct?"

"Da."

"And what is the distance from Boston to Bangor, Maine?" Kopalev leaned back in his chair and consulted a map of the United States posted behind his desk. The map was enormous and took up one entire wall. Vasiliy did the calculations along with the agent. He knew the answer before the man spoke.

"It is roughly a three hour drive."

"Very good. Take your two comrades and get up there immediately. Recover that letter. The agent was involved in a plane crash. Even if she escaped, she must have suffered injuries. She probably wandered away from the wreckage and is even now lying dead somewhere near. If that is the case, find her and relieve her of that letter before someone else does. It is not enough to keep the communiqué from President Reagan. It must be kept from *anyone* who would have the ability to publicize its contents."

"And if she somehow survived?"

"Your mission remains unchanged. Get that letter. Whether the CIA operative lives or dies is of no concern."

21

May 31, 1987
7:30 a.m.
Bangor, Maine

The ringing of the telephone worked its way into Shane's consciousness gradually, pulling him out of a deep sleep. He had been dreaming about a young red-haired woman, mysterious and sexy. In his dream they were sharing his bed, and he was doing things with her he had not done with anyone since the breakup of his marriage more than a year ago.

He burst into wakefulness like a swimmer surfacing, the dream already fading, Shane reluctant to let it go. He glanced at the clock on the living room wall as he crossed to the kitchen. Seven thirty. He had gotten barely five hours of sleep and felt exhausted and weak. His entire body ached, leg muscles complaining, back stiff, joints popping. And he needed coffee.

He picked up the phone and snarled, "What?" into the receiver. It came out harsher than he intended but he didn't much care.

"Shane, this is Marty Hall. I understand you had quite an adventure last night." Marty was the air traffic manager at Bangor Tower, an older man with a mop of thick white hair and a heavily lined face who had spent his entire adult life working his way up the FAA ladder. Shane barely knew Marty because they rarely had the opportunity for interaction beyond the occasional nod and smile as they passed in the hallway of the facility's base building stationed next to the control tower.

"Hi, Marty. Yeah, you could say that." Shane remembered Chuck McNally's statement that he would have to come in and talk to the NTSB accident investigators and cursed under his breath. He wanted nothing more than to lie back down on his couch and sleep for another couple of hours. Or days.

"Listen, Shane, I know this is your weekend, but the crash team is going to be here at nine and would like to talk with you as soon as possible. Think you can get in here by then?"

He sighed. This was not unexpected. "I'll be there," he said. Then he hung up the phone and cursed out loud. There would be no going back to sleep today.

He padded past his bedroom on the way to take a shower and saw the door ajar, as he'd left it. He eased it open and peeked in at his injured guest. She was lying on her side in the fetal position. He took two steps into the room and saw her breathing deeply and steadily. She looked impossibly small and helpless.

Her back was to him, so it was difficult to see how the bandage on her leg was holding up. Shane thought for a moment about trying to take a quick look at it while she slept, then imagined her waking up to see him bent over the bed, staring at her bare legs.

He recalled the feeling of looking down a gun barrel last night and decided the bandage was probably holding just fine. He eased the door closed and continued to the shower.

22

May 31, 1987
7:40 a.m.
Hampden, Maine

The early morning air was cool and crisp, and the slanting sunlight reflected off the windshields of dozens of vehicles parked in the truck stop lot. Anatoli Simonov stepped out of the rented Chevy Caprice and shaded his eyes against the glare. The relative warmth reminded Anatoli how far he'd come from his childhood in Siberia, where the bitter cold was so overwhelming it was like being stabbed in the lungs if you tried to breathe too deeply.

But the desolation felt familiar. Dysart's Truck Stop was located south of Bangor, Maine on Interstate 95, and apart from the cluster of buildings at the truck stop and the big paved parking lot, he was surrounded by a massive expanse of mostly unpopulated landscape, the city of Bangor still just a rumor to the north.

"Come on," Bogdan Fedorov urged, climbing out of the back seat along with a second KGB operative. "We have much to do, and standing around admiring the view is accomplishing nothing."

The three men hurried across the tarmac and into the truck stop for breakfast.

* * *

They ate mostly in silence, preferring to interact with the locals as little as possible. It was easy to blend in with the Americans visually, much more difficult when you spoke in heavily Russian-accented English, as Anatoli's two companions did.

Anatoli had long ago achieved a certain familiarity with the language, so he ordered for everyone, and their conversation ground to a halt whenever their waitress—a heavy-set middle-aged woman with rust-colored hair and an aggrieved demeanor—approached to refill their coffee.

An ancient black-and-white television suspended in one corner of the dining room was tuned to a local channel, the volume cranked to a decibel level roughly approximating that of an air raid siren. Local programming had been pre-empted to carry continuous coverage of a breaking news story: last night's crash of an Air Force B-52 jet.

The men ate their omelets, drank their coffee, and paid close attention as a female reporter gazed solemnly into the camera and said, "It appears as though there was at least one survivor of last night's fiery airplane crash in a heavily wooded area north of Bangor International Airport. Sources close to the investigation have confirmed that a passing motorist witnessed the crash and braved an out-of-control fire to pull a young woman from the wreckage."

Anatoli lowered his coffee cup to the table, unable to believe his good fortune as a graphic was superimposed on the lower right hand corner of the screen. The graphic depicted a head shot photo of a youngish man, perhaps late twenties. The television's distance from the table and the small size of the picture made it impossible to distinguish any details of the man's facial features.

The reporter continued. "Sources tell us this man, Shane Rowley, an air traffic controller living in Bangor, was on his way to work at the time of the crash and managed to rescue the as-yet unidentified woman. Her condition and whereabouts, as well as the whereabouts of Rowley, are at this time unknown, but News 9 has learned Mr. Rowley is scheduled to meet with NTSB investigators as well as Air Force representatives at nine a.m. inside the control tower building at BIA to assist in the investigation. More on this story as it develops. Jane Finneran, WBGR News 9."

Anatoli tried to keep from smiling but just couldn't do it. He tore his eyes from the television for the first time since the news report had begun and saw his fellow operatives smiling as well.

"This would be considered good news, yes?" Fedorov said softly between bites of omelet, flecks of cheese peppering his black beard.

"It most certainly would," Anatoli agreed.

"What is next? Find out where this Shane Rowley lives and force him to reveal the girl's location?"

"We could do that," Anatoli said, "but why wait to take him at his home? This is a matter of no small importance and, according to Colonel Kopalev, extremely time-critical. We know where Mr. Rowley will be spending his morning. Our instructions are to retrieve the letter absolutely as soon as possible. Since we don't know when Shane Rowley will be alone again, I suggest we pay these investigators a visit and remove Mr. Rowley from the meeting. Once we have secured Rowley, we can find a nice, secluded location—that shouldn't be difficult, there is nothing much in this wasteland but trees—and extract the information we require."

He met his companions' eyes and awaited argument.

When he received none, he said, "Now, let us finish our delicious breakfast. It seems this will be a busy day."

23

May 31, 1987
8:20 a.m.
Bangor, Maine

Tracie's eyes fluttered open and she felt a rush of intense panic. She saw no one. Recognized nothing. Had no idea where she was or how she had gotten here.

She sat bolt upright in a strange bed, stiff and sore, and then the memories came rushing back: Major Mitchell shooting his fellow B-52 crewmembers. Tracie returning fire and putting Mitchell down. The desperate attempt by a dying Major Wilczynski to land the big jet in Bangor, Maine. The subsequent plane crash and her rescue by air traffic controller Shane Rowley.

Rowley.

She had fallen asleep in Rowley's bed.

She started to panic again as she looked for the letter from Mikhail Gorbachev she had been charged with delivering to President Reagan. She snatched up her pillow and there it was, right where she'd stuffed it, crumpled and sweat-stained, flecks of blood splattered across it.

She grabbed it with a sigh of relief and then looked around, wondering about the time. A digital clock radio on a dresser across the room said eight-twenty. Tracie tried to recall the last time she'd slept this late and couldn't.

Stretching, she eased off the side of the bed and gingerly placed a little weight on her injured leg. Her thigh throbbed but the pain was tolerable. She leaned more firmly and finally took a couple of shuffling steps toward the bedroom door.

Painful but not overwhelmingly so. Same thing with her headache.

She poked her head into the short hallway and looked around, seeing no one. She smelled fresh coffee and her stomach rumbled. Shane must be in the kitchen.

She decided to take advantage of the opportunity for a shower and slipped into the bathroom. Splotches of dried blood covered her arms and she could feel more blood flaking off her face. Her hair was matted and stringy. She felt as though she had crawled through a mud puddle the size of a football field.

She closed the bathroom door and placed the letter on top of the toilet seat tank, exactly as she had done inside the CIA safe house at Ramstein. Then she undressed, casting a critical eye at the makeshift patch job Shane Rowley had done on her leg last night. She was pleased to note only a slight discoloration of the Ace bandage at the site of the injury. There was no oozing or seeping of blood.

She knew she should remove the bandage and clean the wound again, but didn't want to take the time now. She'd do it later.

Tracie eased into the shower, holding her injured leg awkwardly out of the tub in an effort to keep the bandage dry. It was an uncomfortable position to maintain, hard to stay balanced, but she turned the hot water up as high as she could stand and then showered quickly. She washed her hair with some shampoo she found in a hanging shower caddy and then got out, dripping water all over her host's floor while she searched for a clean towel.

She found one in a stack of them inside a cabinet under the sink. She dried off quickly and wrapped the towel around her body, now clean and pink from the hot shower. She wasn't looking forward to getting back into her filthy clothes, but didn't have much choice—her travel bag had been lost in the crash. She decided to delay the inevitable, instead picking the precious envelope up off the toilet tank, opening the bathroom door and limping down the hallway in search of the coffee.

And, she had to admit, Shane Rowley.

The kitchen was empty. So was the living room. A couple of blankets had been thrown carelessly to one side of the couch and a pillow lay on the far end. It was obvious Rowley had slept here, but Tracie's assumption that her rescuer was somewhere inside the apartment had been off the mark.

She turned and wandered into the kitchen, finding a pile of neatly folded women's clothing on the counter. A handwritten note had been placed atop the clothes.

Tracie furrowed her brow and unfolded the note.

Good morning, Tracie, it read. *I hope you're feeling a little better. Sorry I'm not here, but I got called in to work. I have to talk to the NTSB investigators about the crash. They're going to want to talk to you, too, but you looked so exhausted last night that I didn't have the heart to wake you up before I left. The bureaucrats can wait.*

The coffee is fresh and the water is hot if you'd like to take a shower. I made the assumption you'll want clean clothes, so I dug out some of the stuff my ex-wife left behind in her rush to escape her boring husband and the backwoods of Bangor. You're probably not exactly the same size, but I'm guessing it will fit okay. I have a feeling you could wear just about anything and look stunning.

Make yourself at home, and if you're so inclined, I would love to help you figure out your next move when I get back. If you decide to hit the road before I return, good luck to you, and thanks for my most interesting Saturday night ever.

Shane

Tracie finished reading and then rummaged around in the cupboard above the counter until she found a mug. Then she poured herself a cup of coffee and stood at the counter sipping it as she read the note a second time. *I have a feeling you could wear just about anything and look stunning.*

She found herself smiling as she thought about the handsome young air traffic controller, then she shook her head at her foolishness. Something explosive was contained in the envelope she held in her hand, something someone was willing to go to great lengths to destroy.

She sat down at Shane Rowley's tiny kitchen table, thinking about secret communications and international diplomacy and who might have the desire—and more importantly, the ability—to commit murder in the interest of squelching a communiqué only a handful of people in the world even knew existed.

There seemed to be only one possibility, and if her assumption was right, that possibility was terrifying.

Tracie knew she needed to contact her handler, and she needed to do it before speaking to anyone at the NTSB, or even anyone from the Air Force. A U.S. military officer had brought down that jet last night and had murdered two fellow officers in cold blood, and the only entity Tracie could think of possessing the kind of reach necessary to accomplish that—and the desire to do so—was the KGB.

She wandered back into the living room and flipped on Shane's television. A local news reporter was doing a live broadcast from Bangor International Airport on last night's B-52 crash, and in the lower right corner of the screen was a picture of Shane.

"Sources tell us this man, Shane Rowley, an air traffic controller living in Bangor, was on his way to work at the time of the crash and managed to rescue the as-yet unidentified woman. Her condition and whereabouts, as well as the whereabouts of Rowley, are at this time unknown, but News 9 has learned Mr. Rowley is scheduled to meet with NTSB investigators as well as Air Force representatives at nine a.m. inside the control tower building at BIA to assist in the investigation. More on this story as it develops. Jane Finneran, WBGR News 9."

Tracie stared, her heart sinking. Shane had called a supervisor last night to explain why he wasn't at work and that person, or someone close to that person, must have leaked details to the press.

This was bad. She looked from the television to the letter still clutched in her hand. Whether it was the KGB or some other entity determined to prevent the communiqué from reaching President Reagan, they would have no reason to stop until they accomplished their goal, not after committing multiple murders and destroying an airplane worth tens of millions of dollars.

A chill ran down her spine. She glanced at a wall clock hanging over the TV. 8:50 a.m.

She limped to the pile of clothing in the kitchen, dropped her towel to the floor, and strapped her backup weapon—now the only gun she had left—to her ankle in its holster. Then she stepped into the underwear, jeans and sweater as quickly as she could manage. They were a little loose but would have to do for now.

She took another look at the living room clock. Its hands seemed to be moving at double speed.

There was a lot to do. She only hoped she wasn't too late.

24

May 31, 1987
8:50 a.m.
Bangor, Maine

Shane drove along the roadway leading to the air traffic control facility at Bangor International Airport, which consisted of crumbling chunks of decades-old pavement that had at one time made up the runways and taxiways of the old Dow Air Force Base.

The field had originally been a small civil airport, but had seen three runways hastily constructed at the onset of World War Two, and then a massive 11,400-foot runway added during the darkest days of the Cold War. Dow had been utilized as a Strategic Air Command base for two decades, launching B-52s and other military aircraft until its decommissioning in 1968.

After it was taken over as a civilian airfield and renamed Bangor International, almost all of the runways and taxiways had been closed, deemed too expensive to maintain. The single remaining runway was long enough to accept any aircraft in the world, civilian or military, including the space shuttle.

Many of those closed runways and taxiways were turned into access roads, resulting in some of the widest, if bumpiest, motorways a Maine driver would ever encounter. It was on one of these long-ago taxiways Shane was now bouncing along in his Volkswagen.

The control tower loomed in the distance, ancient and drafty, sticking into the air like a giant's middle finger. Next to the control tower was a squat base building, as old as the tower, which housed the TRACON, the terminal radar approach control facility, in addition to offices and conference rooms.

Several hundred yards from the facility, a Bangor Police Department officer had angled his cruiser across the pavement. The vehicle didn't come close to blocking the wide access road, but the officer standing next to his cruiser, hand resting lightly on the butt of his service weapon, made perfectly clear anyone approaching had better stop.

Shane eased up next to the cruiser. Mirrored sunglasses hid the cop's eyes and his face was impassive. He shook his head. "Sorry pal, no access today."

Shane help up his government ID. "I'm expected. My name is Shane Rowley. I work here, and I've come to assist in the accident investigation."

"Hold on," the cop said. He opened the cruiser's door, picked up a clipboard from the front seat, and glanced at it. After a moment he looked again at Shane's ID and then he nodded, his face still a mask. "Go right on ahead, sir."

Shane, curious, asked, "Have you had a lot of people trying to get up here?"

A trace of a smile flitted across the cop's face. "Not since I turned away the first couple of media vans. I'm sure they're waiting until I get pulled out of here, then they'll be on you guys like flies on shit."

Shane chuckled. "Don't be afraid to shoot 'em if you have to."

As he was pulling away, the cop said, "I wish."

* * *

The parking lot was nearly full, with a half-dozen or so cars Shane didn't recognize taking up the few available spaces.

He found a spot closest to the outer edge and parked, a light breeze ruffling his hair as he crossed the lot to the base building's front entrance. He punched the entry code, then pulled open the door and entered the building.

Inside was a long hallway with doors running down each side. Immediately to the right was a small kitchen area, equipped with an ancient oven, a slightly newer microwave, a dual-tub sink, a coffeemaker, and a small round table nobody ever used. Twenty feet beyond the kitchen on the right a doorway opened into the radar control room, where on a typical workday a controller would spend half his time, with the other half spent working upstairs in the control tower.

On the left side of the hallway were a series of administrative offices: first came the secretary's, occupied during weekday business hours by a sweet, white-haired lady named Mrs. Sanderson, who was maybe sixty years old and who had worked at the facility as long as anyone could remember. This being a Sunday, her office was empty.

Beyond Mrs. Sanderson's office were the rest of the staff offices, beginning with that of the air traffic manager, Marty Hall. Hall's name was just similar enough to the host of the popular game show, Let's Make a Deal, Monty Hall, that it was his fate to be forever known as Monty—at least when he wasn't around.

Shane lifted the carafe off the Mr. Coffee machine and sniffed warily. He could really use another cup of coffee, but the liquid inside the facility's pot was usually so old it had the consistency and taste of used motor oil. Today was no exception, and Shane grimaced and returned the carafe to the hot plate. He decided he wasn't quite that desperate for caffeine.

He left the kitchen and wandered down the hallway, moving toward the sound of voices coming from Marty Hall's office. He stopped at the open doorway and glanced inside. The facility manager was seated behind his desk, with a half-dozen people Shane did not recognize sitting in folding metal chairs arranged in a semicircle around Hall's desk. Everyone seemed to be talking at once and for a moment nobody noticed Shane.

When it seemed like this stalemate might go on forever, and mindful that this was his day off, Shane cleared his throat.

Finally Marty Hall noticed him and waved him in. Everyone stopped talking and turned to stare at the new arrival.

Hall said, "Gentlemen, this is my controller, Shane Rowley, the man who witnessed the crash while on his way to work last night."

Shane nodded at the group while Hall continued. "Shane, this is the NTSB Accident Investigation team. They only just arrived about fifteen minutes ago. I'll let each member of the team introduce himself."

They all did, Shane shaking hands with each in turn, and then the lead investigator pointed to an empty chair and said, "We're still awaiting the arrival of the Air Force representatives. Obviously, they wouldn't be part of the investigation if a military aircraft hadn't been involved, but it's their airplane and they will take part as well. It will undoubtedly complicate matters, but we welcome their involvement."

Shane sat, amused. It was plain by the tone of the investigator's voice that he was anything but welcoming of more investigators, but that he knew full well there was nothing he could do about it.

"How long before you expect the Air Force guys to show up?" Shane asked, picturing Tracie Tanner fast asleep in his bed back home. He felt a strong attraction to the beautiful—if enigmatic—young woman, not that he expected anything to come of it. She had made abundantly clear her desire to leave Bangor in her rearview mirror, and as soon as possible. But if nothing else, he wanted to see her one more time to say goodbye in person, and the longer this interview took, the less likely that was to happen.

"They'll be here soon," the lead investigator said, glancing at his watch.

Shane noticed for the first time that each of the men surrounding Hall's desk had a plastic nameplate pinned to the lapel of his suit, like children on the first day of school, and the man addressing him was named Paul Fiore.

Fiore said, "The Air Force investigators are flying here from Andrews Air Force Base and are in the air as we speak. But I'd like to start now and then catch the other folks up when they arrive. You'll probably have to go over your statement more than once, but my guess is you're going to be telling the story more than a few times, anyway."

"That's fine," Shane said, although it really wasn't. There was no way he was going to get out of here anytime soon.

"So," Fiore said, leaning back in his chair and lacing his fingers behind his head. "Take it from the top. You were driving to work last night and the damned B-52 fell out of the sky next to you?"

"More or less," Shane said. "This part of Maine is so heavily wooded I didn't actually see the plane crash. I caught a flash of the aircraft almost directly overhead, much too low to be on normal approach to Bangor, and then it was gone. A second or two later— barely enough time to register what I'd seen—I heard and felt the impact and knew immediately what had happened. That was when I pulled my car to the side of the road and went into the woods to see if I could find the accident site."

The questioning continued, each investigator asking for clarification of various points at various times.

After maybe twenty minutes, Fiore got around to the subject Shane had expected him to address right off the bat. "I understand you pulled a survivor out of the wreckage. I admire your bravery, Mr. Rowley. It is imperative we speak to this young woman also, and as soon as possible. We've checked all of the hospitals within a fifty-mile radius of Bangor and no one has any record of treating a crash survivor. Where is this woman now?"

This was the question Shane had been dreading. He understood the need of the investigators to question her. After all, who better to describe the circumstances of an airplane accident than someone who'd been aboard the plane?

But by the same token, the girl had made it quite clear she was in serious trouble and did not want to be found.

Shane didn't believe for one second Tracie Tanner had done anything to contribute to that B-52 going down, but he also wasn't about to admit the subject of their search was even now sleeping, injured, in his bed. He took a deep breath and opened his mouth to speak, still with no idea what he would say, when a *Crash* out in the hallway diverted everyone's attention.

And everything went to hell.

Shane craned his head toward the door, as did everyone in the room, just in time to see fellow controller Jimmy Roberts, on duty in the radar room this morning, stomp angrily past the office door in the direction of the facility entrance.

"Who the hell do you think you are? And what the hell is up with all the noise?" Roberts asked, continuing down the hallway and disappearing from view.

Shane heard a *phht* sound, followed in rapid succession by another, and Jimmy stumbled backward into view. He wavered unsteadily in the hallway before crumpling in a heap outside the office door. A spreading ring of crimson stained the front of Jimmy's shirt, and he lay on the floor gasping for breath.

Chaos erupted in the office. Chairs toppled over as everyone stood, jostling and banging into each other, some moving to help the injured man, others backing away from the door.

A half-second later a pair of large men filled the doorway, standing over the fallen Jimmy Roberts. They were dressed in suits remarkably similar to the ones worn by everyone in Hall's office except Shane, and he had the absurd thought that maybe more investigators had arrived.

Then he saw their handguns.

The two investigators closest to the door saw the guns as well and they shoved backward, hard, plowing into Marty Hall, who had gotten up and rounded his desk at the sight of the injured Jimmy Roberts. He toppled directly into Shane, knocking him to the floor.

Shane pushed immediately to his feet, still stunned by the suddenness of the onslaught. The men inside the room were cursing and shouting.

Shane looked toward the doorway and saw the intruder to the right scan the room. The man wore thick glasses and his eyes widened when he looked at Shane. He nudged his friend, gesturing in Shane's direction with his gun, which was big and black and fitted with a sound suppressor on the business end.

"Everybody sit down," the man on the left said with an Eastern European accent. He was muscular, with a blocky head that seemed to melt directly into his shoulders. "No one needs to get hurt."

And Shane exploded. He knew he should do as he was told, slow things down, try to figure a way out of this. But Jimmy Roberts was his friend, they had started out as air traffic control trainees at Bangor on the very same day six years ago, had worked traffic together, gone drinking and fishing together, and double-dated with their wives, back before each man's marriage had crumbled.

Jimmy Roberts was his friend, and Jimmy Roberts was lying on the floor at the feet of these men, dying or already dead.

"No one needs to get hurt?" he spat angrily. "It's too late for that, wouldn't you say? Or do you get a mulligan on your first victim and you only start counting after number one?"

"Easy, Shane," Marty Hall said softly.

The man with the glasses snarled, "Shut your mouth right now."

Shane realized he had taken two steps forward without thinking. He was lost in his rage and his grief and wanted nothing more than to get his hands on the man who had taken Jimmy down. Somewhere in the back of his mind he knew he was making a mistake, but at this exact moment he just didn't care.

And in that instant, things went from bad to much worse.

The guy with the glasses was saying something about everyone calming down and shutting the fuck up, that they only wanted to talk to Shane Rowley—Shane thought, *how the hell do they know my name?*—and then they would go away and leave everyone else alone, and that was when Paul Fiore, the lead NTSB investigator, leapt forward and let loose a roundhouse right, catching the guy doing the talking in the side of the head.

The man went down like a sack of Aroostook County potatoes and the room, which had gone silent, erupted in chaos again.

The no-neck guy pivoted and fired. The slug caught Fiore in the face and his head exploded in a spray of blood, and everyone was screaming and scrambling for cover, trying to escape the hail of bullets as the guy continued shooting.

The man Fiore had punched pushed himself up off the floor, shaking his head, as the square-headed guy began picking off investigators one by one, *like shooting fish in a barrel,* Shane thought.

He dived behind Hall's desk, banging heads with the facility manager and barely noticing the resulting flash of pain.

Hall was panting like he'd just run the Boston Marathon. "What do we do now?" he wheezed.

"Good question," Shane said, trying desperately to think. He knew they had just seconds left before everyone in front of the desk would be dead and the men with the guns came for them.

He looked around for something they could use as a weapon. The metal chairs were scattered around on the floor and Shane wondered how long he might survive if he charged the men using a chair as a makeshift shield.

Not long, he thought.

He squinted against the sunlight streaming in through the window behind Hall's desk, making it almost impossible to see.

The sun. It was coming through the window.

And Shane knew what to do.

He told Hall, "I'll go first, just in case there are still shards of glass sticking out of the window frame. My body should pull most of them out as I go through, but we'll only have a second or two before the guys with the guns react. You gotta follow right behind me."

Hall said, "What are you talking about?" but there wasn't time to explain. The gunshots were dying out and the screams were dying out, which meant the investigators were dying out.

They were out of time.

Shane lifted one of the metal chairs right beside the desk and took a deep breath, then stood quickly and heaved it through the picture window. He dived out the jagged window opening right behind the chair, praying Hall had understood.

He landed on the chair and felt a slash of pain as his elbow struck the metal seat. He rolled onto his back and looked expectantly up at the window, waiting for Marty Hall. The air traffic manager appeared at the window and grabbed hold of the frame, but he was moving much too slowly. He wasn't going to make it.

Shane screamed, "Never mind climbing, just dive out! Dive, get out now!"

He watched in horror as Hall began stuttering like a marionette, bullets peppering his body, slamming it down onto the window frame.

"Goddammit!" Shane screamed in fear and frustration, watching as his boss slumped half in and half out the window, bloody and unmoving.

There was nothing he could do for Marty Hall, or for anyone inside the building. The slaughter had taken no more than a minute, although it had seemed much longer, and Shane knew he had just seconds left before the men with the guns appeared at the window and took him out, too.

He rolled to his feet and started racing toward the parking lot. He would use the cars for cover and try to make his way to his Beetle. Maybe he could start it up and get down to the cop who had set up the roadblock at the access road. It wasn't much of a plan, but it was a hell of a lot better than standing around waiting to be killed.

Shane sprinted into the lot, half expecting to be shot in the back, and ran straight into a third man in a suit. The man was holding a gun fitted with a sound suppressor that looked identical to the ones carried by the two men inside the facility, and he placed it squarely against Shane's forehead as he skidded to a stop.

The man eyed him coldly and Shane knew he was going to die.

25

May 31, 1987
9:10 a.m.
Bangor, Maine

Tracie jammed the accelerator to the floor and turned the stolen Datsun toward Bangor International Airport. The little car was built for fuel economy, not speed, and it reacted sluggishly.

She pounded the steering wheel in frustration, wishing she had stolen a livelier car, but hadn't wanted to risk hot-wiring a vehicle equipped with an alarm system. The ancient cream-colored Datsun, pocked with rust spots and plastered with bumper stickers, had seemed the safest choice.

She had glanced around the apartment parking lot, trying not to be too obvious, and when she hadn't spotted any observers, picked up a brick-sized rock and tossed it through the driver's side window. Then she flipped the door lock, opened the door, and threw a blanket she had taken from Shane's apartment across the seat.

From there it had taken less than thirty seconds to hotwire the car—*chalk one up for CIA training*—and chug out of the parking lot. She guessed Bangor International was roughly a ten-minute ride from Shane's apartment, and the woman broadcasting the live news report had said Shane's NTSB interview was to take place at the ATC facility at nine.

It was now shortly after that. She hoped she wasn't already too late.

Tracie knew the KGB had operatives working in many major U.S. cities. Assuming Boston was one of those cities, or even New York, the KGB's agents could have driven up Interstate 95 overnight. They could be here right now. They could have seen, or learned about, the news report detailing Shane's actions last night as well as the NTSB's intention to interview him today.

They likely would even have learned where and when the interview was to take place. The KGB was not known for their subtlety. Shane would be a sitting duck.

The entrance to Bangor International Airport loomed ahead on the left. Tracie wheeled the Datsun onto the access road, cutting across two lanes of oncoming traffic, serenaded by squealing brakes and honking horns. She ignored them and accelerated toward the control tower.

Two-thirds of the way along the access road she could see a police cruiser slewed across the road, hazard lights flashing, no doubt to prevent the media and curious onlookers from gaining access to the control tower complex. Tracie suddenly realized she had no idea what she was going to say to the cop to avoid being turned away, especially considering she was driving a car with a smashed-out window.

She toyed with the idea of simply blowing past the cruiser, but the Datsun was so underpowered the idea was laughable. She would be stopped before she ever got close to the facility.

She would have to think of something. If worse came to worst she would pull her weapon on the officer and force her way in, and worry about the repercussions later.

She slowed to a stop next to the cruiser. The cop was nowhere in sight. She suddenly got a very sick feeling in the pit of her stomach.

Tracie lifted herself up as high as she could in the driver's seat and craned her neck, looking out the passenger side window into the cruiser. That was when she saw the officer. He was sprawled across the front seat, unmoving, blood staining his uniform shirt.

Shit. Tracie put the gearshift in neutral and yanked on the emergency brake, then leapt out of the car and hurried to the cruiser. She pulled open the door and knelt, placed two fingers gently on the side of the cop's neck. Felt for a pulse. Found none.

He was dead. Shot multiple times at close range. The KGB was already here.

Dammit.

The cop's body was still warm, so they hadn't been here long. Tracie considered finding a phone and calling an ambulance and then immediately rejected the idea. The officer was dead and the wasted time might cost more lives.

She cursed again and sprinted back to the Datsun. She slammed the door and gunned the car toward the control tower, racing along the decrepit access road, driving much too fast. The vehicle bounced and jolted, slamming down into potholes so deep she was half afraid an axle might snap. She kept going.

The car sped around a corner, and a couple of hundred yards away Tracie could see the control tower and FAA base building. She slowed slightly, trying to come up with some kind of action plan, when a side window in the base building shattered. The glass exploded outward as a metal folding chair flew through the window, followed a heartbeat later by a tumbling body. It looked like Shane Rowley.

He dived through the window and landed on top of the chair, then rolled onto his back and looked up at the window. A second man appeared. The man was older, and slower, and as he tried to climb out, his body began to stutter as bullets ripped into him from behind, and then he fell and slumped across the frame.

Shane scrambled to his feet and ran along the narrow alleyway between the base building and the control tower. He burst into the parking lot and was met by a man holding a silenced handgun. The man was facing away from Tracie, but she could see him raise the gun and shove the barrel into Shane's forehead.

And she didn't hesitate.

She drove her foot to the floor and aimed the Datsun straight at the pair. The gunman didn't seem to have heard the sound of the little car's engine, or perhaps didn't comprehend the significance. Shane was facing the vehicle and Tracie hoped he would understand her intent.

The car screamed toward the parking lot and the two men grew steadily larger in the windshield. The gunman seemed to be talking, asking Shane a question or maybe threatening him.

Nothing in Shane's demeanor gave away the fact that a speeding car was hurtling toward them.

At the last moment Shane dived to the side, just as it seemed to occur to the man in the suit that something was wrong.

Shane hit the pavement and rolled. He disappeared from sight as the Datsun plowed into the man with the gun, catching him in the side with a sickening thud. His body flew up and over the hood. He crashed into the windshield and then tumbled over the roof in an ungainly somersault.

Tracie watched in the rearview mirror as the man dropped onto the pavement and lay still. She slammed on the brakes and skidded to a stop just shy of a big vehicle with U.S. Government plates. Then she jammed the car into reverse and began backing up, one eye on the gunman, still crumpled in an unmoving heap in the middle of the parking lot, one eye searching for Shane.

She spotted him crouched between two parked cars just as the base building's front door crashed open and two more men exited the building at a dead run. The men wore suits similar to the downed gunman and each was holding a gun. They turned right and ran toward Tracie and their injured conspirator.

And Shane.

Tracie leaned across the front seat and shoved the passenger door open. "Get in here, now!" she screamed. She reached down and unsnapped her gun. The men were closing fast, shouting something unidentifiable.

She leaned out the smashed window and twisted, pointing the gun in the general direction of the pursuers. She squeezed off two quick rounds and the men hit the deck, flopping face-first to the pavement.

Shane dived through the opened passenger door, a sprawl of arms and legs, landing on the floor-mounted gearshift and unintentionally pushing the Datsun into neutral. By now the two men had risen from the pavement and were almost on top of them. Tracie jammed the car into first gear and popped the clutch and the little vehicle spun its wheels and then took off.

One of the men had reached the driver's side door and held doggedly to the doorframe as he ran along beside, screaming at Tracie, trying to aim his gun.

She jerked the wheel from side to side, zigzagging out of the parking lot, trying to break his grip. Finally the man tumbled away from the vehicle. He rolled into a grassy field next to the roadway.

Shane was screaming, "What the hell's going on here? What the hell's going on here?"

"We'll talk about it later," Tracie answered, realizing she too was screaming. Her hands were shaking as adrenaline flooded her system. She lowered her voice and tried to calm down, to think clearly.

"Right now," she continued, "we have to get out of here. We've got barely any head start and those guys know what vehicle we're in. They'll be right on our tail. If they have any kind of decent wheels at all, they'll catch us in no time."

The Datsun screamed past the dead officer's cruiser, Tracie keeping the gas pedal pinned to the floor. She briefly considered switching cars with the cruiser but didn't dare take the time to stop. They rocketed toward the phalanx of news vans and curious onlookers, the surprised faces growing rapidly larger in the now-cracked windshield.

She glanced right and saw Shane making a visible effort to get himself under control. He had lifted himself into a sitting position and now buckled his seat belt—a smart move under the circumstances. Tracie saw blood sprinkled across his face and clothing. He didn't seem to notice. He took a deep breath and ran his bloody hands through his hair.

Tracie blasted into the intersection of the airport access road and cross street, barely slowing, somehow managing not to T-bone a passing car and kill them all. She turned right, toward Bangor proper and Interstate 95, risking a glance in the rearview mirror, certain the two men in the suits would be right on their tail, but they were alone. For now.

When Shane spoke again his voice had modulated, although it was shaking and he was panting. "First off," he said, "thank you for saving my life. I think I was down to my last couple of seconds on earth when you ran that guy down. That was some quick thinking and some unbelievable driving on your part."

She shook her head and started to answer, but he interrupted.

"Second," he said. "What the hell have you gotten me into?"

26

I-95 buzzed beneath the tires of the Datsun as the wind whis-tled through the little car and buffeted the occupants. Outside, evergreens flashed past, the northern Maine terrain beautiful but monotonous.

After leaving the airport and their attackers behind, Tracie had driven straight to the interstate, but rather than turning south as Shane had expected her to, she had instead driven past that off-ramp and headed north.

"Where are we going?" he asked, confused.

"Those goons know I have to get to D.C. as soon as possible. They'll assume we high-tailed it in that direction. Once they get their act together and come after us, that's the way they'll go. If we'd gone south before changing vehicles, they'd have been on us before we knew what hit us. We'd be dead before we made it ten miles."

"But they didn't even follow us out of the airport."

"Yes, they did. Trust me. The only reason they didn't run us down before we even got off airport property is because they had to go back and toss the guy I ran over into the back of their car. They couldn't afford to leave him there, and he's injured, so that slowed them down. Once they hustled him into their car, though—and I guarantee it didn't take very long—they started out after us. Going north instead of south will buy us a little time, give us a chance to catch our breath, acquire a new vehicle, and formulate some sort of plan."

Shane raised his eyebrows. *"Acquire* a new vehicle? Don't you mean *steal?"*

"Acquire, steal. Tomato, tomahto."

He shook his head. "'Acquire a vehicle?' 'Formulate a plan'? Who the hell *are* you? And what kind of trouble are you in? Because that was a goddamned bloodbath back at the airport. There are dead people lying all over the inside of the tower base building, some of them my friends."

When she didn't answer, Shane pressed the issue. "Come on, Tracie, I know I owe you for saving my life, but the way I see it, my life wouldn't have needed saving if I hadn't hauled your ass out of that burning airplane last night. So I think you owe me, too. How about some answers?"

She chewed her lip as she drove, clearly conflicted about what—or how much—to share.

He kept quiet, letting her fight her inner battle.

Finally she spoke, but it wasn't to shed any light on the situation. "You can't go home until this is over," she said reluctantly. "Thanks to the news media, those guys know your name, which means they can find out where you live. They probably already have. They want to use you to find me. They may well be tossing your apartment right now if they have the manpower."

"What?"

"I'm sorry," she said. "You've gotten mixed up in something big, something I don't even understand completely, and you won't be truly safe until it's over."

"All the more reason, then, to answer my questions."

Tracie nodded. "I know. But let's find a new car first and get something to eat. Once we get started southbound we're going to have a long drive ahead of us and I'll try to fill you in on as much as I can, then." An exit ramp was approaching rapidly and she flicked the turn signal and exited the highway.

"Fair enough," Shane said. "So let's do it. What are we looking for?"

"An All-American strip mall."

* * *

May 31, 1987
9:45 a.m.
Old Town, Maine

They found one within a quarter-mile of leaving the interstate, a long, low, L-shaped cluster of concrete-block buildings that could have been stamped out of a cookie-cutter mold and dropped into any city, town or suburb in the United States. Probably a couple of decades old, the businesses looked tired, not quite defeated but struggling mightily.

There was a Laundromat, a mom and pop convenience store, a drugstore, a Chinese restaurant, and a half-dozen other businesses, with two or three empty storefronts scattered among them.

"Perfect," Tracie muttered after looking it over for a few seconds. She drove into the complex and parked the Datsun roughly in the center of the lot, alongside a group of cars clustered in front of the Laundromat.

"I thought we were going to get some food," Shane said. "The Chinese joint is all the way down at the other end of the mall."

"That's true, and we are," Tracie said. "But once we're done eating, we're going to 'acquire' a car, remember? Too many customers do take-out at your typical Chinese restaurant. We wouldn't want to be in the middle of hot-wiring Suzy Homemaker's station wagon and have Suzy walk out of China Lucky with her Kung Pao special, catching us right in the act, would we?"

"Us?"

"Okay, me. But you'd go to jail, too. The point is we're less likely to be caught in the act by someone who's fluffing and folding inside the Laundromat than by someone picking up their takeout order."

"What if they throw their laundry in the washer and then go out for a drive, or to get a cup of coffee or something?"

Tracie shrugged. "Then I guess we're screwed. There are no guarantees in life, right? But it's clouding up out here and there's a cold breeze. Hopefully most people would want to stay inside the warmth of the Laundromat than go out and freeze their butts off."

"Hopefully."

"Yep. Anyway, that's my theory, so unless you have a better one, let's hike across the lot and share a meal, shall we? And speaking of freezing, you probably noticed that driving at highway speeds in Maine in a car with a smashed window makes you a lot colder than you might have expected, even in late May. It'll feel good to warm up a little."

Shane hesitated. "Uh, well, I hate to seem un-chivalrous, especially since you just ran over a guy holding a gun to my head, but I've only got a few bucks in my pocket. I'm not sure I can afford a meal, and it might be kind of hard to keep a low profile with an angry restaurant owner chasing us into the parking lot."

"I've got enough cash for now and I can get more. Come on, it's my treat."

They shared a combination platter, Tracie skillfully and consistently deflecting any questions about her background and about what she had been doing aboard the doomed B-52 and why men with guns were chasing her around Maine.

"You promised you'd answer my questions," Shane reminded her, surprised but pleased to be eating Teriyaki Steak at this time of the morning, only now realizing how hungry he was.

Tracie nodded. "I can't tell you everything. I just can't. But I'll fill you in on what I can, I promise. Not here, though. We'll have that conversation in the car, away from potentially prying ears."

Shane looked around the dining room. It was dark and mostly empty. "Who's going to hear us in here?"

Tracie shook her head. "Later," she said, and that was that.

* * *

May 31, 1987
10:30 a.m.

She paid the check and they strolled back into the parking lot. The clouds had continued to gather and there was a chilly bite to the air, more like early March than late May. Shane watched as Tracie's sharp eyes scanned the parking lot. She was obviously looking for any sign of trouble.

"I thought you said those guys would go south," he said.

"I'm sure they did," she answered. "But if they hauled ass for ten or twelve miles, pushing hard, and didn't catch up with us, I think it's a least a possibility that they would have doubled back and maybe started prowling the areas surrounding the Bangor exits, looking for the Datsun."

"That's reassuring," he said as they walked back toward the knot of cars parked outside the Laundromat.

She shook her head. "Everything looks fine. I don't see anything unusual, do you?"

He glanced around. "Nope. So what do we do now?"

"Now we try to pass for a normal young couple as we look for a car with unlocked doors. I really don't want to drive around in this Arctic air again with another broken window."

She took his hand like it was the most natural thing in the world. They wandered across the parking lot, keeping several rows of cars between themselves and the Laundromat windows.

"What if everyone's cars are locked?" Shane asked.

"Yeah, right," Tracie said, grinning. "Sooner or later we'll find an unlocked vehicle, and I'm betting on sooner. When we do, we'll 'acquire' it."

She was right. The words had barely left Tracie's mouth when Shane spotted a white Ford Granada, unlocked and empty.

Tracie took a casual look around, and when she found no one paying them the slightest attention, said, "Okay, let's go."

She hurried to the driver's side door. She slid into the car and pried the plastic cowling away from the lower portion of the steering column almost before her body had even stopped moving.

Shane watched in amazement as she pulled a pair of wires free and then touched the bare ends together. There was a spark and the Granada started up, running roughly for a second or two and then settling into a contented purr.

"I always wondered how they did that," he said.

Tracie turned to him with a dazzling smile. "I've picked up a few skills," she said. "But it's time to go." She wheeled the Ford toward the exit and freedom.

Shane twisted in his seat and looked out the rear window, certain the car's angry owner would be sprinting across the lot in hot pursuit. But there was no one, the lot was quiet, and then they were on the road. Three minutes later they were back on I-95, this time headed south.

Shane slumped in his seat. "That was nerve-wracking," he said. "I'm really not comfortable with stealing a car. What if we get pulled over? We'll get busted for Grand Theft Auto."

"We're not going to get pulled over," Tracie said. "I'm going to be the most careful little driver you ever saw, and once we get a few exits south of Bangor, we'll stop somewhere and exchange plates with another car. The police will have no reason to stop us."

"Okay, fine, but why can't we just *go* to the police and tell them someone's after you? That way we stay on the right side of the law, instead of becoming wanted car thieves."

"We're not thieves," Tracie said, exasperation evident in her tone. "The owner will get his car back in short order, good as new. Probably. And in the meantime, we stay alive. I can't go to the police because…well, I just can't."

"Not good enough," Shane said. "You promised you'd give me some answers. Well, we ate, we 'acquired' another vehicle, and we're on our way south, maybe driving into some kind of ambush around the next corner. It's time for you to tell me what's going on. It's past time."

So she did.

27

May 31, 1987
4:55 p.m.
Portland, Maine

After leaving the Bangor area behind, Shane and Tracie drove for a long time without seeing much beyond the occasional small town, looking isolated and lonely in the distance. They passed Waterville and then the state capitol of Augusta, eventually reaching Portland, where they stopped for gas, to use the restrooms and to grab another bite to eat.

Then they continued on.

Shane spent most of the drive in silent contemplation of the incredible turn his life had taken in less than a day. A fiery plane crash. A secret document. A beautiful CIA operative. KGB spies. Murder.

The whole scenario was outlandish. It was like something out of a Tom Clancy novel.

Twenty-four hours ago, Shane would have dismissed it all as a nonsensical nightmare. But that was before he'd seen a room full of professional investigators gunned down in cold blood, had a silenced pistol shoved between his eyes, helped steal a car, and gone on the run.

He shook his head. He realized with a start he hadn't given a single thought to the deadly diagnosis he had received yesterday, the one that had shaken him up so badly, since seeing the airplane burning in the forest.

Until now.

The miles continued to melt away under the tires of the Granada. Shane found himself struggling to keep his eyes open. He blinked a few times, stifling a yawn. They had spent the entire afternoon in the car, with just the short break in Portland at midday, and it was now late afternoon. The skies had cleared as they moved south and the sun blazed high in the sky, but Shane felt like he could drop into a deep sleep at any moment.

"Go ahead and relax," Tracie told him, amused. "Once the adrenaline from the conflict melts away, that high is replaced by a feeling of lethargy. It's your body's way of coping. It's not every day you have to fight off psycho gunmen. At least I assume it's not."

"You assume correctly," Shane agreed. He chuckled and then sobered, thinking about the slaughter that had taken place back at the Bangor Airport. "You don't think the cops believe *we* killed everyone back in Bangor, do you?"

Tracie considered the question. "Right now, I doubt they know *what* to believe. Witnesses saw us leave the airport, undoubtedly followed immediately by the gorillas chasing us, but that doesn't mean much one way or the other. Unless there is someone still alive who can describe exactly what happened—"

"And I don't think there is," Shane interrupted. "As far as I know, the only people they didn't kill were the controllers in the radar room working airplanes, and those guys wouldn't have seen anything, because they were inside a dark room in a separate part of the building."

"If that's the case, then it would be in our best interest not to get picked up by the police. They would eventually have to release you, but it would take a long time to verify your story, and they wouldn't be in a very forgiving mood, not with a half-dozen or more murdered people—one of them a cop—on their hands."

Shane rubbed his face, still just as tired but now nervous as hell, too. He exhaled forcefully and looked across the front seat at Tracie. "So, what's the plan?" he asked. "Where are we going? What do we do now?"

"Well," she said, looking at her watch. "For the rest of today, we'll have to maintain a holding pattern. I've got some cash and a few goodies stashed away inside a safe-deposit box in a bank just outside New York City. The first priority is to retrieve that, but since today is Sunday, we'll have to wait until tomorrow to get at it. We'll have to find an anonymous motel somewhere between here and New York and hole up for the night. I'll call my boss and fill him in on what's going on, and then tomorrow we get up bright and early, make a little bank withdrawal, and then continue toward D.C."

Shane stared hard at Tracie, who gazed straight out the wind-shield, pretending not to notice him watching her.

"A little bank withdrawal," he said.

She glanced across the front seat, a Mona Lisa smile on her face. "That's right."

"What could you possibly have stored in a safe deposit box that will help us out of this jam?"

"I told you, I have some cash."

"You told me. You also said, and I quote, 'a few goodies.' What's that supposed to mean?"

"Oh, you know, a little of this, a little of that."

"You're talking about weapons."

"Well, maybe. You know, a girl has to be prepared for anything."

She returned her attention to the highway and Shane watched the scenery roll by as the Granada continued churning south. *What sort of girl just happens to keep a cache of weapons and money handy? What else might she have stored in that safe-deposit box?*

He thought about the events of last night, about her insistence on avoiding the hospital despite being injured in a deadly plane crash.

About her stoic toughness as he cleaned and dressed her deep thigh wound, wearing gym shorts and little else.

About those long legs, slim and smooth and sexy.

Then he started thinking about things that had nothing to do with secret communiqués or spies or airplane crashes.

He daydreamed about sexy secret agents for awhile, and eventually he fell asleep.

28

May 31, 1987
8:10 p.m.
Washington, D.C.

Winston Andrews was well into his third gin and tonic when he realized he was gulping rather than sipping. He pondered that realization for a moment and eventually concluded he didn't care. His Georgetown condominium felt cold, empty and lonely since Emily had died—was it really almost three years ago?—and he could no longer come up with a single reason to sip rather than gulp.

The endgame was coming, Winston could sense it, and he was surprised to discover he didn't mind all that much. He and Emily had never had children, so when she succumbed to lung cancer—the ultimate irony, Winston thought, given her status as a nonsmoker and lifelong health nut—the only thing left to occupy the long hours in the day was work.

And that was fine, as far as it went. Winston had always been nearly fanatical about his work. But now, push was coming to shove, and Winston was no longer particularly interested in dealing with the shove. Approaching seventy, he had devoted his life to United States intelligence services since playing a critical role in the U.S.-Soviet collaboration to defeat the Nazis in World War II.

Winston had spent virtually that entire war on the ground in Russia, making and cultivating contacts with the Soviets while they were suffering horrific losses of life, more than twenty million people dying before the defeat of Hitler had been accomplished. By 1945, when the Axis nations finally surrendered, Winston Andrews—genteel, Ivy League-educated Winston Andrews—had emerged as the most knowledgeable American alive regarding the affairs of the Soviet Union, both politically and militarily.

Winston had served in the CIA for the next four decades, keeping his contacts inside Moscow active and even, to the utter astonishment of his superiors at the agency, developing new contacts as the older ones died, retired, disappeared or faded away.

During the darkest days of the Cold War in the 1950s and 60s, Winston was considered a star, funneling to the highest levels of the United States government classified intel regarding Soviet military buildups, aggression in foreign countries, KGB activity, and the Soviet Space program.

You name it, Winston Andrews knew about it. His information helped shape the foreign policy decisions of an unbroken string of eight presidents from Truman to Reagan. He wasn't a Democrat or a Republican—although if pushed, Winston might reluctantly admit toward a liberal bias—he was simply an intelligence gatherer.

But Winston Andrews harbored a secret. While funneling all of that sensitive information regarding the Soviets to the U.S., he was simultaneously funneling information regarding the United States intelligence services to the Soviets.

This was Winston's secret. *This* was how he had developed the deep connections in Moscow that others had never been able to accomplish. *This* was how he was able to retrieve sensitive information regarding the Soviets almost in real time.

He knew there had been the occasional whisper questioning his loyalty over the course of the last forty years, suspicions muttered, his work examined through narrowed eyes. But the intelligence he delivered was so consistently valuable, so up-to-the-minute, so sensitive, that the whispers and suspicions never developed into anything more. They invariably died away, often for years at a time.

Winston supposed—hell, with the clarity provided by gulping three gin and tonics, he more than supposed, he *knew*—that most people would consider him a traitor to his country if they learned his secret, but he didn't see it that way. Above all, Winston Andrews was a pragmatist. The more information the two superpowers with opposing political philosophies and mutual suspicion possessed about each other, the less likely they were to blow each other up.

"Mutually assured destruction," was the term describing the concept. It signified each nation's knowledge that the other could retaliate for any aggressive act, nuclear or otherwise, by wiping their enemy off the face of the earth. It sounded like a terrifying prospect because it *was* a terrifying prospect, and as an academic, Winston knew nothing could diminish the likelihood of mutually assured destruction as effectively as information.

So he did what he had to do, year after year, decade after decade, through Republican administration and Democrat, and regretted none of it. Winston liked to believe the fact that both countries were still standing forty years after his first tentative information exchange was proof positive his theory had been right.

He pushed himself up from his leather recliner, wobbling unsteadily, and tottered out of his office for another drink. He had no regrets about anything he'd done over the past four decades, but what was happening now was different. This was a situation unlike anything he had ever experienced. Lives were directly at stake. In fact, lives had already been lost, and that loss of life could be traced right back to Winston Andrews.

Winston could accept the notion of sacrificing a few in the interest of saving many. He had built a career on that concept. But in the past, that loss of life had been largely theoretical, at least to Winston. He had no doubt Soviet citizens had died thanks to intelligence information he had generated. Probably Americans had lost their lives, too, due at least in part to information he had passed on to Moscow.

But as far as he had been aware, there had never been a direct connection.

Until yesterday.

Until he had learned of a plan set in motion by some in the KGB to prevent a secret communiqué, written by Soviet General Secretary Gorbachev and addressed to President Reagan, from reaching the White House. Despite his best efforts, Winston had been unable to ascertain what was contained in the letter and, in fact, strongly suspected the KGB didn't even know.

But their plan had backfired. The plane crash ordered by the KGB had occurred not in the middle of the Atlantic as planned, but on U.S. soil, just a few hundred miles away, in Bangor, Maine. Now, news organizations were reporting that an unidentified female passenger, whose whereabouts were currently unknown, had survived the crash.

The passenger wasn't unidentified to Winston, though.

The passenger was his agent, Tracie Tanner, a young operative he had discovered and helped train, talented and smart.

And things got even worse from there. A brutal massacre had taken place at Bangor International Airport: seven people slaughtered in cold blood, one a law enforcement officer. He shuddered at the thought of the carnage, a chill running down his spine that was unrelated to the temperature in his office.

Winston had no way of knowing whether Tracie was still alive. It was possible the KGB, whom he was certain had engineered the attack at the airport, had killed or captured Tracie and taken possession of the letter.

He didn't think that was the case, though. Tracie Tanner was perhaps the finest operative he had ever supervised over forty years in charge of the CIA's Soviet Intelligence Division. He doubted a small group of Russian operatives working on U.S. soil would have had the ability to eliminate her, unless she was badly injured or they simply got lucky.

He was in the process of mixing another gin and tonic when the shrill ringing of a telephone caused him to slop gin onto the bar in surprise. It wasn't his house phone, it was one of his special telephones, the one that received incoming calls only rarely, and only from a select few Russian intelligence officers. Even the majority of his contacts inside the USSR were not privy to this number.

This was the call Winston had been dreading. He could predict, almost word for word, how the conversation was going to go, and it wouldn't be good.

He sighed deeply and reluctantly climbed the stairs to his second floor office. There was no need to hurry; the caller wasn't going anywhere. And he wouldn't give up.

Winston walked to the phone, which he had placed squarely in the middle of his desk in anticipation of this call. "Hello?"

"Are you secure?" the caller asked, not bothering to identify himself. No introduction was necessary. Winston recognized the distinct baritone immediately, the voice raspy from a lifetime of abusing strong Russian vodka and unfiltered American cigarettes. It was Vasiliy Kopalev, the highest-ranking KGB member Winston had ever dealt with.

"Of course," he answered, hoping he sounded stronger and more confident than he felt.

"Good. I am certain you are aware of the events of today?"

"I know what I've seen on the news."

"Then you know our operation has, thus far, been an abject failure."

"It would seem so."

"We need to know where your agent is, Mr. Andrews. We need to know right now."

"I understand, but she has not yet contacted me. She has been quite busy, though, as I'm sure you are well aware. If she is able, she will be in touch soon."

"Are you being honest with me, Mr. Andrews? The critical nature of this mission cannot be overstated."

Winston's heart sank. There was no way out of this. Kopalev's presence on the other end of the line was indication the KGB intended to play their cards right to the end.

He hesitated long enough for Kopalev to bark, "Mr. Andrews!"

"Yes, yes, of course I'm being honest with you, Vasiliy. The moment I hear from my operative, you will know it."

"Sooner is better than later. We must gain possession of that letter."

"I understand. As I said, when I hear from my agent, you will hear from me." The line went dead and Winston returned the handset to its cradle, lifting the telephone off the desk and placing it into a drawer, which he then locked.

Tracie Tanner. His protégée, the daughter he never had. To be delivered up to the KGB, after which she would most certainly disappear forever. His stomach roiled, the gin sitting in his gut like an unexploded bomb.

He sat at his desk, head in his hands, for a very long time. Then he stood and walked downstairs to finish making that drink.

29

May 31, 1987
9:40 p.m.
New Haven, Connecticut

They made it as far as New Haven before stopping for the night.

Shane felt almost as tired upon waking from his nap as he had before falling asleep. He offered to switch places and take a turn behind the wheel but Tracie declined, saying, "I do some of my best thinking when I drive, and right now I have a lot to think about. Besides, we've gone about as far as we need to today."

She steered the car off I-95 and then seemed to drive aimlessly around New Haven looking for a suitable motel. She checked out three run-down establishments, all equally unappealing to Shane, eliminating each from consideration for reasons he could not discern.

Finally she selected one. The winner in the overnight housing sweepstakes featured a central parking lot separating two rows of attached wood-frame rooms that looked like mirror images of each other, right down to the peeling paint and crumbling cement foundations.

The motel appeared virtually identical to the other three as far as Shane could tell, and he looked at her quizzically. "This is the best we can do, huh?"

She smiled. "I'm a little low on cash, so we're going to have to slum it for tonight. Once we hit the bank tomorrow, money won't be as much of an issue, but for now I'm afraid we'll have to pass on the Four Seasons."

"Not to worry," he said. "I'm a cheap date. But just out of curiosity, if we were only going to stay at a roach motel, what was wrong with the first three places you scoped out?"

"None of them had the features I was looking for."

"And what features would that be?"

"Oh, you know, a little of this, a little of that."

"You already used that answer once today."

"I know," she said brightly, looking like the cat that ate the canary.

"Has anyone ever told you that you're one frustrating person to deal with?"

"More often than you might think."

"I doubt that."

Tracie parked the car in front of an office that looked like it had been built by the architect who designed the Bates Motel. An old-fashioned MOTEL sign hung in the front window, the glass tubes filled with red neon gas. The "L" had burned out, leaving MOTE flickering weakly in the darkness. Above it, another sign said NEW HAVEN ARMS.

Shane looked at the MOTE with distaste. "I hope that's not a warning of what's waiting for us in the rooms."

"Ah, come on, how bad could it be? Where's your sense of adventure?" she said, stepping out of the car and stretching.

Shane reached for the door handle to join her and then stopped, admiring the view through the windshield as she reached for the sky. The night was mild and she hadn't bothered to pull on her jacket and her blouse lifted as she stretched, revealing a taut belly. He had already gotten an up-close and personal look at her legs last night while cleaning her injury, and he decided this young woman was the complete package.

She bent down suddenly and looked in the driver's side window, catching him staring, and laughed. She waggled her index finger.

"Naughty boy," she said through the closed window. It looked to Shane like her face colored a little, but maybe that was his imagination.

He clambered out of the car after her. "Sorry about that," he said, although he really wasn't, and he knew *she* knew he wasn't. "So, what's the plan?"

"What do you mean, what's the plan? Come on Romeo, haven't you ever shacked up with a girl of questionable repute in a run-down motel before?"

"Sure," he said. "But when you say it like that it sounds so cheap."

They shared a laugh and she turned toward the door. "Just follow my lead," she said, and entered the office.

The décor was Spartan and had gone out of style sometime before John Glenn orbited the earth. A potted plant stood in one corner covered in dust. It looked like it was dying despite the fact it was made of plastic. A small couch, the fabric ripped and torn, lined the wall next to it. To the left of the entrance was a single rickety wooden chair.

They moved to the front desk and Tracie dinged a small bell. Through an open door behind the counter came a rustling sound and then the scraping of a chair, and a moment later a rumpled-looking scarecrow of a man appeared. He was dressed in loose-fitting jeans and a stained Rolling Stones T-shirt, and he gazed at them suspiciously through red-rimmed eyes, as if not quite able to believe a customer had actually entered the place.

"Help you?" he asked, making clear through the inflection in his voice it was the last thing in the world he really wanted to do.

Tracie flashed a smile and Shane thought she could have been a beauty queen if she wanted to. Or an actress.

"We'd like to rent two rooms," she said, and the clerk actually took a step back, blinking in surprise. Shane knew how he felt.

"*Two* rooms?" he said and then paused, like he was waiting for the punch line.

"That's right, and I know exactly which ones I want."

"Oh-kayyy," the clerk said, now clearly convinced the world as he knew it had been thrown off its axis.

"We would like to rent the rooms at the far end of the parking lot, one on each side, facing each other," Tracie said, still smiling, enjoying the clerk's confusion.

Scarecrow-man shook his head, not even attempting to hide his skepticism. "Sign here," he mumbled, lifting a worn logbook up from under the counter and sliding it across at Tracie. "That'll be fifty bucks total."

She dug the money out of her pocket, signed the log book—Shane watched as she wrote "Sally Field" next to one room and "Kathleen Turner" next to the other, and the clerk shook his head again—and then received two keys. Each was attached to a red plastic fob with the words "New Haven Arms," as well as the room numbers, stamped in faded gold lettering on both sides.

"Thanks," she said, flashing another dazzling smile at the clerk, although she had to have known by now charming this guy was impossible.

They turned toward the door and the clerk mumbled, "Checkout time's ten a.m., Miss Field."

Tracie waggled her fingers in response and then they were back in the parking lot, the smell of the nearby Atlantic Ocean floating across the night air as they walked to the Granada.

"Two rooms?" Shane asked.

"Security," she said, the answer puzzling him. Was she afraid of him?

If he was going to hurt her, he could have done it last night when she was passed out on his couch or in his bed. *Besides,* he thought, remembering the pistol she had waved in his face. *She's the one with the gun.*

Tracie laughed. She seemed to know exactly what he was thinking. "Not security from you, silly."

She started the car and drove slowly to the back of the lot, then nosed into the parking space directly in front of the last room on the right.

"Then from who?" Shane asked. "You don't think those guys from the airport can find us, do you? I mean, how could they possibly know where we would be?"

"How, indeed," she said thoughtfully.

Shane shrugged, exasperated. This was one strange young woman: beautiful and alluring and sexy, with a girl-next-door innocence about her, but also tough as nails and somehow world-weary, as if being chased by cold-blooded killers represented just another day at the office.

"Okay," he said, shaking his head. "I give up. Which room do you want me to take?"

She flicked her thumb in the direction of the room across the parking lot, directly behind the Ford. Shane held his hand out for the key and Tracie looked at the room numbers stamped on the plastic fobs, then handed him one. He took it without a word, annoyed, then opened the car door and stalked off across the lot.

When he reached the other side, he stuck the key in the door, surprised by the motel's poor lighting. The doorway was bathed in shadows despite the fact the moon was full. He opened the door and realized Tracie was right behind him.

"I thought you wanted me to take this one," he said.

"I do. I also want me to take this one."

"Then why the hell did we rent two rooms when you said you're almost out of money?"

"I told you," she said. "Security."

Shane stared at her. "You really are worried about those guys."

"Not worried, exactly, but let's just say I like to maintain a healthy dose of concern at all times. It's what keeps me alive."

30

May 31, 1987
9:55 p.m.
New Haven, Connecticut

The room was more or less what Tracie had expected: small and cramped, with outdated furnishings and a bed topped a mattress that was probably as old as she was, covered by an off-white set of threadbare blankets and a fading blue bedspread. She had stayed in a hundred similar rooms all over the world—and many that were much, much worse.

It was clean at least, more or less.

Shane bounced on the bed like a little kid, grinning. "Wanna take it for a spin?" He waggled his eyebrows like Groucho Marx and she burst out laughing.

"As tempting as you make it sound," she said, "I have work to do. I really need to call my handler. In fact, this phone call is way overdue. I should have contacted him last night, but I was down and out and then today we've been too busy trying not to get killed. Before I do that, though, we need to set up the room across the way."

Shane looked at her quizzically. "Set it up?"

"Yep. You can put all that excess energy to good use, although maybe not he way you intended. We're going to haul all the pillows over there, as well as any extra blankets you can find."

"What for?"

"Bait."

Shane picked the two lumpy pillows off the bed while Tracie investigated the tiny closet. In it was a small ironing board, and ancient iron, and an extra set of bedding: two sheets and two blankets. She grabbed the blankets and sheets, wondering if anyone frequenting this rundown piece of shit motel had ever had occasion to iron an article of clothing, or if the iron even still worked.

"Take the blankets and the bedspread off this bed," she told Shane. "We can use those across the way as well. We'll leave the sheets, though. I don't think I'd want to even sit on the bed without something covering it." She wrinkled her nose.

"Take this bedding? What about you? What are you going to sleep on? I'll sleep on the floor in my clothes and you can have the bed, but without blankets it won't be very comfy."

Tracie smiled. He was being a perfect gentleman, despite his half-joking proposition of a moment ago.

"We're going to trade off sleeping," she said. "Nobody will have to sleep on the floor, because one of us is going to stay awake all night, watching the room across the way. Even when you're sleeping you'll have to stay in your clothes, anyway, because if we have to move we'll need to be able to do it quickly."

"What will we be watching for?"

Tracie chewed on her lower lip, a reaction to stress she'd been trying unsuccessfully to break for as long as she could remember.

"Hopefully nothing," she said in a tone that didn't even convince herself.

Shane stared at her for a long moment. She thought he was going to reply but didn't. Then he stripped the covers off the bed, rolled them up into a ball, and hugged the pillows and bedding to his chest. He opened the door and they trooped across the parking lot to their second room.

Tracie examined the lot as they crossed, pleased with her choice of motels. The sight line between the two rooms was perfect, the lighting in the parking lot was abysmal, and only a couple of the other rooms appeared occupied, both of them far off in the distance next to the office.

They entered the second room and found a mirror image of the one they'd just left, right down to the faded coloring on the decades-old bedspread. She pulled the spread to the foot of the bed and then did the same thing with the blankets and top sheet. She placed her blankets on the right side of the bed and told Shane, "Hand me yours."

When he passed them over she placed them lengthwise on top of hers, folded the whole pile back on top of itself, and then scrunched everything up in the rough approximation of a sleeping body.

She stepped back and examined her handiwork with a critical eye.

"Hmph. Guess it'll have to do," she muttered. "Good thing it's dark out there."

She walked around the bed, darting past Shane with the grace of a dancer. "Toss me the pillows," she said.

When he did, she arranged them lengthwise along that side of the bed, creating a second sleeping body. Then she pulled the original blankets back over her creation, covering the two lumps.

She took one more look and then shrugged. "What do you think? Does it look like two sleeping people?"

"Maybe to Ray Charles," Shane said and she punched his arm.

"Wise ass. It only has to fool them for a couple of seconds."

"Then what happens?"

"I happen."

"What does that mean?"

"It means they get interrogated."

"By you?"

"That's right."

"But this is all for nothing, because nobody's coming."

"Hope so."

"You and me both," Shane said, concern in his voice.

She winked at him and walked to the bathroom, flipping the switch on the wall. Then she pulled the door almost all the way closed. A thin shaft of dirty yellow light slashed across the main room, illuminating just enough of the beds, she hoped, to convince any interested visitors that two people were actually sleeping in them.

"That's going to have to do," she said.

"Now what?" Shane asked.

She pulled her dwindling supply of cash out of her pocket and studied it. "You said you had a little money, right?" she asked hopefully.

Shane said, "Yeah, I've got around twenty bucks."

"Good," she answered. "I'll go out with you and start the Granada, then I want you to take it and find an open hardware store. We need duct tape."

"Duct tape. What do we need duct tape for?"

Tracie grinned and waggled her eyebrows as he had done when they entered the first motel room. "Use your imagination."

* * *

Back in the original room, Tracie picked up the phone and dialed a complex series of numbers from memory. She waited for an accompanying series of beeps and then dialed more numbers. There was a thirty-second silence and then the earpiece buzzed, indicating the line was ringing.

The call was answered on the second ring. "Green twenty-seven," a voice said.

"Red eighteen," Tracie answered.

"Thank God you're okay," Winston Andrews said. "When I didn't hear from you last night I started to think maybe you had crawled off into the woods and gotten yourself eaten by a bear." He seemed to be enunciating carefully, like he was trying not to slur his words.

"Nope, I'm still kicking."

"Do you have the cargo?"

"I have it."

"Any damage?"

"It's like me: a little beat up but fine."

"How close are you?"

"Still a few hours out. We're going to hole up in a cheap motel for the night and come into D.C. tomorrow."

"We?"

"I have a civilian with me. It's the guy who rescued me from the

143

burning B-52. He's got a bulls-eye on his back now and will until this thing is over. I thought it best to keep him close."

"That's a serious breach of mission protocol."

"I know that. I'll deal with the consequences later."

Andrews sighed heavily. Through the phone's earpiece the sound was like a strong gust of wind. Tracie had worked with her handler a long time, and she was convinced he'd been drinking.

Like he had a lot on his mind.

Like he was worried.

"Where are you?" he asked.

"In the New Haven area, somewhere safe," Tracie said, hoping against hope he would let the issue drop.

"Tell me the exact location and I'll pull some strings," Andrews said. "You know, keep you out of trouble. You left one hell of a mess up there in Bangor. Every cop along the Eastern Seaboard is looking for the dirtbag who shot one of their brethren point blank in the chest and drove off. They're out for blood, and it seems they don't much care whether they shoot one of the Russian guys or you."

Her heart sank, and not because of the police who could be after them. Her worst fears had just been confirmed. Andrews was involved with the Soviets. She had always wondered about that, had heard whispered rumors over the years. The fact he wanted to know exactly where she was verified her suspicions.

Tracie hesitated, trying to put just the right amount of indecision into her response. "Me revealing my location on an unsecured line is against mission protocol, too."

"I understand that, but I'm trying to keep you alive. I have some connections in the New Haven area. Tell me where you are and I can call in a few favors, divert the attention of the law from your area until you're safely out of there tomorrow."

Tracie sighed loudly and gave in. "Okay. We're holed up in Room Twenty-One at the New Haven Arms, just south of I-95. It's a cheap little dive, well off the beaten path. There's no way anyone could track us here. We'll be fine."

"I hope so," Andrews said. "Just the same, I'll call my people in the area and make sure the cops stay away from there overnight."

"Thanks. We should see you by late afternoon tomorrow."

"Roger that," Andrews said. "Stay safe."

He broke the connection and Tracie sat on the edge of the bed, staring out the dirty picture window at the dark parking lot. She couldn't decide whether to be angry or sad.

She settled on both.

31

Shane pulled the Granada into the spot it had previously occupied in front of the dummy motel room and then trotted across the pavement to Room Twenty.

The door swung open and he knew immediately something was wrong. Tracie barely acknowledged him. Her face was troubled and she was obviously deep in thought.

"What is it?" he said. "What's the matter?"

She smiled forlornly. "You mean aside from this whole mess?"

Shane nodded.

"I just got off the phone with my handler, a man named Winston Andrews, an intelligence specialist who's been the company's foremost expert on Soviet covert activities since well before I was born."

He placed a paper bag on the ancient dresser between the two beds. "Okay. And?"

"And I'm almost certain he's involved with the guys who are trying to kill us."

Shane froze. "Why do you say that?"

"He asked where we were staying, claimed he could use his influence to divert the attention of the police away from this area. They're looking for us and are pretty pissed off about the dead cop back in Bangor. Anyway, Andrews said he would help keep the police from shooting our asses off."

"So what's the problem? I'm pretty fond of my ass and I'd hate to see anything happen to yours. We could certainly use all the help we can get."

"*This* is the problem." Tracie picked the telephone's black plastic handset off its cradle and brandished it in front of him, dropping it back onto the receiver with a thud.

"The telephone connection in his home office is secure. It's a dedicated CIA line, encrypted, nearly impossible to hack into. But this—" she pointed again at the offending motel phone—"is anything *but* secure. Anyone could have been listening in. Andrews violated Rule Number One of covert operations. He should never have asked me to reveal our location on an unsecured connection when there's a Russian hit team chasing us all over the East Coast."

"Maybe..." Shane's voice trailed off as he struggled to come up with a reasonable explanation, knowing he was wasting his time. Tracie would already have found one if it existed.

"No," she said grimly. "He's involved. It's the only thing that makes sense, the only reason he would care where we were. Obviously the KGB is up to something big, something potentially game-changing, or else they never would have risked exposing so many of their U.S. assets in such a desperate manner for one simple op."

Her eyebrows knitted together in concentration. "This letter I'm tasked with bringing to Washington—no one besides Gorbachev himself knows what's in it. I think he's trying to send a warning directly to the president."

Shane was skeptical. "I don't know," he said. "It sounds pretty farfetched, like something out of a Hollywood movie. *The Manchurian Candidate* or something."

"It sounds farfetched, I'll give you that. But I can't imagine what else could have the KGB this spooked."

"But they've only thrown three guys at us. I mean, it's pretty daunting from our perspective, but what are three guys to the KGB in the grand scheme of things?"

"Three guys is a lot," Tracie said, her face burning with intensity. Shane was amazed. She barely resembled the All-American-looking girl he had gotten used to riding with.

She paused, thinking something over, and Shane wondered if he had just been dismissed. Then she said, "How much of your American History do you remember from high school?"

"I don't know. Some, I guess. I mean, it was interesting so I mostly paid attention."

"You've heard of the McCarthy hearings?"

"Of course. Joe McCarthy was a U.S. Senator back in the 1950s who started a big Communist scare, claiming the commies had gained influence in all levels of U.S. society, governmental and otherwise."

"Exactly," Tracie said, nodding, still intense. "McCarthy had a lot of people running scared, but eventually it was determined there was no way the Soviets could possibly have infiltrated our government to the extent McCarthy was claiming. He was discredited."

Her laser stare bored in on him as if willing him to understand. He didn't.

"Don't you see?" she said. "There weren't a huge number of Soviet Communists in the United States, at least not such a large number they could do any real damage. But that doesn't mean there weren't *any*. The Soviets probably have an agent or two in many of our major cities, enough operatives to pass along whatever intel they can gather, but not the numbers to really accomplish much. Maybe a few dozen people total, similar to the number of assets we have in Russia. The numbers just aren't that great.

"So when they expose three of those few dozen people in such an obvious and risky way, it's significant. It means something if you're paying attention. And like I told you before, attention to detail is what keeps me alive."

"So what are we going to do?" Shane asked.

"Well, if what I believe is true, we've probably got a minimum of, say, two hours before anything happens. The goons chasing us will have expected us to head toward D.C., but they had no way of knowing how far we would have gotten. They're probably ahead of us because they'll assume we wouldn't stop—"

"Which we wouldn't have," Shane interrupted, "if you didn't need to get at your cash."

"Exactly. So they'll have to double back once Andrews relays our location to the Russians. That's why I say we should split the night into two-hour shifts. One of us keeps watch while the other sleeps. If it's alright with you, you can start with the first watch, since I really don't think anything will happen for awhile."

"Of course I'll take the first watch. I'll do whatever you want. But in the meantime, there's something else we need to talk about."

"And that is?"

He cut a look at Tracie. "You need to open that letter. I mean, like right now."

"The letter is classified."

"I understand that."

"It's Top Secret."

"I understand that."

"It's for the president's eyes only."

"I understand that."

"I'm expressly forbidden to open it, Shane."

"I understand that, too, and under normal circumstances I would never suggest you disregard protocol. And I'm well aware that you've been doing this black ops stuff—"

"Clandestine operations," she interrupted.

"What?"

"I don't do 'black ops.' I do clandestine operations, missions that by necessity must remain deniable by those in positions of authority all the way up the political and military food chains."

"Whatever," Shane said. "And thank you for making my point for me. As I started to say, I understand you've been doing these types for things for years and I've only been exposed to this shit for a day, but it's pretty obvious to me you're just stumbling around in the dark unless you know what you're up against. If your fears about your handler are anywhere close to being accurate, reading that letter might make the difference between living and dying. More to the point, *only one person in the world* knows what it contains, and it seems to me becoming the second person to know might be the best way to figure out how to proceed. Hell, it's probably the *only* way."

Shane took a breath, amazed he hadn't been interrupted, amazed she had not yet shot him down.

"I know," she said quietly. "I've been thinking the same thing.

Opening this little time bomb"—she patted her pocket light-ly—"could get me executed for treason, but I don't see any way around it. I've been sitting here trying to work up the courage to do it."

She took a deep breath. "I guess now's the time."

She held up Mikhail Gorbachev's correspondence. The enve-lope was soiled and wrinkled from its travels but even from across the room Shane could see it remained sealed. Tracie ran her fingers over the surface as if trying to divine its contents via osmosis.

Finally she tore one end off the envelope, careful not to damage the contents, then removed two handwritten sheets of paper, which she held up for Shane's inspection.

He took one look and felt like an idiot. The letter was written in Russian. Of course it was. Mikhail Gorbachev was General Secretary of the Soviet Union; why would Shane have assumed the damned thing would be written in English?

He shook his head. "Oh, for Christ's sake. What do we do now?"

"I can read it," Tracie said. "You can't be in my business and work in and around the Soviet Union without demonstrating some proficiency with common Russian dialects."

She pulled the letter back and squinted down at it, concentrating.

"To President Reagan," she began, and then continued haltingly.

"Dear Mr. President. Please accept my apologies for this most unusual method of communication. The contents of this letter are of the utmost importance, critical to the security of both of our countries and, in fact, the entire world. The information I am about to impart to you is so explosive, I am afraid I cannot trust the usual diplomatic channels for delivery. You will soon understand why."

Tracie lifted her head and looked at Shane. He face was trou-bled, her beautiful eyes haunted. She looked back down at the letter and continued reading.

"As you know, Mr. President, changes are sweeping the globe. Many inside the Kremlin insist on resisting these changes and are intent on preserving the Soviet Union in its current incarnation at all costs.

"I do not agree with the assessment of these people, but they form much of my government, and their plan for assuring the continued survival of the Union of Soviet Socialist Republics is one that has a direct impact on you personally.

"Mr. President, a plan to assassinate you has been set in motion by a powerful minority at the highest levels of the KGB. Your travel itinerary for June 2 has been acquired and your outdoor speech celebrating the District of Columbia urban renewal has been targeted. An operative placed on top of a nearby building and armed with a high-powered sniper rifle has been assigned to assassinate you as you deliver your remarks at ten o'clock.

"Please treat this information with the gravity it deserves, Mr. President. Relations between the word's two great superpowers have improved during the terms of your presidency, and I cannot allow the progress we have made to be nullified by the single-minded fanaticism of those inside my government who refuse to recognize the future, even as it approaches.

"Understand this assassination is being undertaken without my approval. But understand also that my administration does not currently possess the means to stop it. I hope you see now, Mr. President, why I am being forced to contact you via these drastic and unprecedented measures. I am subject to constant surveillance. There is no other alternative.

"Good luck, Mr. President. Cancel that appearance and avoid a catastrophe that will launch a third world war.

"Sincerely, Mikhail Gorbachev"

Tracie looked again at Shane. Her face had gone white. "June second. That's the day after tomorrow," she said.

* * *

Shane had to remind himself to breathe. He gazed at Tracie, still seated on the bed staring at the letter. The Top Secret document she'd risked her career, her freedom, maybe even her life to open.

"You have to alert someone," he said.

"I can't," she answered simply. "Not until I know whether Winston Andrews has been compromised. If I'm right about him, I can't trust *him* with this information, and if that's the case, I have no idea who above him in the chain of command I *can* trust. If I'm wrong, and the night passes quietly, no Russians show up to kill us and gain possession of this"—she held up the letter—"then first thing tomorrow I'll tell Winston everything."

Shane whistled quietly. "Holy shit," he said. "So what do we do now?"

"Now we wait. Try to get some sleep and see if we get any visitors in the night." Tracie stood slowly from the bed, wincing as she placed her weight on her injured leg.

Shane said, "I don't think there's any way I can sleep right now, not after this. If you're pretty sure we have some time, why don't we clean and re-bandage that leg wound of yours? If those guys show up like you think they might—"

"They will," she said dejectedly.

"Okay, well, if they do, you already said we're going to have to move fast. Right now you look like you're eighty years old."

"Thanks for the sweet-talk."

Shane laughed, relieved the black mood permeating the room had been lifted, even if only slightly. "Okay, let me rephrase that. You *look* fantastic, but you're *moving* like you're eighty years old."

"Hmph," she said. "I'll take what I can get, I suppose. But there's one problem. We don't have any bandages."

"You underestimate me," he answered. "I found a twenty-four hour drugstore as well as a home-improvement place while I was out. I picked up some Ace bandages as well as first aid cream in addition to the tape you wanted. Now, get out of those pants and let me check out—uh, I mean fix—those legs of yours."

Tracie smiled and limped to the bathroom while Shane reached into the paper bag, removing the first-aid supplies. A moment later the bathroom door creaked open and she returned, carrying her jeans. A motel towel that at one time had been white and was now the color of dirty dishwater was wrapped around her slim waist.

She eased onto the bed, primly covering herself, looking more like a shy young girl than the kick-ass CIA spook Shane now knew her to be. He wanted to crack a joke but decided she seemed uncomfortable enough without him making things worse, so he bit his tongue and began unwrapping the bandage covering her wound. Blood had seeped into the gauzy material before clotting, more or less, and the bandage felt stiff, stuck to the wound.

He stepped into the bathroom and returned a moment later with a washcloth soaked in warm, soapy water. He dampened the soiled bandage, working carefully to remove it. Then the cleaned around the puncture wound in much the same way he had done last night, dabbing and probing, doing his best to ignore the lacy pink panties he could see under the insufficient cover of the towel. Tracie squeezed her eyes shut, teeth gritted against the pain, muscles tensed.

There was no sign of infection, and when he had cleaned the injury to his satisfaction, Shane patted the area dry with a second towel. Then he began wrapping the fresh Ace bandage around her thigh, trying to make it tight enough to provide support and prevent the wound from bleeding again, but loose enough for some semblance of comfort.

He concentrated on his work and when he had finished, he looked up to find Tracie's eyes open, unblinking, staring into his. She eased up off the cheap headboard bolted to the wall and leaned forward, moving slowly, deliberately, and then they were kissing, and Shane thought about those pink panties and reached down and pulled off her towel, throwing it to the floor while she fumbled with his belt buckle and the snap on his jeans, and then they were together.

32

June 1, 1987
3:30 a.m.
New Haven, Connecticut

Tracie sat perched on a rickety chair, watching the mostly-empty parking lot through a slit in the drapes while Shane dozed. He had fallen asleep despite his protestations he wouldn't be able to, and now he lay sprawled across the bed, covers tangled around his waist, snoring lightly.

Tracie wondered if she should feel guilty for sleeping with him in the middle of this insanity. After all, they had been thrown together by chance, and when this was all over—assuming they survived; assuming the *president* survived—Shane would go back to his air traffic control job in Maine and she would return to Langley for another assignment. She had no way of knowing where that assignment might take her, but she was pretty certain it would not be Bangor, Maine.

So, yes, she thought, she probably should feel guilty. But she didn't. Her life for the last seven years had consisted of training, work, and more work, most of it clandestine and dangerous, and over the course of those seven years she could count her sexual relationships on the fingers of one hand. And she wouldn't need most of her fingers.

Then along came what at first glance appeared to be a simple job, a piece of cake once she had escaped East Germany. All she needed to do was babysit an envelope, deliver it to Washington, and then move on to her next assignment.

Somewhere along the line, though, things had become immeasurably more complicated, and in the middle of everything, here was this solid, earnest, well-meaning guy who was gorgeous to look at, self-deprecatingly modest, and who had, oh by the way, crawled inside a burning airplane to save her life.

The attraction she felt for Shane Rowley was immediate and consuming, and she simply hadn't been able to stop herself from coming on to him when he finished bandaging her leg.

She hadn't planned what happened between them, not exactly, but her injury certainly wasn't something she couldn't have dealt with on her own, either. She had handled much more severe wounds by herself, out of necessity, and could easily have waved Shane off when he insisted on cleaning and bandaging her leg.

So maybe what happened hadn't quite been spontaneous. Maybe somewhere deep in her subconscious, Tracie *had* intended to seduce him all along, but either way he didn't seem to mind. She smiled, thinking about the frenzied lovemaking of their initial encounter, and then a slower, more sensual round just a few minutes later.

She glanced across the room at Shane's sleeping form, and when she looked back out at the parking lot, the smile froze on her face before turning into a frown of concentration. A late-model Chevrolet Impala was creeping past the motel office, lights off.

From this distance and in the poor lighting, she couldn't make out the color, but the vehicle looked black or dark blue, or maybe green. It wasn't the car the Russians had used earlier—she had scanned all of the cars in the Bangor Tower lot by force of habit even as she had been rescuing Shane, and this Impala had not been among them—but that didn't mean anything. They would undoubtedly have changed cars by now, just as Tracie and Shane had.

She glanced at her watch. It was 3:45 a.m.

The Impala eased into a parking space several slots away from their Granada. Its driver killed the engine. For several long moments nothing happened. The car's occupants were being cautious, eyeing the surrounding environment, alert for any movement or anything out of the ordinary.

Tracie knew they couldn't see her in the darkened room. She waited, tense, weapon held in her right hand, ready to move.

Finally, both front doors on the Impala opened at the same time and two men stepped out. The car's interior lighting had been disabled. The men were dressed entirely in dark clothing, identical watch caps covering their heads, grease paint tamping down any sheen from their white faces.

Tracie's heart dropped, and the sadness she had felt earlier returned with a vengeance. Winston Andrews, her mentor and father figure, had betrayed her.

She forced herself to push her feelings aside. She needed to focus. She could come back to them and mourn her lost relationship with the traitor Winston Andrews later.

If she survived.

The two men outside moved slowly, scanning the parking lot while moving steadily toward the dummy motel room with the Granada parked nose-in toward the door.

Tracie backed silently away from the window and bent over the bed. She gently shook the slumbering Shane.

"It's going down," she whispered. "Stay here and keep quiet. If things go bad, get the hell out of here. Find a police station and turn yourself in."

He rubbed the sleep out of his eyes and nodded once.

Tracie crossed the tiny room in a few steps and slipped into the bathroom. Built into the rear wall was a window just large enough for her to wriggle through. She had cut the screen away earlier and the window stood open for easy access, the cool early-June night air filling the room with the tang of ocean salt.

She stepped onto the closed toilet seat cover, braced an arm on either side of the window frame, and boosted herself through. She dropped to the ground noiselessly, the long wooden motel building shielding her from sight of the parking lot. Three steps took her to the back end of the structure. Less than thirty seconds had elapsed since she had moved away from the picture window.

She peeked around the corner. Sixty feet away, shrouded in shadow, the two Russians had arrived at the front of the dummy motel room. One of the men was bent over the doorknob working on the lock, while the other stood facing outward, keeping watch.

The lock was cheap and Tracie knew if the Russian had any experience at lockpicking—and there was little doubt he did—the two men would be inside the room in a matter of seconds. She had to hurry.

A string of ornamental shrubs, brownish-yellow and dying, lined the rear of the parking lot, forming a barrier between the motel property and the trash-strewn alley behind it. Tracie ducked down below the tops of the shrubs and raced behind them, using them for cover, limping only slightly. She melted into the darkness at the rear of the dummy room and then made her way back along the side until she reached the corner. She bent down, hands on her knees, and worked to quiet her breathing.

A couple of seconds later she heard a muffled grunt of satisfaction and eased her head around the corner just in time to see the lock-picker begin easing the door open, He worked slowly, clearly concerned a squeaky hinge might awaken the occupants.

She waited patiently, just out of sight, as the two men stood in the doorway. The first man faced into the room, unmoving, door partly open, and she became concerned she had not done a good enough job of disguising the blankets on the bed to look like sleeping people. Then she realized the Russian was letting his eyes adjust to the darkness in the room before proceeding.

It made sense. It was what she would have done.

At last the first man disappeared inside, while the second man maintained his position at the door, facing outward with his back to the room. He held his silenced weapon against the side of his leg. The gun would be invisible should a car happen to drive into the lot, but Tracie could see it clearly, its black matte finish muted by the dirty half-light.

Within seconds the assassin inside the room would discover they had been duped. Tracie had to make her move before that happened or she would lose the advantage of surprise.

Still she waited. She would get an opportunity soon. The Russian hit team was being sloppy, careless because their intel had come directly from their high-ranking CIA connection. They were confident that their targets would not suspect a thing, that the doomed man and woman would feel safe and secure inside their anonymous New Haven motel room.

Instead of maintaining an active scan, the Russian at the door stared impassively into space, clearly bored, occasionally glancing left and then right. The third time he looked in the direction of the motel office, Tracie moved.

She broke from the cover of the motel building, moving silently but speedily. Before the guard could react, Tracie grabbed his gun with one hand. She used her other to place her own gun against his head, nestling the barrel in the soft tissue between the skull and jawbone. She pushed hard.

"Don't move," she said softly.

The man didn't move.

Tracie ripped the Russian's weapon out of his hand. He would have a backup, probably in an ankle holster, but she didn't have time to worry about that.

"Move into the room as quietly as you can," she whispered.

The man pivoted slowly and eased through the open door, Tracie right on his heels. The first Russian had arrived at the bed and stood next to it, his back to the doorway. The lookout cleared his throat and the first Russian froze for just a second and then whirled, sensing danger.

He wasn't quick enough. Tracie trained the lookout's gun on the assassin's chest, her hand unwavering, her Beretta still pressed against the first man's head.

"Drop your weapon," she said quietly. "Do it now or you die, and so does your friend. I won't say it again."

For a long moment nothing happened, as if the Russian was calculating his odds of survival should he attempt to shoot his way out of the room.

Tracie let him do it. His gun was pointed at the floor. Hers was pointed at his chest. He would inevitably reach the same conclusion she had: that he was out of options.

A moment later the gun dropped with a muffled thud to the thinly carpeted floor.

"Now kick it over to me," she said, and he did, undisguised malice in his hooded eyes. The gun skidded to a stop a couple of feet to her left. For now she ignored it. She didn't have a free hand to hold the third gun and it was far enough away from either of her captives that they would not be able to make a play for it without catching a bullet in the head.

She flicked her gun toward a small chair at a writing desk next to the TV stand. "Go sit down," she said, wondering how she was going to immobilize the assassin without giving the lookout an opportunity to jump her or go for her gun.

"I'm right behind you," a voice said and she jumped, barely resisting the impulse to squeeze the triggers on both weapons. She recognized it as Shane's voice and wondered briefly how he had made it to the doorway without her noticing.

The Russian assassin was a cool character—he was facing Tracie and must have seen Shane standing in the doorway behind her, but he had given nothing away with his cold, calculating eyes. He'd been waiting for an opportunity to take advantage of the unexpected visitor to make an escape attempt. Now it was too late.

Tracie spoke to Shane, still talking quietly. "You were supposed to wait in the other room." She couldn't decide whether to be glad he was there or angry he had ignored her instructions.

"I thought you might need help and I was right."

She nodded reluctantly. "Okay, the duct tape is in my right jacket pocket. Take it and secure our friend here," she nodded in the direction of the assassin, "to the chair. Tape his wrists to the arms of the chair first, then his ankles to the legs. Use plenty of tape and wrap it as tightly as you can. When you do his ankles, be sure to remove the gun in his ankle holster."

Shane eased past. Tracie kicked the door closed and shuffled forward, prodding the lookout with her weapon. Her arms were beginning to tire from the strain of keeping both guns raised and trained on their targets. The pair moved forward, locked in a bizarre dance, and finally she stopped when they had moved to within a few feet of Shane and the other Russian.

She watched closely as Shane slid the chair out from behind the desk and turned it around. The Russian sat and Shane got to work.

It took only a couple of minutes to immobilize the man and finish disarming him. Finally Tracie felt comfortable lowering the weapon in her right hand.

She told Shane, "Tape his mouth shut."

He wrapped the duct tape around the man's head and when he'd finished, Tracie said, "We're going to split these two up and

I'm going to get the information I need. This guy's not going anywhere. Come with me and help me tape down this one," she nodded toward the lookout, "and then come back here and babysit our murderous friend. It won't take me long to get what I need."

She shoved her gun into the ribs of her captive and moved to the parking lot. Shane picked the third and fourth guns up off the floor and walked out behind her, closing and locking the door. Then they hustled across the lot to the second room.

Within seconds, Shane had dropped the guns onto the bed and taped the man to the chair while Tracie held her weapon on him.

"I need a little private time with this guy," she said to Shane. "If Mr. KGB over there," she nodded at the room across the parking lot, "does anything other than sit quietly, shoot him."

Shane hesitated for just a moment and then nodded without a word. He pulled the door closed quietly as he left and Tracie was alone with her captive. She stared at him without speaking. He returned her gaze, trying to look defiant but only managing uncertain.

She smiled thinly. "What do you say we get to know each other?"

33

June 1, 1987
3:55 a.m.
New Haven, Connecticut

The iron was ancient, two decades old if it was a day, a cheap model with just a dew heat settings and a long, fraying power cord. Tracie could see a hint of bare copper wire nestled behind the rubber plug and wondered how long it would be before the damned thing sparked and burned the entire wooden motel structure to the ground.

It appeared today would not be that day, however. She plugged in the iron and held it by its cracked handle as she stood directly in front of her captive. She said nothing, drawing out the moment.

The Russian wasn't speaking, either. He was making an effort to control his fear but was failing. His shaking hands gave him away. His eyes darted around the room, doorway to Tracie to iron and then back to doorway, starting the cycle all over again.

Tracie raised her hand to her lips and licked her index finger, then tapped it against the business end of the iron. It emitted a short, sharp hiss. In the silence of the motel room it sounded like a staccato laugh. The lookout tried to remain impassive but she saw his eyes widen in fear.

She nodded. "Let's begin, shall we? I'm sure you can guess what's about to go down here. I'm not anxious to hurt anyone but I need answers and I'm going to get them. One way or the other."

The Russian remained quiet, his jaws clamped shut. Tracie could see the muscles working behind his cheeks as he ground his teeth together. The tension in the air was electric.

"You know," she said, "it seems only fair I should start with you. It's thanks to your sloppy surveillance that you and your buddy across the way are in this situation. He's probably pretty unhappy with you right now, don't you think?"

The lookout remained silent. He was stocky and muscular, like a football lineman, but his eyes gave away his terror.

Tracie continued, "It doesn't really matter, anyway. The only way I can be sure I'm getting the truth is to interrogate both of you, so if it makes you feel any better your buddy will get his turn, too."

Again the man refused to respond. It didn't seem to make him feel any better.

Tracie shrugged and then snapped her fingers. "Oh, I almost forgot. I wouldn't want you to accidentally bite your tongue off, at least not before giving me the information I need. It's so hard to understand someone when he's trying to talk with no tongue, especially when he's not speaking his native language. Know what I mean?"

She walked into the bathroom and pulled out the roll of toilet paper. She removed the roll from the metal cylinder and took the cylinder back with her. She stood directly in front of her captive, moving close, invading his personal space. He smelled like stale sweat and onions.

She held the cylinder out in front of him. "Last chance. You're going to talk to me either way. The only question is how much pain you're going to endure before you do."

The man hesitated. "I…"

Then he closed his mouth again.

Tracie shrugged. "All the same to me," she said conversationally. "To be perfectly honest, after what you two did to the cop and the accident investigators up there in Bangor, I kind of prefer it this way."

She leaned toward the lookout. "Open up." The conversational tone had disappeared, replaced with an ice-cold, deadly menace.

He closed his eyes and shook his head almost imperceptibly.

Tracie slammed the butt of her gun against the side of his head.

He grunted in pain, stunned, and opened his mouth to moan. She shoved the cylinder into place between his upper and lower teeth, then quickly slapped the base of the iron against the right side of his face, holding it there for one beat, then two, and then three. It sizzled and the smell of burning flesh filled the room.

The man bit down hard on the toilet paper holder, convulsing against his duct-tape bindings like an electric current was pulsing through his body. He tried to lean away from the burning pain but she kept the iron pressed tightly to his head. An agonized sound, something between a groan and a wordless scream, issued from deep inside the man's chest, and when Tracie removed the iron, an angry red mark had been seared into his cheek, its curved triangular outline clearly visible.

He panted and moaned and shook his head.

Tracie was unmoved. "Ready to talk?" she asked.

The man refused to respond and she lifted the iron to slap it back into place. He moaned in panic and began nodding enthusiastically.

She removed the toilet paper holder from between his jaws and said, "I know about the plot to assassinate President Reagan. I know where and when the shooting will occur. What I don't know is which D.C. rooftop your operative will shoot from. You're going to tell me."

The lookout raised his head, resignation in his eyes, and said, "Nyet...I cannot..."

Tracie cursed. "We don't have time for this," she spat, and forced the toilet paper holder back into the man's mouth. He mewled like an injured kitten.

She slapped the iron against the left side of his face and left it in place for twice as long as she had the first time.

When she finally removed it, the man sat in a puddle of his own urine, his bladder having released while he struggled. Trace slapped the side of his face with an open palm and the man opened his mouth to scream and she neatly plucked the holder out of his mouth once more.

"Let's try this again. Which rooftop?"

"The Minuteman Mutual Insurance Company building," the man mumbled, his Russian accent magnified by the pain. Tears rolled down his crimson cheeks. A thin line of drool leaked from the corner of his mouth. The smell of burning flesh filled the room and Tracie tried not to gag.

"Are you telling me the truth? Because if I find out you're lying to me, I'll burn your skin right down to the jawbone. Do you understand me?

The man was panting and shaking. Sweat poured down his face. "I understand," he said.

Tracie thought about Winston Andrews and about his betrayal, and another question occurred to her, one that didn't bear any direct relation to the KGB assassination plot but one she could not help asking.

"Was killing us part of the assignment?"

The man hesitated but only momentarily. Tracie passed the iron in front of his right cheek and the man spoke quickly. "Yes...I mean, no...I mean it did not matter. Once it was learned you were still alive, the mission was to retrieve the letter at all costs."

"And once you gained possession of the letter, what were you to do?"

"Take it to someone."

"Take it to whom?" She prodded him again.

"Mister Andrews," he said.

She paused, thinking. "How many of your other operatives will visit this motel tonight?"

"None," the man said, shaking his head in resignation. "There is a two-man team driving north from Atlanta, but they will not arrive in the area until tomorrow. They are meant only to provide backup."

"Okay," she said. "One last thing and then I'll leave you alone. What's the procedure for reporting in after you secure the letter?"

"After we retrieve the letter we are to phone our contact."

"Comrade Andrews."

"Da. We are to advise him of mission status and then begin driving back to Washington to deliver the letter to him in person."

Tracie reached for the telephone on the writing desk. It was an ancient black rotary model, attached to the wall with a long cord so guests could use it without getting out of bed if they wished.

"You're going to make that call right now," she said, holding the phone in front of him.

He recited the number and she dialed. It was different from the one she used to call Andrews, which made sense, she thought. The traitor down in D.C. would need to know which side of the fence he was talking to before he picked up any ringing telephone.

Before she spun the plastic rotary dial on the final digit, she leaned down and got in the Russian's face, moving once again closer and closer until she could smell his sour sweat and his rancid breath.

"One warning," she said, her voice soft and deadly. "If I so much as suspect you are trying to pass a message to Winston Andrews—and I'll know, I've worked with Andrews a hell of a lot longer than you have—getting burned by an iron will be the least of your problems. I'll shoot you in the face and then dump your worthless corpse in the Atlantic Ocean. Do you understand me?"

The Russian paled and nodded. "I understand," he said in his heavily accented English.

Tracie dialed the last digit and held the handset between her own head and the Russian's angled so he could speak into it but so she could still hear everything that was being said.

The call was answered on the first ring, as if Andrews had been sitting right next to the telephone. Undoubtedly he had.

"Go," he said without preamble.

"We have retrieved the letter."

"Very good. Casualties?"

"Your CIA asset and the young man are both dead."

There was a brief silence and then Andrews said, "Dispose of the bodies and then get back here with the letter. Do not let it out of your sight."

"We will be there as soon as possible."

The line went dead and Tracie replaced the telephone on the bedside table. A numb sense of shock filled her. Her handler, the man she had worked with for years, had just spoken of her murder with no more emotion than if he were discussing a change in the weather.

She turned back to the Russian. "I'm going to go and ask your comrade the same questions I just asked you. Do you understand what will happen to you if I find out you've been lying to me about any of this?'

"I understand," he said, defeated.

"Is there any part of your story you would like to change? If so, now's the time."

He shook his head.

She nodded once and then walked out the door.

*   *   *

Tracie was gone longer than Shane had expected her to be, and when she returned, her face was pale and drawn.

She stepped through the door and he asked, "Are you alright?"

She ignored the question. "Did this one give you any trouble?" she asked.

"No."

"Good," she said, and her face softened just a bit. "Nice job. Do me a favor now, and go keep an eye on the lookout. Our talk was very fruitful. It required a little persuasion to convince him to open up, but eventually we reached an understanding."

Shane stared at Tracie. Her voice was cold and hard and bore little resemblance to the one he had heard moaning and gasping in pleasure just a couple of hours before.

"Of course," he said. "What are you going to do?"

"I'm going to make sure the first guy told me the truth."

34

June 1, 1987
4:50 a.m.
New Haven, Connecticut

They moved quickly, Tracie directing the action. She had returned fifteen minutes after sending Shane to watch the lookout, her face grim but satisfied.

"I got what we need," she said, "and now we have to move. Help me get this guy to the other room."

After Shane had secured the man, she instructed him to wipe down all of the surfaces they may have touched. "I'm going to call the spooks on these two once I'm sure who we can trust at the agency," she said, "so fingerprints won't be an issue. But just in case someone finds them before I do that, I want to make sure you're protected. My prints are untraceable but I doubt you would be so lucky."

While Shane toured the room with a worn bath towel, scrubbing every surface he could think of, Tracie double-checked Shane's bindings to satisfy herself they would hold. Then she applied a second layer of tape over each man's mouth, winding it tightly around their heads and patting it into place.

Despite the fact the two men had been there to kill them, Shane almost felt sorry for them as he watched. They looked like twins, their cheeks flaming crimson, shiny and burning above their beards, and the tape's sticky adhesive must have felt like an additional torture session.

Tracie didn't seem to notice.

Once she seemed satisfied both men would stay immobilized, she gathered up the weapons and picked up a DO NOT DISTURB placard off the inside doorknob and told Shane, "Let's go."

She said nothing to the Russians, neither of whom had spoken since the end of the interrogation, and both men stared straight ahead, ignoring Tracie and Shane and, it seemed, each other.

They paused at the door, Tracie doing one last quick check of the room, Shane pondering how quickly his life had turned upside-down. After a few seconds, she hung the sign on the exterior doorknob, then eased the door closed and locked it from the outside.

They hurried across the rapidly lightening parking lot to the second motel room and Shane repeated his print-scrubbing exercise with the bath towel while Tracie packed their meager supplies in the Granada.

Tracie hung another DO NOT DISTURB sign on that door and then they slid into the car and drove to the motel office.

After paying for a second day's rental of both rooms, they hurried back to the car and drove out of the New Haven Arms lot, Tracie at the wheel. They turned toward New Haven proper in search of an all-night restaurant. It was 5:05 a.m.

* * *

They found one almost immediately, tucked away under an I-95 overpass.

The Original Greasy Spoon seemed to embrace the 1950s with an enthusiasm bordering on obsession. Shane knew Tracie was almost out of money and he thought he might have just enough cash left for two cups of coffee and a couple of blueberry muffins. He was right, and they walked out of the diner and back into the 1980s with their breakfast less than three minutes later.

Tracie asked Shane if he wanted to drive. He hadn't bothered to offer because even with all the traveling they had done yesterday she had not so much as considered giving up the wheel.

"Sure," he answered, surprised and pleased although he was not entirely sure why. It was as if he'd passed some kind of test back at the tumbledown New Haven Arms in the surreal few hours they'd spend there.

She climbed into the passenger seat and sat demurely, smiling at him while he dropped into the driver's seat.

"What?" he asked. "What's so funny?"

Then he went to start the car and realized. There was no key.

"Okay, you win. Would you mind starting this piece of junk for me?"

"No problem," she answered, pleased. "We'll make a proper criminal out of you yet."

She leaned over his lap to hot-wire the ignition and he flashed back to their time together in bed at the motel before the Russians had arrived. Her silky skin, her luscious lips, the curve of her naked hip under his hand, the way her breathing had quickened as he stroked her inner thigh, the sweet sound she made when—

He realized she had spoken to him and he cleared his throat. "Uh, sorry, I missed that," he said, embarrassed.

"I asked if you were going to start driving or whether you planned to sit there the rest of the day replaying your mental movie of us together in the sack."

"I wasn't..."

"Don't even try to deny it. I'm a trained interrogator, remember?" He could hear the smile in her voice.

"Okay, okay, I admit it. Just don't come at me with an iron."

She laughed, the sound light and girlish, light-years removed from the icepick chill she had displayed when dealing with the Russians.

Shane smiled and dropped the car into gear, turning left, right and the left again, climbing the ramp onto I-95 south, thoroughly confused by this young woman sitting to his right.

Thoroughly enchanted by her as well, although he knew he could not afford to be.

She ate delicately as Shane drove, picking tiny pieces off the muffin with her fingers and placing them on her tongue before chewing soundlessly and swallowing, brow furrowed in concentration. Shane had to be careful not to get so caught up watching

Tracie out of the corner of his eye that he drove off the highway and into the guardrail.

He let her think for awhile and when it became clear she had no intention of starting a conversation, said, "So, what did those guys tell you back there?"

"I know where the assassin is going to be stationed."

"How can you be sure they told you the truth?"

"They both gave the same location. There's no way they would have done that if one of them had been lying."

"Unless they agreed on a story beforehand, in case they were caught."

Tracie shrugged, conceding the point. "True enough," she said. "But I don't think so. Those guys were one hundred percent certain they were going to walk in on us in our sleep, put a bullet in each of our heads, and walk away with the letter. That's why they were so sloppy. They had no reason to suspect we were on to them, and thus no reason to make up a story. Plus, they wouldn't have expected us to know anything about the assassination."

She paused. "I'm confident I got the truth out of them."

"Okay," Shane said. "So what's the plan from here?"

"The plan? I wish I knew." She sighed heavily. "First stop is New York. We'll pick up my supplies and then head straight to D.C. I'll find a safe place to stash you, and then I'll have to pay a visit to my traitorous boss, Winston Andrews. From there, I stop an assassination. I'm not exactly sure how yet."

"Stash me? I don't think so. You said yourself I'm neck deep in… whatever is going on, and I've nearly been killed twice now in less than twenty-four hours. I have a stake in everything too, Tracie, in case you've forgotten. Plus, you can't do everything yourself. You need help, and I'm going to help you. Period. End of story."

35

"I don't understand," Shane said. They had pulled off the highway at a random exit, bought fresh coffee, and then hit the road again. Steam curled out of the plastic lids and dissipated into the air.

"It doesn't make sense. What possible advantage could there be for the KGB to launch World War Three?"

"It actually does make sense," Tracie said. "It makes perfect sense if you consider the situation in context. Maintaining tyranny is dependent upon wielding total control, but the world is opening up. Citizens who have been under the thumb of the communists for decades are beginning to get a glimpse of the freedoms they have long been denied, and they're starting to realize those freedoms are within reach. They want them.

"The Soviet Union is crumbling, Shane. I know because I've seen the evidence firsthand. They have arguably the finest, most modern military in the world, next to ours, and yet the rest of the Soviet infrastructure is in a shambles, as is their economy. It's getting harder and harder for the Soviets to keep their satellite countries in line, and more and more expensive to do so at a time when resources are shrinking.

"This makes perfect sense," she repeated, a reluctant sense of wonder in her voice.

171

Shane shrugged, frustrated. "Call me stupid but I still don't get it. Czechoslovakia wants to break away from the Russians. So what? How does that tie in with the KGB assassinating the president of the United States?"

Tracie sat for a moment, thinking. Shane could see her working through it.

"Okay," she said at last. "It's obvious from this letter," she tapped the grimy envelope, "that Gorbachev can see the changes coming, and that he knows he is helpless to stop them. He admits as much. Whatever the future holds for the Union of Soviet Socialist Republics, in ten years' time it is going to look very different than it does right now."

"So?" Shane said. "Things change all the time. I still don't understand why they have to kill Reagan."

"Because," Tracie said, rubbing her eyes. She suddenly looked very tired. "The Soviet Union is no different than any other government, at least as far as the inner workings are concerned. Politicians disagree philosophically, squabble, grab power, consolidate that power, whatever. Obviously there's a faction—in this case, a group of high-ranking KGB officials—who will stop at nothing to prevent the destruction of their power base and their personal empires. This faction *wants* to start a war, and the bigger the better. You think Czechoslovakia is still going to want to want to step out from under their protector's umbrella once the world's two great superpowers start lobbing nuclear warheads at each other?"

"But all wars end eventually. What happens then?"

"Whoever is behind this mess doesn't care what happens then. Assassinating Reagan and starting World War Three will give those people inside the Kremlin plenty of time to consolidate their power and stockpile resources so that no matter who wins—and even if everyone loses, which seems likely—*they* are provided for. Additionally, their precious Soviet empire remains intact that much longer, or at least has not fallen completely apart, which seems the most likely outcome the way things are going right now."

Shane stared out the windshield at the cars on I-95, metal boxes hurrying toward unknown destinations. "But if Gorbachev is so opposed to this plan, why not just stop it from inside his government? He's the man in charge, after all."

"Gorbachev's skating on thin ice over there. He has instituted reforms that have outraged the political hard-liners, people who would like nothing better than to go back to the days of Khrushchev, or even Stalin. Gorbachev recognizes that he doesn't have the muscle politically to take on those hard-liners directly, so instead he's going through the back door. He doesn't trust anyone within his government to deliver his message intact—he certainly can't ask the KGB to do it—so he tried to handle it clandestinely, on his own."

"Why not just go public with what he knows? That would stop the whole thing in its tracks."

"If he tried to do that he'd be gone by the next day. He would either be arrested or killed. He would likely disappear in the middle of the night and never be heard from again. The Soviet political system is not like ours—there isn't even the illusion of openness. The truth is considered an asset only when it advances the Communist cause. If Gorbachev went to the press with the details of this plan, even his supporters would consider him a traitor to his country.

"No," she said slowly, thinking out loud. "This is really the only way he could have handled it, and he's taking one hell of a big chance as it is."

"Okay, that's it," Shane said. "We're hours away from the assassination of the president and the start of a war maybe no one will survive."

He eased down on the accelerator and the car surged forward. "We've got to get you to a phone. You have to call your superiors at the CIA and tell them about this. Never mind Winston Andrews. Call the CIA director himself if you have to."

"I can't," Tracie said simply, shaking her head.

Shane pulled his foot off the gas and stared at Tracie in amazement. He ignored the honking of a horn behind him. A middle-aged woman flipped him off as she pulled around the Granada and he barely noticed.

"What do you mean, you can't? You have to!"

"No," she said. "I can't. Nothing's changed, Shane. *I don't know who can be trusted.* I trusted Winston with my life, put it in his hands dozens of times, and it turns out he's involved with the

Soviets, apparently has been for years. I have no way of knowing who else in the power structure is compromised, and that includes Director Stallings. If I alert the wrong people, or even if I alert the right people but the wrong people get wind of it, the letter gets destroyed, you and I get neutralized, and the president of the United States gets assassinated."

"*Everyone* can't be involved."

"Of course not. I'm sure only a small percentage are involved. But I can't take the chance of the one person who *is* involved finding out. The stakes are just too high."

"Call the cops then. The Secret Service. Alert the media. We have to do something."

Tracie sighed. "I'd like nothing better. But do you have any idea how many 'tips' the authorities get every day about assassination attempts against the president? Dozens, especially when he travels or makes public appearances. We won't be taken seriously, Shane, trust me on this. We'll be detained and the speech will go on as planned."

He stared at her, his stomach turning over slowly. The blueberry muffin he had eaten earlier felt like a ticking time bomb and his mouth tasted sour and acidic, like he might be about to puke.

"What are we going to do, then?"

"We continue to D.C. I have to interrogate Andrews, force him to give up the names of everyone involved in this thing. Once I have those names, I'll know who's clean. *Then* we pass along this damned letter."

Shane punched the gas and the Granada leapt forward again. They were still hours away from Washington and time was ticking away.

Something was still bothering him, though. "What if Andrews refuses to give up the information you need?"

Tracie stared straight ahead, steely-eyed and determined. "He'll talk."

36

June 1, 1987
4:20 p.m.
Washington, D.C.

Winston Andrews' two-story townhouse was located in George-town, a couple of blocks northeast of the Potomac River and Virginia, a couple of blocks west of the D.C. political sprawl. Built of weathered brick and covered in climbing ivy, the house looked lush and full and green in the summer.

Tracie and Shane had been forced to pass the time in the New York City area waiting for the bank containing Tracie's safe deposit box to open for business. At nine o' clock sharp, they had parked outside a squat concrete bank building, and the moment the manager had unlocked the front door, Tracie entered.

Shane stayed with the car while Tracie carried in a cheap canvas backpack they had picked up at a roadside Five and Dime store. She returned fifteen minutes later with the pack bulging, then tossed it into the back seat where it landed with a metallic clank.

"Don't ask," she said, and Shane didn't ask.

After that they had taken turns driving, following the interstate, pushing the speed limit as much as they dared. Getting stopped for speeding would be a problem, but arriving in Washington too late to prevent the assassination of the president of the United States would be a bigger problem.

They stopped at a highway gas station just after noon, where they filled up the tank and bought a couple of cold burgers, then got right back on the road and ate as they drove.

Conversation was sporadic. Shane could see plainly that Tracie had been shaken to the core by her betrayal at the hands of Winston Andrews. It was eating at her, seemingly bothering her even more than the idea that the two of them were all that stood between the KGB and likely outbreak of World War Three. She chewed her lip and muttered to herself, shaking her head when she thought he wasn't looking.

"Can't talk about it," was all she would commit to when he tried to get her to open up.

Shane thought he understood. The relationship between a field operative—Tracie refused to use the term, "spy," but to Shane it seemed appropriate—and her handler was of necessity extremely close, especially when clandestine operations were involved. She had told him back at the New Haven Arms while they relaxed in bed that often the handler was the only person alive besides the operative herself who possessed all the details of an assignment, making the handler the only lifeline if the operative ran into problems in the field.

So Tracie had placed an inordinate amount of trust—faith, really—in Winston Andrews. And he had turned out to be a traitor both to Tracie and to his country, accepting without question what he thought had been her execution in a dive motel by the two KGB agents as the cost of doing business.

Shane wondered what was going to happen when they arrived at Andrews' townhouse. After having seen the results of her interaction with the two Russian spies back in New Haven, he guessed life would suddenly become exceedingly unpleasant for the man.

The sun had lost its daylong battle with an overcast layer, and the slate-grey sky hung dour and menacing over the mid-Atlantic as they entered the D.C. metro area. Tracie was behind the wheel for this leg, and after exiting the highway, navigated the streets with practiced ease.

Fifteen minutes later she pulled to the curb in a quiet, leafy neighborhood, letting the Ford idle while she sat taking in the activity, of which there was little.

"Which one is it?" Shane asked, and she pointed out Andrews' home.

"He lives alone?"

She nodded wordlessly.

"He won't be expecting you, so you have the advantage of surprise," he said.

"That may or may not be true," Tracie answered, the first time she had spoken more than a couple of words at a time in several hours. "It all depends upon the communication schedule he had set up with the Russians. If he expected them to check in between New Haven and here, say at the halfway point or something, he'll obviously be aware by now that something's gone wrong."

"How likely is that?"

She shrugged. "No way of knowing. He wouldn't have had that kind of arrangement with me, but then again, he and I worked together for a long time."

Her voice was hard-edged and bitter. "But with these guys, he may have wanted a more hands-on relationship."

She shrugged again. "Doesn't really matter. Nothing we can do about it either way."

They sat for another moment.

"What's the plan?" Shane asked.

"The plan? Reintroduce myself to my old friend and have a little heart to heart."

37

June 1, 1987
4:50 p.m.
Washington, D.C.

Tracie knew she needed to move now, but couldn't shake her depression. She'd been brooding for hours in the car, the weight of Andrews' betrayal throbbing in her gut like a physical ailment. She liked to think of herself as a keen judge of character—staying alive often meant sniffing out the difference between sincerity and bullshit—and she had never viewed Andrews as anything but a patriot.

It was like losing a parent. Hell, in some ways it was *worse* than losing a parent, because Winston Andrews' deception had been so willful, so heartless, so...*complete.* Death happened, it came calling on everyone eventually, and although the death of a loved one could bring pain, the actions of Winston Andrews had brought that and much more: the hurt of personal betrayal, and anger, and a confusion Tracie simply could not seem to work past.

She had signed on at CIA not out of any desire to put her life on the line. Not because she had some addiction to danger. Certainly not because she wanted to fly around the world nonstop for years on end, working in the biggest hellholes, putting out the biggest fires, always knowing that if things went sideways there would be no one to come to the rescue, always knowing if she were captured or killed she would be cast aside by her government, sacrificed on the altar of political expedience.

No, she had signed on at CIA out of an abiding love for her country, a knowledge that despite our weaknesses and faults as Americans—we had them, of course we did, we would not be human if it were otherwise—we possessed the greatest system of government in the world, enjoyed freedoms and opportunities unprecedented in human history.

She had wanted to give something back, and fighting in the most significant philosophical conflict of the twentieth century—Democracy versus Communism, freedom versus repression—had seemed the best way to do that. She thought of herself as an "All-American girl" in the truest sense of the word.

She had been a fool, she now realized. She had looked up to Winston Andrews as a mentor and a friend, had considered him a fighter for the cause of freedom, just as she was. And all the time she was traipsing around the globe, crawling through mud puddles, freezing her fingers and toes inside substandard equipment, getting shot at and knifed, coaxing information out of unwilling subjects, taking lives, working nonstop with never a moment to enjoy life like a normal twenty-seven year old single woman, in all that time, Winston Andrews had been sitting here in Washington, playing both sides against the middle, sipping cognac and committing treason, making deals with Communists and traitors.

And laughing at her.

That was the worst part. He had to have been laughing his wrinkled old ass off at her. Little Miss Idealist, taking orders without question, doing exactly as she was told, all in the name of freedom and the advancement of American ideals.

What a joke. He had played her for a fool and she had followed along blindly. Willingly.

Tracie felt her eyes filling with tears and blinked them back. There was nothing she could do about her monumental stupidity now, and this wasn't the time to worry about it, anyway. Winston Andrews had made a fool of her, but that had been his choice, not hers. She still believed in her country even if he didn't, and the clock was still ticking down to the assassination of President Reagan, and it had fallen to her to stop it, not out of choice but necessity.

How many others were involved? That was the question. If Winston Andrews had been co-opted, anyone could be. It was time to find out what Andrews knew, and Tracie had been watching the neighborhood long enough. Activity was minimal. No one had come or gone at Andrews' townhouse, so he must have been working from home today, something he often did.

And he was likely alone. Tracie felt certain he would not have gone to Langley or received visitors with Gorbachev's letter unaccounted for.

It was time to move.

She turned to Shane and saw him watching her closely.

"Are you alright?" he asked, his voice gentle.

She thought about it for a moment before answering. Then she said, "Yes I am." And she discovered she meant it.

She took a moment to tell him how she intended to gain access to Andrews' home and what she needed from him to help make it happen.

Then she opened the door of the Granada and stepped into the muggy late-spring air.

38

June 1, 1987
5:25 p.m.
Washington, D.C.

Shane walked up the front steps and pushed the buzzer. Whatever Winston Andrews' faults, and it seemed there were plenty, being a lazy homeowner was not one of them. The grass around the flagstone walkway had been trimmed with military precision, and the home's wooden shutters appeared freshly painted, the purity of their near-blinding whiteness providing a stark contrast to the tired-looking weathered grey of the shutters on the surrounding homes.

Shane rang the bell and listened closely.

Nothing.

He waited maybe thirty seconds and pressed the buzzer again, worried Andrews might not even be home.

Tracie had felt certain he would be. "He won't go anywhere until he gets his hands on the letter he thinks is coming," she had said, but Shane wasn't so sure. Maybe he had found out somehow that the Russians had been taken down, or maybe he simply got cold feet and skipped town.

He lifted his hand to buzz the house a third time when through the closed door came a muffled voice. "Yes? What is it?"

Tracie had said he wouldn't open the door, not even a crack, and she had been right. There was a peephole in the middle of the heavy oak door, eye height, and Shane pictured a suspicious old man peering through it, sizing him up.

"Thank God you're home," Shane said, following Tracie's instructions. "I wonder if I could use your phone. I've been bitten by a dog and I need medical attention."

"Bitten? Where? I don't see any blood."

"It's on my lower leg. See?" Shane turned around and pointed toward the porch floor. Tracie had said the fisheye lens in the peephole would likely not show the floor clearly enough for Andrews to be sure whether Shane really was injured or not, and in any event the point was not to convince him but rather to keep him occupied long enough for her to do what she needed to do.

"Please," Shane said. "I feel queasy, like I'm gonna be sick. If you won't let me in, could you please at least call an ambulance for me? The blood, it's soaking into my shoe…" He sank to one knee, like an athlete offering up a quick prayer before a game.

There was a short pause, and then the disembodied voice said, "All right. Stay where you are, I'll be—"

A second later the door swung open and Shane rose to his feet. A tall, deeply tanned white-haired man, trim but not skinny, faced him with a mixture of annoyance and resignation on his lined face.

Tracie stood behind Andrews, backpack slung over one shoulder, barrel of her gun placed against the side of his skull.

"You appear to have made a remarkable recovery," the man said to Shane drily. "Please, won't you come in?"

"Yeah. It's a miracle," Shane answered grimly, brushing past the older man and into the house. He turned and closed the front door, suddenly gripped by a fast-building fury. This was the man who had wanted Tracie and him dead. This was the man who had betrayed his country. This was the man responsible for the deep despair in Tracie's soul.

The anger came out of nowhere, rising in him like a physical being, making him want to strike out.

"Easy," Tracie muttered, and Shane realized he had wrapped both hands tightly into fists and was holding them rigidly at his side.

He blew out a breath forcefully. "Sorry about that. I don't know where that came from." He released his hands and shook the tension out of them.

"I do," Tracie said. "I feel the same way, believe me."

Shane smiled weakly and said, "Didn't take you long to get in here."

"I told you it wouldn't. All I needed was a minute or two's worth of diversion to pick the lock on the back door. Nice job with that."

Andrews watched the exchange, an unreadable look on his face. "I'm unarmed," he said, ignoring Shane and speaking to Tracie. "Any chance you can take that cannon out of my ear?"

She lowered the gun to his ribs and held it there with her right hand while patting Andrews down with her left.

"One wrong move," she said, "and I'll blow your ass into next week. All I need is an excuse."

"Understood," Andrews said. He seemed mostly unaffected by the threat. Shane thought the entire bizarre scene might be the strangest thing he'd ever seen, and that was saying something, given the events of the last couple of days.

"Where to?" Andrews asked.

"Your office," Tracie said, and the older man turned and walked through a luxuriously appointed dining room—Oriental rug covering gleaming hardwood floors, crystal chandelier hanging over a massive maple dining table, fieldstone fireplace in one corner, fully stocked bar in the other—and began climbing a set of stairs.

Tracie followed, gun still in her hands but now pointed at the floor, and Shane brought up the rear. He could feel the sensation of pressure building at the base of his skull and thought, *not now, dammit, not now.*

About a third of the way up the stairs, Tracie said, "You don't seem all that surprised to see us still breathing."

"That's because I'm *not* particularly surprised," Andrews said. "I helped train you, remember? I was never convinced the Russians would be able to take you out of the picture, and even when their team checked in and reported that they had completed the mission, I didn't completely buy it."

Tracie stopped dead on the stairs, Shane bumping into her from behind. Andrews seemed to feel the movement stop behind him and he stopped, too.

In a puzzled voice, Tracie asked, "If you suspected I might have gotten the jump on the Russians, why was it so easy to get in here?

Why weren't you better prepared? You had to know if I survived the ambush in New Haven, I would come straight to you—nobody else knew we were there."

Andrews glanced at Tracie with a paternal half-smile that Shane instantly wanted to knock off his face.

"Because it doesn't matter anymore," the old man said. "Things have progressed to the point now that they cannot be stopped. The slaughter by the KGB of law enforcement and civilians in Maine will prompt an investigation so thorough I could never survive it. My cover will be blown and I'll end up in prison, if not in front of a firing squad. This is the end for me, my dear, one way or the other."

Andrews continued trudging up the stairs and Tracie followed. At the top of the stairway a short hallway led to a home office. In one corner stood an antique redwood desk, roughly the size of a small aircraft landing strip. The top was bare, and in the center stood an empty glass, two ice cubes melting inside. A ring of condensation had formed around the base.

A bank of telephones covered a rack next to the desk, and alongside that, against one wall, was an array of electronic equipment, none of which looked familiar to Shane.

There was no sign of any work in progress in the room, no correspondence on the desk, no paperwork anywhere. The office felt tidied-up, antiseptic. The low hum of cooling fans, presumably protecting the electronics, was barely perceptible in the background.

Andrews stood in the doorway, bushy white eyebrows raised, hands in his pockets, awaiting instructions.

Tracie asked Shane to pull Andrews' chair out from behind his desk and drag it into the center of the room. When he had done so, she bent and ran her hand along the underside of the seat. Satisfied there was no weapon hidden there, she told her mentor to sit.

"For what it's worth, which is clearly not much," Andrews said, settling into the chair and folding his hands in his lap, "I have no idea specifically what information is contained in that letter. When you were dispatched to East Germany to act as courier for an emergency communiqué from Mikhail Gorbachev, I was as much in the dark about its contents as you were. As anyone was."

"Bullshit," Tracie said simply. "This is the biggest operation the KGB has attempted in years, probably decades. You've been working with them at least that long, therefore you knew about it. It's that simple."

"You give me far too much credit," Andrews said. "I've been aware the assassination of a high-ranking American is in the works, that much is true. But I've not been privy to the specifics of the operation."

He gazed at Tracie appraisingly. "But you have, haven't you? The fact that we're even having this conversation means you've opened the letter. What does it say? My KGB contacts have their suspicions, but no one seems to know for certain."

"What it says," Tracie began, her voice cold and her face stony, "is none of your business. You're a traitor and an embarrassment to the agency. An embarrassment to your country. You're still alive for one reason and one reason only: I need to find out how deep inside the government this conspiracy reaches."

"The letter is a warning to President Reagan, isn't it? Gorbachev wants to stop the assassination attempt," Andrews said, ignoring Tracie statement.

Her face boiled red and Shane could see how close she was to losing control. "How can you sit there, calmly discussing a presidential assassination?" she asked. "An event that, if successful, will in all probability launch World War Three? How?"

"So the president *is* the target," Andrews answered, still seemingly unruffled, a note of wonder in his voice.

"I understand you view me as a traitor to my country," he continued, "but what you don't realize is that my work as a buffer has saved tens of thousands of lives, hundred of thousands probably, and prevented outright war between the United States and the USSR many times over. My role has been to prevent the destruction of the country I have spent my life serving, and to my way of thinking, I've done exactly that."

"Your work as a buffer?" Tracie asked, nonplussed. "You mean your unsanctioned, illegal, treasonous work? Is that the work you're referring to?"

Andrews shrugged. "Most of the work you do is unsanctioned and technically illegal, too."

"There's no comparison. I'm serving my country. I'm certainly no traitor."

Andrews said nothing and she continued. "You claim to have prevented war between the two countries, but you're assuming people in the highest positions of responsibility would have responded to situations in a certain way had you not acted, when you have no justification for those assumptions. And if you've contributed to the beginning of a third world war *now*, what the hell has been the point?"

Andrews started to answer and Tracie held up a hand.

"This is not a debate," she said. "You don't get equal time. This discussion is over. I told you once, you're still breathing only because I need information. And you're going to give it to me. Right now."

Andrews smiled sadly but did not answer.

Tracie shrugged her backpack off her shoulder and it dropped heavily to the floor. She knelt and unzipped it, all the while holding her weapon on Andrews, who sat quietly, making no move to interfere.

Shane ran a hand over his face and sighed shakily. The pressure at the base of his skull had increased steadily until it was now a dull throb, radiating waves of pain outward into his neck and shoulders as well as through his head. He had been here before. The pain would get much worse before it got better. He cursed the timing, wished he had the pain medication back home in his medicine cabinet.

Tracie paused, gun leveled against Andrews, one hand buried in her backpack. She could sense that Shane was suffering and watched him closely, her eyes flicking back and forth between Andrews and Shane.

"Are you all right?" she finally ventured.

Shane nodded, closing his eyes against the discomfort. "More or less. I could use a glass of water, though."

"You look like you need to lie down. You're white as a ghost."

"I'll be okay." He wondered if his words sounded as unconvincing to Tracie as they did to him. Judging by the look on her face, they probably did.

"Go get some water," she said quietly. "I can handle this from here."

"No," Shane shook his head. It felt like someone had let loose a baseball inside his skull. Soon it would feel like a bowling ball. "I'm okay. I'll stay."

Tracie returned reluctantly to the search of her backpack, her hand emerging a few seconds later with a red-handled pair of pliers and a set of handcuffs, both of which she tossed onto Andrews' desk. They landed with a clunk on the polished surface and spun to a stop.

"Careful with the desk," Andrews said mildly. "It's an antique."

She smiled at him acidly. "So are you, and wait til you see what I'm going to do to you."

Andrews grimaced, looking at the pliers. "A bit barbaric, wouldn't you say?"

"You didn't leave me a lot of time to prepare for this. I've been too busy trying to stay alive. Besides," she said, making a show of looking at her watch, "the hours are slipping away. The time for subtlety is long past, not that I particularly care what happens to you, anyway."

Her lie was blatantly obvious to Shane, he could see through it even with the black waves pounding through his head. It had to have been even clearer to Andrews after more than half a decade spent working with Tracie.

She wrapped her hand around the back of the chair and yanked it across the Persian rug with Andrews still sitting in it, bringing it closer to the desk. He nearly tumbled onto the floor but regained his balance and for the first time looked angry. Or maybe what Shane could see on his face was the beginning of real fear.

Tracie held his left hand in her right and thumped it down on the surface of the desk, snapping the pliers with her left for emphasis.

"Why don't you try asking me what you want to know before beginning to pull out my fingernails?" Andrews said.

"I already told you what I wanted to know, and you insisted on playing games with me," Tracie answered. "I don't have time for games. And, by the way, when I'm done with your fingernails I'll be taking your teeth. I don't want to hurt you, Winston, but time is running out, and the *only* thing that matters is stopping this madness. So I'll do what I have to do, and by the time I'm done with you, you'll be begging to tell me everything."

ALLAN LEVERONE

Her face was grim but determined, the sight chilling Shane, who flashed back to the faces of the two Russians after her interrogations twelve hours ago.

"You want to know who else is involved with the Soviets, is that correct?"

"See? I told my new friend," she nodded at Shane, "that you were relatively sharp for a dinosaur. Start talking and maybe you can save a few of those choppers, so when you have dinner at Leavenworth while you're serving your life sentence, you won't have to suck it through a straw."

"There aren't many KGB collaborators in positions of power above mine," Andrews said softly, "but there are a few. Listen to me. No one's going to believe you when you claim there's a Russian hit man out to kill President Reagan. A far better strategy for you to follow right now would be to prepare for the new reality. Things are going to change in the world, and quickly. Position yourself to benefit from the upcoming war. I can help you with that."

"You make me sick," Tracie said, her voice dripping with venom. "Stop dragging your feet and just give me the fucking names. Last chance."

"Okay, you win," Andrews said. He bent his head in defeat, running his hand over his face like he was exhausted. Finally he dropped his hand to his lap and he looked up at Tracie, mouth closed. Shane could see the muscles in his jaw tense as he ground his teeth together.

He looked almost expectant, like he was waiting for her to answer a question, which didn't make sense because *Tracie* had been the one asking questions of *him.*

"Well, " she said. "Who are you working with? Goddammit, Winston, I need to know…" Her words began to fade as she realized something was wrong.

Andrews' eyes bulged out and his face reddened. His body stiffened in the chair and he began to struggle to breathe, almost panting, unable to fill his lungs.

"Winston, no!" Tracie cried as he began convulsing. His body pitched sideways off the chair and he cracked his head on the edge of the heavy wooden desk. He hit the floor and flopped around like a fish out of water. Tracie knelt next to him and Shane stood

188

frozen, helpless, unable to comprehend even what was happening.

A thin line of drool, whitish and foaming, trickled out of the corner of Andrews' mouth and sprayed into the air as the convulsions caused his head to snap back and forth.

"What's wrong with him?" Shane asked anxiously, his headache momentarily forgotten.

"Cyanide," Tracie said. "He must have had a capsule in his pocket. He's poisoned himself."

Shane recalled him keeping his hand in a fist. He had assumed it was a reaction to the stress of being unmasked as a traitor. Obviously it had been something else.

Tracie reached under his head with one hand and supported him at the neck, trying to force his mouth open, presumably to clear his breathing passage, unable to do so. Andrews' mouth was clamped shut in what must have been a muscular reaction as he slipped into unconsciousness.

"Dammit, dammit, dammit," Tracie said. "I should have seen this coming." She felt for a pulse in his neck and then shook her head.

She rose and turned to Shane. "There's nothing we can do for him. He's going to be gone in seconds."

Shane said nothing, stunned at the ugliness and brutality of the scene, at the speed at which the poison had done its job. Finally he shook his head and asked, "What do we do now?"

Tracie's eyes were twin pools of shocked hopelessness. She shrugged. "I have no idea. It was imperative I find out who else is involved in this conspiracy. Without knowing that, I won't be able to get within fifty feet of the president. I'll be intercepted, the letter will disappear. Without that proof, my story is nothing more than a wild fiction."

She stared at Shane. "We're screwed."

39

Tracie picked up her intended instruments of torture and tossed them into the backpack. She pulled out a rag and ran it over the surface of the desk, then looked around the room pensively before asking Shane, "Have you touched anything in here?"

"I don't think so," he said, still trying to comprehend what had just happened.

She zipped the backpack closed, still clutching the rag in one hand, and said, "There's nothing more we can do. Let's get out of here. I need to get somewhere where I can sit and think."

She peered up at Shane. "And you really look like you need to lie down."

"I'm fine," he said automatically, his thoughts still focused on Winston Andrews and the shocking abruptness of his suicide.

Tracie trudged out of her CIA handler's home office and Shane followed her down the stairs. "What are we going to do about him?" he asked.

"Nothing."

"What do you mean, 'nothing'? We're just going to leave him dead on the floor?"

"Unless you want to invite the police over and answer lots of invasive and time-consuming questions about what you're doing

190

here, and why the owner of the house is dead on the floor with a lethal poison clogging his system. *Maybe* you'll be able to convince them you didn't kill Andrews, but I guarantee you won't do it before spending a full day—if not a lot more—in custody. I don't have that kind of time to spare."

"I suppose, but still…"

"Don't worry about him. He's beyond caring about his present situation. If it makes you feel better, I'll let someone at the agency know about this as soon as I can. But everything comes back to the same logjam: I don't know who I can trust. If I alert CIA before figuring out what to do about this letter," she patted her pocket protectively, "and the wrong person takes the call or hears the message, we get eliminated and the president gets killed. I just can't afford to take that chance."

Shane nodded, forgetting Tracie was in front of him and couldn't see him.

"Besides," she continued. "When he doesn't show up for work, they'll call over here and when Andrews doesn't answer they'll send someone to check on him. He'll be found, probably by tomorrow night, even if we do nothing."

Tracie stopped in front of the picture window in the town-house's elegantly appointed living room. She peered out into the Georgetown neighborhood. A couple of houses away, a young boy rode a tricycle up and down the length of his driveway. Otherwise the street appeared empty.

"Let's go," she said, and they stepped out the front door. He watched as she wiped down the inside and outside of the door-knob, then used the rag to pull the door closed behind them. Thirty seconds later, they were accelerating away from the home containing the dead body of Tracie Tanner's handler.

* * *

"Pull over," Shane said suddenly. They had been driving for no more than ten minutes, working their way through Georgetown toward a motel on the outskirts of D.C. He had known the nausea would strike suddenly and it had.

"What are you talking about?" Tracie asked. "What's wrong?"

"Just pull over, right here, right at this corner." Shane clamped a hand over his mouth like that might make a difference as Tracie swerved to the curb. He pushed the door open before the car had even stopped rolling, vomiting mostly stomach acid into the dirt and trash littering the gutter.

He leaned out the door, retching, waiting for the nausea to pass, humiliated. At last it did and he eased back into the seat. He pulled the door closed and accepted a tissue from Tracie without a word. He wiped his mouth. His head felt like someone was attacking it with a jackhammer.

While he knew from recent experience the feeling wasn't going to go away any time soon, he suspected now that he'd thrown up that he would begin to feel marginally more human shortly.

For a little while.

"I'm all set," he said quietly, looking straight out the windshield, refusing to meet Tracie's gaze. He could feel her watching him, holding him in her intense stare with those captivatingly beautiful eyes. Somehow that made things much worse. The car didn't move.

"You can start driving any time now," he said, and then gave up and turned to look at her, waiting for the question he knew was coming.

"What's going on?" she asked quietly. "Something is wrong. What is it?"

"I'm dying," he said.

*   *   *

June 1, 1987
7:30 p.m.
Washington, D.C.

"It's a brain tumor. Inoperable and it's growing like a weed." They had checked into a motel on the outskirts of D.C., close to the city but cheap and anonymous. It was maybe a half-step up on the quality scale from the New Haven Arms.

The minute they checked in, Tracie pulled the bedcovers down, plumped up the pillows, and helped Shane into bed. He hadn't needed the help, not really, but her touch was so comforting he wasn't about to try to dissuade her, especially feeling as poorly as he was.

"The tumor is growing and I'm dying and there's nothing anyone can do about it." Shane shrugged. He sat propped against the cheap motel headboard as Tracie stared at him, horror written on her delicate features.

"Can't they treat it somehow? What about surgery? Chemotherapy?"

"The tumor's too advanced. There's no way to remove it or kill it without also wiping out most of my grey matter. And I don't have that much to spare," he said, trying to make her smile.

It didn't work. Her eyes began to fill with tears and he said quickly, "Most of the time the pain's not that bad. I go for days on end without feeling any different than I ever did. Then, out of nowhere, it'll strike."

"Like now."

"Yes, like now."

"How much worse is this headache going to get?"

"There's no way to tell. Over time, obviously, the headaches are going to get worse and worse, but each individual one is a crapshoot. I'm hoping this time that it won't get too much worse than it is right now. I can still function, more or less, except for those brief time-outs when I have to puke my guts out." He was trying to keep things light, still embarrassed.

Tracie looked away and shook her head.

He said, "I'm really sorry about this. I was hoping nothing would happen until our little road trip was all over."

"My God, Shane, you don't have to apologize. *I* should apologize to you for dragging you into this mess. It's not bad enough you're suffering from a terminal illness, I have to pull you away from your family and your job and haul you into the middle of an international incident."

Shane smiled weakly. "Are you kidding me? I haven't had this much excitement in...hell, probably ever. When your plane crashed, I was driving to work, I already told you that. What I didn't tell you was that I had come from an appointment with the oncologists that afternoon. They told me there was nothing more they could do, that they would help make me comfortable when the time came, but that I needed to get my affairs in order. That was exactly how they said it, too: 'Get your affairs in order,' like we were in some bad Hollywood movie or something.

"So, needless to say, I was feeling pretty sorry for myself that night. But then, when your plane crashed and I worked my way through the woods and saw you stuck inside that B-52, somehow still alive but about to be burned to a crisp, it served as the wake-up call I think I needed. It shook me out of my self-pity, reminded me other people have problems, too, and that I could still actually make a difference to someone. It made me realize that I might be dying, but I'm still here for now. I'm not dead yet."

He looked up and Tracie had moved next to him, tears running silently down her face. He took her hand and she squeezed it ferociously.

"Besides," he said. "We're all dying. Some go quicker than others, but nobody gets out alive."

Tracie looked away, her eyes bleak. "What about medication? I'll go to the drugstore and try to get you something for the pain."

He shook his head. "It won't matter. Just talk to me. That'll give me something to think about besides the pain."

"Of course." Her voice sounded gravelly and she cleared her throat. "What would you like to talk about?"

"With Andrews dead, what happens now? I've only known you for a couple of days, but that's long enough for me to know you're not just going to shrug your shoulders and give up and accept that the KGB is going to assassinate the president of the United States. Have you decided who at the CIA you're going to give Gorbachev's letter to? I'm telling you, go right to the top, to Aaron Stallings."

"I'm not giving it to anyone," Tracie answered, her lips set in a grim line. "Nothing's changed. I still don't know who I can trust. If they could get to Winston Andrews, they could get to anyone, even Director Stallings."

"You keep saying that."

"It keeps being true."

"So, what are you going to do?"

"I'm going to catch the assassin."

Shane leaned back on the pillow and closed his eyes as the waves of pain rolled through his head. He pictured the tumor as an invading army, the attacking troops dressed all in black, his body repelling them time after time, fighting hard but eventually weakening in the face of the tumor-army's endless supply of reinforcements.

"How do you propose to do that without any backup? It seems impossible."

She shrugged. "Why? Between the letter and the information our KGB friends supplied in New Haven, I have everything I need to run an op: I know where the hitter is going to set up, I know the method he's going to use to take down the president, and I know he's going to strike at ten o'clock tomorrow morning. This will be no more difficult than a dozen other missions I've completed—all successfully, I might add."

"But isn't the CIA prohibited from working inside the boundaries of the United States? Aren't you only supposed to operate in foreign countries?"

"That's true," Tracie admitted. "But this situation is one in a million. It seems highly unlikely anyone in Congress could have envisioned this precise scenario. I'll take my chances and worry about the fallout later. I'm certainly not going to sit by and allow the president's assassination because I'm afraid to act."

Shane nodded. He saw Tracie watching him closely and tried not to wince from the pain. "I figured you were going to say something like that. But I still can't imagine taking out a professional assassin without a team to work with, especially with no time to develop a plan."

"Even with the support of a team," she said, "there are no guarantees. Things always go wrong, that's a given. It's just that this time there won't be anyone to pull my butt out of the fire if I get in trouble."

"Yes there will."

"You?"

Shane nodded.

"Absolutely not. That's out of the question. You're NOT going to be there."

"That's what you think."

"There's nothing you can do for me."

"Bullshit. I can at least drive a car. I'm going."

Tracie shook her head, her lips compressed into a thin slash across her pretty face. She had placed her fists on her hips and her eyes looked like chips of flint. Her red hair hung in fiery ringlets, cascading over her shoulders. Shane thought she might just be the sexiest thing he had ever seen.

He reached for her right wrist and pulled her down onto the bed, her lithe form molding onto his like they'd been meant to be together. Maybe they had.

She whispered, "What about your headache?"

He said, "What headache?" as the tumor armies continued their assault, wave after wave of pain rolling through his skull.

But right now, none of that mattered. He didn't care about the tumor. Didn't care about the pain. Didn't even care that a KGB assassin was close by right now, waiting to pull the trigger on the president of the United States.

He needed Tracie and, what was more, he knew she needed him. Tomorrow she would undertake what might become a suicide mission, her protestations to the contrary notwithstanding. But tonight there was nothing to do but pass the time and wait.

It was eight p.m.

He began caressing her, his hands moving of their own accord, breaking down her half-hearted resistance, until soon everything melted away and nothing existed but their dance.

* * *

June 1, 1987
8:20 p.m.
Washington, D.C.

Tracie lay still, listening to Shane breathe, the sound slow and steady. Peaceful. He had fallen asleep quickly, not surprising given what she now knew about his health. She savored the proximity of his body, warm and comforting under the blankets, wanting nothing more than to join him in sleep.

But there were things to do first. She sighed softly and slipped out of bed. Dressed quietly. Then she walked out the door, locking it behind her.

40

June 1, 1987
11:50 p.m.
Columbia Road, Northeast of Georgetown University,
Washington, D.C.

Nikolai Primakov eased his plain white panel van into an empty parking space. The spot was perfect—a block and a half away from his destination. Close enough to be within walking distance, but far enough away for the vehicle to go unnoticed.

Tomorrow would be a long day, a history-making day. Nikolai pulled a pack of Lucky Strikes out of the breast pocket of his shirt and tapped out a cigarette. He lit it and took a deep drag. Lucky Strikes were the closest thing he could find in this country to the Soviet-made Belomorkanals—unfiltered, strong and cheap—that he smoked when he was home.

Outside, the dim light from a quarter-moon coated the buildings of the city in a gauzy sheen. Millions of stars twinkled overhead.

Nikolai examined the horizon and nodded. The weather would be perfect. Clear skies, virtually no wind. The temperature was chilly right now, but the day would warm nicely.

Besides, cold didn't bother Nikolai. He had been born and raised in the bitter chill of Yakutsk, where winter temperatures plummeted to depths the soft citizens of this decadent country couldn't even comprehend, much less withstand. But Nikolai had withstood the temperatures just fine.

He had been comfortable with weapons from a very young age, excelling as a marksman. He'd trained as a sniper in the Red Army, serving with distinction in Afghanistan before being recruited by the KGB for more delicate, and much more important, work.

Nikolai was one of the finest assassins in the Soviet arsenal. Over the course of the last decade-plus, Nikolai Primakov had eliminated somewhere in the neighborhood of forty people; he'd lost track of the exact number years ago.

All of his targets had been enemies of the Soviet state, although surprisingly few had been politicians. Some were, of course, but many more were business leaders, or dissidents, or people who to Nikolai's eye were nothing special, simple people living simple lives who had somehow found themselves on the KGB's radar, marked for removal from this earth.

Their offenses were irrelevant to Nikolai, as were their job titles. When he was given an assignment he carried it out, coldly and efficiently, and then moved on to the next. It was a job, no different than farming or factory work.

He had a talent for assassination, so he was an assassin. End of story.

Tomorrow's job, of course, was an exception. Eliminating the president of the United States was an assignment even Nikolai had to admit was special, even though it was a mission no one could ever know he had performed.

He checked his watch. Nearly midnight. It was time to go.

Nikolai took one last deep drag on his Lucky and opened the door, flicking the butt onto the pavement where it dropped into a thin film of condensation. It hissed and died away. He slipped into a windbreaker with the Capitol Floor Refinishing logo sewn onto the breast pocket and stepped out of the van.

Capitol Floor Refinishing did not exist. It was a cover created specifically by the KGB for this mission. The temperature was cool, but not so cold Nikolai actually needed his jacket. However, creating the illusion of legitimacy was critical to mission success, so he shrugged it on over a uniform shirt with the same logo, opened the van door and slid to the ground.

He stepped to the rear of the vehicle and glanced around for any sign of law enforcement. All clear. He opened the rear doors, revealing only one item secured in the back of the van—a wheeled cart with the Capitol Floor Refinishing logo prominently displayed on its canvas sides.

To the casual observer, the cart would appear identical to those used by janitorial services everywhere. The top portion was filled with tools and equipment necessary for the business of refinishing floors. There was an electric hand buffer, brushes and cloths of all sizes and shapes, and a healthy assortment of hand tools and small power tools, none of which Nikolai would be utilizing tonight or tomorrow.

Hidden under the top portion of the cart were the items he really needed, the tools necessary for the business of ending lives. There were four sandbags, each roughly the size of a cement block. There was a Soviet-made Dragunov SVD rifle, disassembled and secured inside a hard plastic traveling case, along with three cartridges filled with 7N1 steel-jacketed sniper rounds, though Nikolai was confident he would require just one shot. There was a PSO-1 Optical sniper sight with Bullet Drop Compensation turret and quick-release mounting bracket.

There were shooting glasses, binoculars, a small pillow, candy bars and water. There was a Makarov PB silenced semiautomatic pistol with three eight-round magazines, an NR-40 combat knife, and a change of clothes in which Nikolai intended to effect his escape upon mission completion.

Unlike the floor refinishing equipment, these were the items with which he was intimately familiar, items he had used—or identical to items he had used—on dozens of successful missions. They were hidden under the diversionary floor tools beneath a canvas separator, which would be folded up and used for camouflage once Nikolai was in position on the roof.

The cart would stand up to casual inspection, which was sufficient for Nikolai's requirements. He would not permit a more thorough inspection by anyone, under any circumstances.

Nikolai wrapped his arms around the cart, straining under its weight, and lowered it to the sidewalk. He stumbled to his knees and the cart landed hard, clattering but remaining upright.

He breathed a sigh of relief. Scattering the tools of his trade on the sidewalk just a few hundred yards from where the U.S.

president was scheduled to make an appearance tomorrow morning would not be conducive to a successful mission.

A casual look around confirmed for Nikolai that there were still no police in the area. He locked the van and began pushing his cart along the sidewalk. He crossed Columbia in front of an empty Plexiglas-enclosed bus stop and continued halfway down the block, eventually arriving in front of the Minuteman Insurance building just before midnight.

His timing was perfect. Three men stood in front of the entrance, dressed in the identical charcoal-colored slacks of Cote Cleaning, the company contracted to provide janitorial service for the building. They wore button-down shirts similar to his, except with Cote Cleaning sewn onto the pocket instead of Capitol Floor Refinishing.

He dragged the cart up the stairs one at a time. It was big and bulky and Nikolai had begun to sweat lightly despite the cool temperatures. As he approached the top of the stairs, the last janitor was being ushered through the front door by a uniformed security guard. The guard closed and locked the door. He was large and blocky, with greying brown hair trimmed in a military-style buzz cut. He wore a white uniform shirt and dark blue pressed trousers, a handgun displayed prominently in the leather holster at his hip.

Nikolai knocked and the guard reluctantly opened the door, squinting as he gave Nikolai the once-over.

"Who're you?" he asked with an aggrieved air, as if Nikolai's sudden appearance represented some kind of personal affront. He stood half-in and half-out of the doorway, blocking access with his bulk.

"Nick Kristoff," Nikolai answered with an easy smile. "I am here for floor refinishing project."

There was no way to hide his thick Russian accent, so Nikolai didn't even bother to try. His English was passable, but would never be anything more. He had neither the time nor the inclination to master the language, particularly since he figured one day soon the Americans would be learning to speak Russian. It was inevitable.

"Floor refinishing, huh?" the guard said skeptically. He frowned. "Nothing like that on my board for tonight." He held up a clipboard for Nikolai's inspection as though it might mean something to him. Idiot.

"Capitol Floor Refinishing," Nikolai said helpfully, pointing to the logo on the side of his cart. "We were contracted to service floors in entire building. You would like to see work order?"

"Yeah, I would like to see work order," the guard answered in a tone which was just mocking enough to be clear to Nikolai, but not so obvious the guy couldn't make a plausible denial later if he were called on it.

Nikolai didn't care about mocking tones, obvious or otherwise. He unzipped his windbreaker, making a show of shivering. "Cold," he observed, and the guard said nothing.

He pulled a folded document out of his breast pocket, making sure the Capitol Floor Refinishing logo on his shirt flashed at the guard. Positive reinforcement. He handed the paperwork to the guard and re-zipped, then stood rubbing his hands together while the man peered at the "work order."

The forgery would stand up to the guard's—or anyone's—inspection. It had been created by top forgers inside the KGB, men who did nothing all day but reproduce important items for the Soviet Union. Currency, licenses, permits, work orders. You name it; the KGB forgers could reproduce it. The work order looked real, right down to the signature of Minuteman Mutual's office manager. There was absolutely no chance this drone would identify the work order as being forged.

What there *was* a chance of—and the one way this mission could fall apart before it even got started—was the guard smelling a rat and deciding to phone the manager at home to question the legitimacy of the project. Given the time of night, and the relative stations in life of the guard and the manager, Nikolai didn't think the likelihood of that happening was very high.

But if it did, Nikolai would be forced to take out the guard, something he absolutely could not afford to do here on the front steps of the Minuteman Mutual building, not fifty feet from Columbia Road. He had already decided that if the guard made any mention of double-checking with his superiors, Nikolai would slip his NR-40 combat knife—identical to the one currently hidden inside his cart, right down to the curved blade and lethal, razor-sharp cutting edge—out of its sheath strapped above his ankle and force his way inside the building. He would then bring the man to the interior stairwell, where he would kill him and hide the body.

He hoped it wouldn't come to that.

It didn't. The guard glanced at the paperwork, sweeping his eyes over it for maybe five seconds, not bothering to hide his utter disinterest.

Then he handed it back to Nikolai and said, "Come on in, then," in a tired voice. He stepped back, and just like that Nikolai was inside.

Nikolai smiled again and nodded. One of the reasons he had been so successful in his current line of work—in addition to his proficiency with dozens of weapons and his total lack of compunction when it came to taking human life—was his physical appearance. Nikolai Primakov was utterly unremarkable, from his thinning sandy hair to his gold-rimmed glasses, to his wiry frame, to his average height, to his lack of identifying scars or blemishes.

He was easy to underestimate.

He blinked owlishly at the guard and said, "I would like to start on top floor. Where is elevator, please?"

The guard shook his head slightly. "*The* elevators are right over there, on the far side of the lobby." He gestured vaguely at the far wall.

Nikolai pretended not to notice the guard's derisive correction of his phrasing and peered across the lobby. He nodded, as if he hadn't known for weeks where the elevators were located. He suspected he was more familiar with the interior of this building than the guard had ever been.

"Thank you," he said, bowing his head submissively and trundling his cart across the shiny marble floor.

He was completely alone when he reached the elevators. Thanks to his exchange with the guard at the front door, all three janitorial workers who had entered in front of him were by now dispersed throughout the building. He pressed the button with the up arrow and turned to look in the direction of the front entrance while waiting for the elevator car.

The guard hadn't moved. He stood staring at Nikolai through narrowed eyes, his forehead wrinkled like a Shar-Pei puppy's.

Nikolai hoped the man wouldn't become a problem.

41

June 2, 1987
12:05 a.m.
Washington, D.C.

Tracie rolled over and checked the bedside clock. Its iridescent numerals bathed the room in an eerie green glow, giving the unfamiliar surroundings an alien, almost lunar cast. She slipped out of bed, barely rippling the mattress, moving with a feline grace and economy of motion that belied her tension. Shane continued to sleep, breathing heavily, smoothly.

She padded to the bathroom, peed without flicking on the light, and then returned to bed, knowing she likely wouldn't sleep any more tonight.

She hadn't lied to Shane, not exactly, when she told him taking down the Russian assassin would be just another operation. But what she hadn't told Shane, what she suspected he knew anyway— he was a lot of things, including one amazing lover, but he wasn't stupid—was that a typical CIA op would have taken place only after dozens, if not hundreds, of hours of preparation, and would only have been green-lighted after briefings, surveillance, and meticulous planning. And it would have involved a hell of a lot more people than one lone agent.

Her mission later today would be the exact opposite of that: a rushed intervention based on the uncorroborated words of a

Soviet politician sitting thousands of miles away, and information offered up under duress by a pair of Russian spies.

There had been no preparation. Tracie had never even set foot inside the building she would enter to stop the assassination.

And she would be alone. Utterly and completely alone.

She slipped under the covers. Next to her, Shane snored softly, the rhythm of his respiration steady, almost hypnotic. She supposed it stood to reason she would find herself going solo on the most important mission she would ever undertake. She had always been alone. Career-wise, personal-life-wise, every kind of wise. She had steadfastly refused to allow herself to get close to anyone, preferring to rely on her own devices, always.

Until the last couple of days.

Until falling like a lovesick teenage girl for the handsome Maine air traffic controller who had appeared out of nowhere, like the hero in some ridiculous romance novel, a hero who had saved her life at the last possible moment, literally sweeping her off her feet. He was good-looking and self-deprecating and generous and kind. His smile took her breath away. When they were together it was all she could do not to throw him to the ground and rip his clothes off and ravage him.

And she knew he felt exactly the same about her.

And he was dying.

And when he was gone she would once again be alone.

She ran her hand gently over his chest, twirling the wiry hairs in her finger. She wondered how long it would take before he ceased to have any semblance of a normal life, before the cancer took him and he had no life at all.

She thought about what he'd said, how no one really knows how long they have, how we're all dying, some quicker than others, and realized it was truer of her than most. Covert CIA work was dangerous and the careers of operatives tended to be short. So did their life spans.

Hell, there was the very real possibility that *she* wouldn't survive beyond a few more hours. She was trying to put up a brave face—for herself as much as for Shane—but the fact of the matter was trying to take out a KGB pro, who had undoubtedly been planning this assassination for weeks if not months, with no backup and no real action plan, was the very definition of a suicide mission.

And wouldn't *that* be ironic? Fall in love, find out the man who had stolen your heart had mere weeks to live, and then die before he did. It was almost humorous in a cynical, black-hearted way. It was a play Shakespeare might have written had he been born four hundred years later than he was. Romeo and Juliet for the twentieth century.

Tracie smiled at the thought and was surprised to feel her eyelids getting heavy. She glanced at the clock with the ghostly green numerals. 12:15 a.m.

She closed her eyes and slipped away.

42

June 2, 1987
12:20 a.m.
Minuteman Mutual Insurance building

The seventh floor of the Minuteman Mutual Insurance building was used for storage—cleaning and maintenance supplies, reams of paper, cast-off typewriters, word processors, office furniture, boxes and boxes of pens. Everything necessary for the operation of an American insurance company in the late twentieth century.

Nikolai assumed the janitors had already armed themselves with whatever materials they needed to begin their shift, so his only real concern was of the guard becoming suspicious and checking on the progress of the "floor refinishing" project. He pulled his cart quickly down the hallway, stopping in front of a door with a red-lettered sign that warned, ROOF – AUTHORIZED PERSONNEL ONLY.

He had disabled the alarm on a previous visit, so there was no way anyone would realize the door had been breached. Picking the lock was easy. Within thirty seconds of removing his lock-picking tools from the cart, he was tugging open the metal door. He removed a heavy electric belt sander from the cart and set it on the floor, using it to prop the door open.

Roof access was accomplished via a cement stairway slicing like an artery between reinforced cinderblock construction walls. The building had been erected close to a century ago, but the

Victorian-era elegance of its interior did not extend to the portions the public would never see, and Nikolai knew it would take no small effort to muscle the cart up those narrow stairs.

He stepped through the doorway and then turned and grabbed the cart by its metal frame. He lifted the front and pulled. The angle was all wrong. It was hard to get any leverage, he was straining, but after a moment he was rewarded by the sound of the cart's front wheels clattering onto the first step.

He lifted and pulled and gained the second step.

Lifted and pulled. Third step. The rear wheels squeaked and complained and then slid onto the first step.

Nikolai breathed deeply while maintaining a grip on the cart. As he began pulling again, a disembodied voice from somewhere down the seventh-floor hallway said, "Hey! What the hell do you think you're doing up there?"

Nikolai froze. Cursed softly in Russian.

He released his grip on the cart, hoping it wouldn't lurch back down the stairs and nullify his hard-earned progress. It didn't.

He wiped a sheen of sweat from his forehead and reached down to his ankle, slipping his combat knife out of its sheath under his pant leg. He positioned it in his right hand, blade resting against his inner forearm, handle nestled in his palm. He turned his arm so the knife would be invisible to whoever was in the hallway, then placed what he hoped was a look of innocent confusion on his face.

He squeezed past the cart and descended the stairs, then walked through the doorway. Approaching briskly along the hallway was the guard who had examined his forged work order.

Nikolai had known the man was suspicious of him but hadn't really thought he would pursue him.

He had been wrong.

The guard's face was dark, his eyes hooded, and his hand rested on the butt of his weapon as he challenged Nikolai again. "What are you doing, boy? What business does a floor cleaner have on the roof?"

Nikolai walked forward slowly, non-threateningly, smiling and nodding to placate the guard even as the man moved to intercept him. He was still at least eight meters away. Too far for Nikolai's purposes.

"I am sorry," Nikolai said meekly.

Six meters.

He continued, "I do not know where…"

Four meters. Still too far.

The guard slowed, confused. "Do not know where…what?" He spread his hands in a show of frustration.

"I do not know where…" The man was now directly in front of Nikolai, and although his hand still rested on the butt of his gun, it was as useless to him as if Nikolai had taken it away and thrown it off the roof.

He was a dead man. He just didn't know it yet.

With a practiced flick of his wrist, Nikolai dropped the knife into his hand, spinning it effortlessly so the blade faced outward. The guard recognized the danger much too late and took one stumbling step backward just as Nikolai attacked, his arm a blur. He plunged the knife into the guard's ample belly and slashed upward between the bones of the rib cage.

The guard gasped.

Drew in a shuddering breath as if to scream.

Didn't.

Half-coughed and half-gasped.

Stared to scream again.

Nikolai covered the man's mouth with his right hand as he used his left to shove the guard's hand away from his gun. He clubbed the guard behind the ear with the butt of his combat knife and the man dropped to the floor like a felled tree.

Nikolai swore again, angry and annoyed. The man would be dead within minutes, if he wasn't already, but he was bleeding all over the place.

There was suddenly a lot to do. If he didn't get this mess cleaned up, it would be the first thing the employees noticed when they showed up for work tomorrow morning. The only positive Nikolai could think of was that the janitorial crew should be focusing their efforts on the portions of the building accessible to the public. The likelihood was slim that anyone else would appear on this floor before morning.

Still muttering, Nikolai reached under the guard's armpits and dragged him the short distance to the roof access door. A trail of blood marked the journey. He dropped the guard to the floor and grabbed his cart with both hands. The stairway was too narrow to haul the guard up in without first moving the cart, so Nikolai would be forced to forfeit his progress after all. He yanked the cart angrily back down to the seventh floor hallway where it wobbled dangerously and nearly tipped over.

Chert voz'mi. Things were not going according to plan.

Okay, take it easy. Relax. You have plenty of time to get this situation under control.

Nikolai composed himself, slowing his breathing, clearing his mind. Finally, still muttering but now refocused, he hooked his arms once more under the guard's armpits and dragged the man up the stairs to the roof.

He emerged, breathing heavily, through a dented steel bulkhead that had once been painted grey but was now pocked with rust and faded almost down to the bare metal. The roof was flat as a flood plain and covered with gravel. Various protuberances—vents and air-conditioning units and pipes whose purposed were unknown to Nikolai—jutted up out of the surface, combining with the gauzy moonlight to make the surface appear stark and menacing.

Nikolai ignored it all. He had seen the roof in surveillance photographs and even picked the lock and climbed up here himself during two of the three trips he had made into the building to familiarize himself with its layout in preparation for this mission. He pulled the guard through the entrance and turned toward the rear of the building. Once clear of the bulkhead he placed the body alongside as close as possible to the base, concealing the cooling corpse as much as possible.

He hurried down to the seventh floor. In the hallway he examined closed storage closets until finding one with a sign that said, JANITORIAL SUPPLIES. He opened the door and found a wheeled plastic cart in one corner. It was shaped like an oversized bucket with a wringer built into the side. A mop had been placed in the wringer, its handle reaching almost all the way to the ceiling. The bucket was half filled with dirty water.

Nikolai thanked his lucky stars for the innate laziness of American workers.

He stuck his head out the door and glanced down the hallway.

No one there. How likely was it the janitorial workers would notice the guard was missing?

Not terribly likely, Nikolai decided.

He rolled the cart down the hallway and stopped at the spot where he had gutted the unfortunate guard. The man was big, the spillage substantial. There was plenty of evidence to clean. Nikolai dipped the mop into the dirty water and got to work, swishing it through the blood, smearing some around the floor but removing the heaviest of the stain, which had only just begun to dry at the edges.

Nikolai examined the floor and decided the stain was still too obvious. He rolled the cart into the restroom at the far end of the hallway. Dumped the dirty water and watched it disappear down the sink. Refilled the bucket with fresh, hot water and some hand soap, then rolled back to the murder scene.

Tried again.

Much better.

One more pass and the evidence of the slaughter was now no more than a light brown stain that could have been the remains of a coffee spill. Nikolai wrung out the mop and moved quickly along the hallway toward the roof access door, erasing from the tiles most of the blood trail he had created when he dragged the guard up to the roof.

He stopped when he reached the door. There was no reason to waste time mopping the stairway. The door would be closed soon—barring any further interruptions—and no one would see the evidence until it was much too late to matter.

He examined the hallway with a critical eye.

Not perfect but it would do.

He hurriedly returned the mop and bucket to the janitor's closet. Stepped out and closed the door.

Still no unwanted visitors.

He turned and sprinted to the roof access and once more began the laborious process of pulling the tools of his murderous trade up to the roof.

This time he was uninterrupted.

43

June 2, 1987
7:00 a.m.
Washington, D.C.

Shane's head hurt, that was the first thing he noticed. His eyes were closed and he lay on his side and it felt as though someone was shining a flashlight squarely into his face. He opened his eyes slightly, two tiny slits.

No flashlight. Nobody shining anything into his face. The motel room curtain was half-drawn, holding the morning sun partially at bay. From behind he could hear the sounds of furtive movement.

He rolled over and sat up, moving slowly until he could gauge the extent of the throbbing inside his skull. From in front of the bathroom door Tracie flashed a tight-lipped smile in his direction, and just like that he didn't give a damn about his headache. She looked even more beautiful than he remembered, and he wouldn't have thought that possible.

"You're a heavy sleeper," she said. She was dressed in an outfit he didn't recognize, a business suit. It looked like the sort of thing a young female executive might wear.

He rubbed his eyes and ran a hand across his face. He wondered what the hell time it was.

"What the hell time is it?" he asked.

"It's seven o'clock," she said. "I knew you were exhausted so

I tried to be quiet. We're not far from the Minuteman Mutual building so I wanted to let you get as much rest as possible."

"Quiet? You were quiet as a mouse," he said. "Last thing I remember is that noise you make when…well, you know."

"I know," she agreed with a smile.

"Where'd you get the outfit?" he asked. "You look terrific."

"Went shopping last night after you zonked out. Hit the store just before closing. I went out this morning and got breakfast. There's coffee and a croissant for you." She nodded at a brown bag and paper coffee cup on top of the small bedside table.

"Thanks for the grub," he said gratefully, reaching for the coffee.

"No problem." She looked at him closely. "I brought you something for the pain, too. How are you feeling?"

"Never better," he lied. He didn't know exactly how Tracie was planning to stop the assassination but he knew she needed help. The only way she might even consider letting him ride along was if she thought his headache had disappeared.

"Liar," she said mildly.

"So," he said, changing the subject as quickly as he could. "What's the plan for today?"

"Well, let's see," Tracie answered, cupping her chin in her hand and pretending to think. "Dress up in my new outfit, have breakfast and, oh, I don't know, maybe foil an assassination plot. You know, the usual."

She was keeping things light but Shane could sense her tension. "I don't understand," he said. "You know where the shooter is going to be—on the roof of that insurance building—but how in the world are you going to access it? The building will be locked down tight as a drum, won't it? And for that matter, how is the *Russian* going to get into position? Won't he be spotted?"

"All good questions," Tracie answered. "Undoubtedly the buildings will have been swept in anticipation of the president's visit, but the sweep will have been accomplished yesterday. It will have been routine, matter-of-fact. As far as we know there's no reason for the Secret Service to suspect anything might be wrong. And don't forget, this is D.C.—presidential movements are routine here.

"Once the sweep has been completed," she continued, "it will be a relatively easy thing for the shooter to access the building's roof. This hit has been in the works for while, so either someone will have been paid off—say, a maintenance man or a janitor—or a master key will have been bought or made. The guy dresses like he belongs, nobody notices him. It will be pretty easy, really."

Shane sipped his coffee and thought about it. Made sense. "But what about you? How are *you* going to get at him?"

"Exactly the same way," she said. "I'm going to look like I belong. That's where this new outfit comes in." She twirled. She was a natural at modeling and Shane wondered if there were things in her past she night have glossed over.

He wolf-whistled and beckoned her closer and she smiled. "Sorry, big boy, we don't have time for what you want. I'll have to take a rain check."

"I can guarantee it would be quick," he said with a smirk. "But I understand."

Then, "So you're going to pretend to be an insurance exec or something? Won't it be obvious to everyone who works there that you don't belong? That nobody knows you?"

"You're on the right track," she said. "But I'm not going to be an insurance employee. I'm FBI. That way it's perfectly natural no one knows me. Meet Special Agent Maddee James," she said with a demure curtsey.

Shane nodded. "Brilliant. But how are you going to get around the fact that you have no ID? Isn't that the first thing the insurance big shots are going to ask for when you walk in there?"

"Who says I don't have any ID? This isn't my first rodeo, cowboy." She reached into the backpack filled with the items she'd liberated from the safe-deposit box outside New York City and rummaged around for a moment.

"Ah," she said, and lifted out a laminated plastic card.

"Let's see," he said.

She strutted over to the bed, all business now, stern FBI persona in place.

He examined the card. "Federal Bureau of Investigation" was stamped across the top in gold lettering set against a blue background. A small headshot of Tracie appeared on the right side, unsmiling, staring directly into the camera. Her hair was pulled back from her face and she looked ready to step out of the picture and arrest someone. On the left side of the card was the FBI seal, with identifying information, including her "name," Special Agent Madison James, inscribed in the space between the photo and the seal.

Shane examined it for a moment and then handed it back, shaking his head. "Planning a second career?" he asked doubtfully.

"This ID, along with some other stuff I retrieved, was my backup plan. All operatives have them—at least they do if they're smart. It's the first thing you learn: if things fall apart, you'd better be prepared to disappear."

"Except you're not using your ID to disappear."

"Don't worry," she said, "it's not my only one, and Maddee James is not my only identity."

He stared at her, amazed, trying to determine whether he was more attracted to her or creeped out by her. *It's not even close,* he thought. *Attracted wins in a landslide.*

"You're definitely the most unusual date I've ever had," he finally said.

Tracie smiled and placed the ID card into a small plastic flip-holder with the identifying information facing out, then slid the holder into the breast pocket of her suit. She was now FBI Special Agent Maddee James.

"That's what all the boys say," she answered and walked away, hips swaying. She turned her head and winked.

"I'm coming with you," he said to her retreating figure, and she stopped.

After a moment she turned to face him. "You can drive," she said, surprising him with her lack of resistance. "But you'll drop me off a block from the insurance building and then stay with the car. No matter what happens. You'll wait for me and then drive us away when the job is done."

Shane grinned and she said, "Do you understand me? You stay with the car no matter what happens."

"You can count on me, babe," he said.

"I want to hear you say it. Repeat after me: *I give my word I will stay with the car, no matter what.*

Shane said, "I give my word I will stay with the car, no matter what." He had no intention whatsoever of doing so.

Tracie's eyes narrowed and she looked at him critically. "Hurry up and get dressed, then. It's time to go."

He slid off the bed and began throwing on his clothes. His head pounded and throbbed and he tried not to wince.

44

June 2, 1987
8:15 a.m.
Washington, D.C.

The traffic was moving fitfully, about what Shane would have expected for drive time in the nation's capital. He followed Tracie's directions, turning rights and lefts, and glanced at his watch. Two minutes after the last time he'd looked.

"How far is it?" he asked.

"We'll be there in plenty of time," Tracie said.

"How do you know where this place is?"

"I grew up in this area. The Minuteman building is pretty distinctive, even in a city filled with landmarks and historic structures."

Shane nodded. The pounding in his head had leveled off, the pain distracting but bearable, at least for the time being.

"How are we going to do this?" he asked.

"*We* are not going to do anything," she said. "*You* are going to do exactly as we agreed. Park the car a couple of blocks away from the building and wait."

"Fine," he said, annoyed. "How are *you* going to do this?"

"Reagan's speech is scheduled for ten," she said. She was speaking confidently, without hesitation, and it was obvious she had given the situation plenty of thought. Shane wondered whether she had gotten any sleep at all last night. "The building doesn't open until nine, so—"

"How do you know that?" he interrupted.

"I went out last night after you fell asleep, remember? I did a quick drive-by of the Minuteman building after buying my outfit. Business hours are posted at the entrance. Anyway, my plan is to arrive the minute the building opens. I'll let the manager know Special Agent James is on the case, so he doesn't see me prowling around and call the cops. Then I'm going to catch an assassin."

"Just like that," Shane said skeptically.

"Just like that."

"How do you know where he'll be?"

"I don't, specifically, but he had to have accessed the building last night. He would have needed time to set up. Once his preparations were complete, he probably napped in an empty office or something. But he'll have to be in position on the roof before the office workers begin to arrive, if only to avoid the risk of detection. I should be able to surprise the guy and catch him flat-footed before President Reagan ever leaves the White House."

Traffic was beginning to bog down, and Shane checked his watch again. "Unless there are two of them," he said. "You can't catch two guys by surprise."

"You can if you do it right," Tracie replied grimly, and he wondered whether she really believed what she was saying.

Ahead, a traffic light turned yellow. Shane slowed, thought about stopping and decided they could make it. He accelerated into the intersection behind an old Buick with a badly rusting rear bumper.

Ahead and to his right a flash of movement caught his eye, and Shane saw a child step out from behind a parked car. The kid walked into the street without looking, directly in front of the Buick, and Shane gasped in surprise.

The Buick's driver slammed on his brakes a half-second later and Shane hit the breaks on the Granada. Both cars slewed forward, tires squealing, and Shane watched as the kid disappeared in front of the hulking mass of the Buick.

The cars shuddered to a halt, the Granada somehow stopping before impacting the Buick. Shane realized he was holding his breath and exhaled heavily. He felt a surge of relief as the kid appeared on the other side of the first car.

The kid, maybe eight years old, had darted away from the Buick and now stood in the middle of the street, head swiveling madly. He took advantage of a small break in the opposite direction traffic and sprinted across the street in front of a yellow taxicab and disappeared.

"Holy shit," Shane said, his voice shaking.

He glanced over at Tracie just as she turned to look at him. Her eyes widened in shock at something over his shoulder and he whipped his head to the left just in time to see a blue pickup hurtling through the intersection's cross street. The driver had locked up his brakes but the truck was moving much too fast to stop in time. He would T-bone them right in the driver's side door.

Tracie lifted her left foot and slammed it down on his right, shoving the accelerator to the floor. The Granada lurched forward and smashed into the rear of the Buick, forcing it forward a few feet before the pickup truck struck the Granada in a shower of shattering glass and screeching metal.

The car spun on an invisible axis and Shane felt his head bounce off the window and his headache exploded anew. He was aware of Tracie screaming to his right, a short, sharp sound, and then everything stopped and the interior of the car was quiet but for a faraway-sounding hissing noise. Whether the sound was coming from the Granada or the pickup truck he couldn't tell.

Shane heard cars screeching to a halt—he knew they were in the middle of the intersection and the fear of a second car striking them flashed through his mind.

He tried to clear the cobwebs and was vaguely aware of Tracie tugging on his arm. "Unbuckle your seatbelt," she said, her voice intense. "We have to get out of here."

Shane nodded and tried his door. It wouldn't budge.

"Not your door, mine," she insisted. "Yours has been smashed. It'll probably never open again."

She pulled on his arm more insistently. "Come on, we have to leave *now*."

A man in a suit pulled open the door on Tracie's side. "Are you folks all right?" he asked, his concern evident.

"We're okay," Tracie said, slipping out the door as Shane worked the buckle on his seatbelt and began sliding across the front seat behind her.

The driver of the pickup stumbled onto the sidewalk. It was a kid, late-teens it appeared, and he looked stunned but uninjured. "I just looked down to change the radio station," he said, "and when I looked up you were right in front of me. I swear I only looked away for a second."

"Are you okay?" Shane asked.

The kid nodded. "But my parents are going to kill me. This truck was a graduation present."

"*Come on,*" Tracie repeated, her voice soft but firm. "We have to get out of here."

The kid heard her and said, "No, you can't leave. We have to exchange insurance information."

She ignored him and started dragging Shane away from the wrecked vehicles. "The police will be here any second," she whispered, "and we have to be gone when they arrive."

"We can't leave the scene of an accident," Shane said, closing his eyes for a moment against the rejuvenated pain bounding around inside his skull.

"We have to," Tracie insisted, speaking a little louder now that they were out of earshot of the teenaged driver of the pickup truck, who had staunchly refused to leave the area of his vehicle.

"We're driving a stolen car, remember? I could eventually get this straightened out through CIA channels, but it would take hours, and we're—" she glanced at her watch and swore softly, "—almost out of time. We might still make it, as long as we disappear before the cops arrive."

They took three more steps and then Shane froze as a D.C. police cruiser eased to the curb, lights flashing, stopping almost directly in front of them.

*   *   *

Tracie grabbed Shane's hand and began walking as casually as possible along the sidewalk, their path taking them past the police car. The patrol officer stepped out of his vehicle and she watched as his eyes bounced between the accident scene and them, then back to the accident scene.

They were almost past him when he swiveled his head and focused his gaze on Shane, his eyes narrowing. Tracie wondered what had gotten his attention.

Then Shane turned and looked at her and she wanted to curse out loud. A thin line of blood had leaked out from his hairline and begun zigzagging down the left side of his face. He must have cut his head in the accident. The injury was clearly not serious, but it had been enough to draw the cop's attention immediately.

The officer lifted one arm to block their passage. "Where do you think you're going?" he said, his natural cop suspicion evident in his voice.

Tracie took a look at the blood and said, "Oh, honey, you must have been cut by flying glass." She drew a tissue out of her pocket and wiped the blood off Shane's face.

She gestured toward the accident scene and added excitedly, "We were walking along the sidewalk when those two cars collided almost right next to us. Someone's trapped inside that Ford. I think they need help!"

The kid who had been driving the pickup truck was still standing next to the vehicles, watching curiously.

The cop took two quick steps in the direction of the wreck and then turned back to them. He pointed a finger and said, "You're not going anywhere. If you witnessed this accident, we're going to need a statement from you."

"Of course," Tracie answered, and the cop hurried off toward the vehicles.

The moment he turned, Tracie pulled Shane in the opposite direction. "Come on," she said. "We've got about ten seconds before that cop realizes we're full of shit. This is our last chance. Let's make the most of it."

They melted into the crowd, trying to disappear behind the growing throng of onlookers. A few seconds later, she could hear raised voices and hoped none of the pedestrians had been alert enough to track their movement and point them out to the officer.

Seconds passed and Tracie risked a look back and saw no one who seemed to be paying any attention to them.

"Are you all right?" she asked Shane.

He shrugged. "I didn't even realize I'd been cut. Smashing my head against the window in the accident didn't do much for my headache, but the cut itself is no big deal. The more important question is what the hell are we going to do now?"

Tracie checked her watch and shook her head, frustrated. "I wish I knew," she said. "We'll never be able to get there in time on foot."

She looked up and down the street. "And there's not a cab or a bus stop in sight. Goddammit."

Then she slowed her pace and watched the scene unfolding in front of them, unable to believe their good fortune.

Less than thirty feet ahead, a dirty green Chevrolet Station wagon pulled to the edge of the street, almost close enough to another parked car to scrape paint. The driver leapt out of the Chevy and trotted into a neighborhood convenience store, leaving his car idling in the D.C. sunshine while purchasing his newspaper or coffee or whatever.

Tracie flashed a smile at Shane. "We're back in business," she said.

45

The Minuteman Mutual Insurance building had clearly been constructed over a century ago and was a throwback to a more elegant time, with ornate granite columns soaring over the Columbia Road sidewalk, an architectural dinosaur somehow managing to avoid extinction into the late 1900s. It looked slightly out of place next to its more modern neighbors, like a dowdy grandmother dressed in decades-old finery. At just seven stories high, the building was stubby by today's standards.

They had driven a couple of blocks west of the Minuteman building in an attempt to avoid the worst of the traffic snarls that inevitably accompanied a presidential appearance. The trip from the accident scene to the Minuteman building's Columbia Road address had taken much longer than Tracie anticipated thanks to that congestion, and she drove the stolen station wagon as fast as she dared.

She circled the KGB assassin's perch and pulled the car to a stop at a curbside spot a block-and-a-half away from the wooden platform that had been erected for Reagan's speech. The president was to dedicate a brand-new twenty-story office building in celebration of the renewal of American entrepreneurial spirit.

The crowd seemed to be thickening as Tracie parked the car

and she said, "I've really got to hustle. We lost too much damned time with that car accident. When I get out, you slide over and take the wheel. Wait for me, but be ready to take off at a moment's notice. You'll know if I've failed because all hell is going to break loose if I'm too late. People will be running everywhere, sirens will be blaring, and you're going to see cops and agents in plain clothes come out of the woodwork."

"You're not going to fail," he said.

She turned and fixed him with a hard look. "If that chaos happens, wait five minutes. If I'm not back in five minutes, I won't be coming back. Find your way to a police station and tell the cops everything."

Shane returned her stare. His face was pale, with dark puffy circles under his eyes. He looked like hell and Tracie knew he must be suffering, but he didn't show it.

He nodded once. "Got it," he said unconvincingly. "But what are you going to do about the letter?"

Tracie hesitated. She had been giving the issue some thought. "I'm keeping it with me," she said. "It's my responsibility to deliver it to the president, and by God that's what I'm going to do. If things go south and I get killed, I doubt the sniper will have the time or the presence of mind to search my body before escaping, so the authorities will eventually find it, anyway."

Shane said nothing, holding her in his steady gaze until she began to feel self-conscious.

"What?" she finally said.

"Nothing." He swiveled his head and looked out the passenger window, then raised his hand and held it to his forehead for just a moment.

"Listen," she said hesitantly. "I need to know you're going to be here when this is all over."

Her stomach felt queasy from the familiar adrenaline effect she always experienced just before going operational. She suspected the mission wasn't the only thing causing those butterflies. She felt exactly the same as she had as a teenage girl before her first date. The feeling was wonderful and horrible at the same time.

"I'm not going anywhere," he said. "This car will be right in this spot when you get back. You don't have to worry about that."

She reached for his hand and he picked it up and squeezed it. She squeezed back, hard. "I...I've never said this before, not to anyone other than my mom and dad," she said. "I'm not sure I even know how to do it. Um, I think, I uh..."

"I know," he said. "I love you, too. I have from the minute you introduced yourself by sticking a gun in my face."

She hugged him fiercely, then stepped out of the car and began hurrying toward the Minuteman Insurance building.

*   *   *

June 2, 1987
9:45 a.m.
Columbia Road, Washington, D.C.

Shane squinted and watched her go. The sun streaming through the dirty passenger-side window ratcheted up the pain in his already pounding head, but it was worth it. Tracie looked fantastic in her new suit, and he tracked her with his eyes until she disappeared in the crowd.

He waited thirty seconds, then shut down the car and placed the key on the driver's side floor. It would be out of sight of anyone passing by unless they stopped at the window and closely examined the interior.

He stepped out of the car and closed the door, leaving the vehicle unlocked. He couldn't risk Tracie returning, needing to access the car and finding it locked, especially since he was supposed to be sitting here waiting to leave. Hopefully any potential car thieves would be reluctant to ply their trade with the police and Secret Service blanketing the area.

Shane stepped onto the sidewalk and trailed along behind Tracie. He had no real strategy in mind other than to follow and try to help her if he could. He knew he was being foolish, knew his presence on the scene would likely cause more problems for her than it would solve, but the thought of the beautiful young woman he had pulled from the burning wreckage of a plane just a few nights ago—the woman he had fallen deeply, hopelessly in love with—taking on a professional KGB assassin with no backup and only the vaguest sense of a plan herself was unthinkable.

Who was to say there was only one man perched up on that roof waiting to put a bullet through Ronald Reagan's heart? Shane was no expert on covert operations, but he had read enough spy novels to know that military sniper units often consisted of two men: one to pull the trigger, and one to calculate wind direction, velocity, and distances, and to act as a spotter.

Maybe that wasn't how the Russians were going to do it, but if it was, Shane doubted Tracie would ever get close enough to the shooter to take him down.

So he followed, struggling to keep up.

He was far enough behind Tracie that she couldn't see him unless she backtracked or stopped and turned around for some reason. Neither action seemed likely because they were almost out of time. The president's appearance was scheduled for ten o'clock and it was now after nine forty-five.

Shane picked up his pace. He felt light-headed and shaky, the headache blasting like a jackhammer inside his head. The Minuteman Insurance building was still a little more than halfway down the block. He wanted to break into a run but didn't dare. If the cops saw a young man sprinting toward the location where the president would be speaking in just a few minutes, he would likely be rewarded with a bullet in the back.

The ironic thing was that Shane didn't even care all that much about getting shot. But he wouldn't be any help to Tracie lying dead on the sidewalk, although the thought ran through his mind that if that scenario were to take place, the president's appearance would certainly be cancelled and at least the leader of the free world would still be alive.

He had to trust Tracie, though. She was a pro and she knew what she was doing. He chanted it as a mantra as he walked.

He hustled along Columbia Road, moving as fast as he dared, feeling time slipping away. Finally he reached the wide marble steps leading to the Minuteman building's front entrance and took them two at a time.

He looked for Tracie but she was nowhere to be seen. He dodged a cluster of men in suits and overcoats moving in the other direction, pushed open the door and stepped into the building.

46

June 2, 1987
9:50 a.m.
Minuteman Insurance building

There was no time to waste. Tracie marched quickly across the lobby—an authoritative woman walking with a purpose—and stopped at a small reception area two-thirds of the way across the floor. A young woman was in the middle of a conversation with the receptionist, a hefty older woman with silver-blue hair wearing an old but clean business suit.

Tracie stepped directly in front of the desk, cutting off the customer. The young woman sputtered, beginning to complain, and Tracie turned and flashed her FBI ID, first at the customer and then at the receptionist.

"I'm FBI Special Agent Madison James," she said. "Please excuse the interruption, but I'm here on critical, time-sensitive government business."

The woman took a quick look at the card and backed off a step. She raised her hands and turned away.

"How may I help you?" the receptionist asked.

"I need to speak with your supervisor," Tracie said.

"That would be Mr. Foley, but he is in a meeting and currently unavailable. Did you have an appointment?"

"No appointment," Tracie said, "but it's critical I speak to him now. Get him."

"I'm sorry, but—"

"Pull him out of his meeting and get him here now. This is the last time I'm going to ask."

"Or what?"

"Or I go get him myself. This is literally a matter of life and death." Of course it was a bluff. Tracie didn't have the first clue where to begin looking for the receptionist's supervisor, but time was short and getting shorter, and she was desperate to light a fire under this bureaucratic battle axe.

It worked. The receptionist took one last frosty look at Tracie's ID, now back in her breast pocket with the photo facing outward, and then punched a button on her telephone with a look on her face that suggested she would rather be eating bugs.

She spoke quietly into the handset for a few seconds, listened, said something else, her face wrinkled in distaste, and then hung up.

"Mr. Foley is on the way," she said, refusing to look at Tracie.

"Thank you for all your help," she replied sweetly, doing her best to look earnest and sound sincere.

"Thank you, also," she said to the customer she had interrupted, this time hoping she actually *did* seem earnest and sincere.

She turned on her heel and moved to the center of the lobby, conscious of the seconds ticking away. Moments later, a middle-aged man with perfectly coiffed silver hair and an air of authority stepped out of an elevator and walked hurriedly toward the receptionist's desk, glancing around the lobby as he did so.

Halfway to the desk he spotted Tracie and turned toward her like a guided missile. The man had impatience written all over his face—*that makes two of us,* Tracie thought—and was dressed in a suit that she guessed cost more than her monthly salary.

As he approached, Tracie flashed her FBI ID and the man waved it away, fluttering his fingers as if shooing away a pesky mosquito.

"FBI Special Agent Madison James," she said, doing her best to sound clipped and officious, guessing the tone would appeal to a man who struck her as the very definition of the word "officious."

"Doug Foley," he answered, taking her hand reluctantly, giving it one moist pump and then dropping it as if perhaps he feared he might catch something contagious. "Would you mind telling me why I had to interrupt my weekly meeting with the claims department? We're very busy here and I don't have time to hold the FBI's hand."

"I wouldn't mind at all," she shot back. "It's about President Reagan's appearance, which is due to begin down the block in just," she glanced at her watch, "nine minutes."

"Yes," he said in exasperation, "what about it? You people were a major disruption yesterday, disturbing my employees and poking around my building. Last night I was promised these disruptions were over with. So what is it now?"

"We've had a report of a man acting suspiciously in the area. The report stated the man might have entered this building. I need to take a walk through to check it out. I just wanted to let you know I'll be here for the next few minutes. Oh, and I'll need a key for roof access. Preferably a master, if you have one."

The manager huffed and looked at his watch distractedly. "Fine, look around, just try not to disturb my people too much this time." He didn't specify whether he considered his employees or the customers—or maybe both—to be "his people."

He pulled a set of keys out of his pocket and fussed with it, finally removing one and handing it to Tracie.

She took it and said, "I'll return the key to your receptionist when I've finished. Thank you for your time."

The manager had begun striding away before she finished talking, barreling back toward the bank of elevators on the far wall.

She lowered the hand she had offered him and followed, moving just as quickly. She didn't trust the speed of the elevators so her goal was the fire stairs, the doorway to which was located in the same corner of the lobby as the elevators.

When Foley stopped suddenly and turned, she almost plowed him over. He blinked in surprise at finding her right behind him. "You say there may be someone inside the building who's been acting strangely?" he said.

"That was the report," she answered brusquely, anxious to get to the roof.

"You know, there was one odd incident this morning," he said, cupping his chin with one hand.

"Yes?"

"That's right. We employ a security staff of one during overnight hours. Break-ins are not uncommon in this neighborhood and it just seems prudent."

He seemed to be waiting for a response, so Tracie nodded impatiently and he continued. "Well, the guard on duty last night, Sean Sullivan, never clocked out at the end of his shift and he was nowhere to be found when we opened up this morning. Nothing is missing, and the janitorial staff reported that he was here to let them into the building at midnight last night."

"Maybe he simply forgot to sign out before he went home," Tracie said.

"I don't think so. Sean has been with us for over five years and has never forgotten to sign out before. He is ex-police and very professional. Anyway, with the report of a suspicious person, I thought you should know. We've been trying to get in touch with our man at home, but so far, no luck."

"Hmm," Tracie said, thinking. "What time do the rest of the employees typically show up for work?"

"The managers and supervisors around eight, and the rest of the staff just before nine."

"Okay, thank you," Tracie began, but the man had once again dismissed her. He turned and punched an elevator button. Tracie pushed through the door to the stairs and began sprinting up them two at a time.

The guard was dead, Tracie was certain of it. There was no doubt in her mind what had happened—the KGB's man had overpowered the guard sometime between midnight and eight this morning.

Her calves began to tighten as she rushed up the stairs. She tried to tell herself maybe she was wrong, that the assassin might simply have neutralized the guard and then tied him up somewhere, but it didn't feel right. There would be nothing for the KGB to gain by leaving a witness alive.

The guard was dead, his body dumped somewhere out of the way. He would be discovered in the next day or two.

The floor numbers were posted in the stairwell next to the doors. Tracie passed the fifth floor and pushed herself harder. Two more to go. She was beginning to breathe heavily. A few seconds later she arrived at the seventh floor landing, surprised to see the stairway suddenly end. There was no roof access.

She paused, taking a moment to get her breathing under control and to think. There had to be a way to access the roof from the inside of the building. If it wasn't via this stairway, then there would be another somewhere. Maybe at the opposite end of the hallway.

She drew her weapon and eased the door open a crack.

Peered into the hallway.

Nothing out of place.

A third of the way down the length of the corridor she could see a sign on a closed metal door that read ROOF – AUTHORIZED PERSONNEL ONLY. She slipped into the hallway, eased the door closed quietly behind her, and began walking rapidly toward the roof access.

47

June 2, 1987
9:52 a.m.
Minuteman Mutual Insurance building

Nikolai was hot. He had been huddled on the roof for two hours on a sunny day in early June.

If there was one thing Nikolai Primakov hated it was heat. Cold he knew. Cold he could deal with. In seventeen years growing up in Yakutsk, and the years of service to the Soviet government, Nikolai had lived and worked in some of the most frigid, forbidding places on earth.

But here, today, the sun caused the heat to radiate off the asphalt roofing gravel, making the temperature skyrocket. He was thankful the mission would soon be complete and he could climb down off this roof and out of the damned sunshine.

Nikolai had burned a lot of nervous energy simply waiting. After killing the guard and dumping his body next to the roof's access bulkhead, he had lugged his cart up the stairs and then hustled down to the seventh floor entryway. There he removed the belt sander he had been using to prop the door open and placed it on the stairs while he used a strip of duct tape to seal the latch open. Then he eased the door closed and retreated back up the stairs to the roof.

With the door's one-way locking system, if the tape were to fail and the latch were to operate as designed, the door would open only from the interior and Nikolai would be trapped on the roof, unable to escape after shooting Reagan. There was an iron ladder fastened to the rear of the building to be used as a fire escape, but Nikolai fully expected that escape route to be blocked within seconds after the U.S. president fell.

Once he had ensured the viability of his escape route, Nikolai returned to the roof and rolled his cart toward the front of the building, struggling to pull it through the asphalt. He stopped next to a gigantic air conditioning unit that rose out of the roof like a monstrous tumor. He snugged the cart up against the west side of the unit, using the massive structure to shield him and his equipment from prying eyes in the closest buildings.

To counteract the possibility of being seen by a worker inside the office building adjacent to the Minuteman Insurance building, Nikolai dug through his cart, pulling out two signs attached to portable metal stands. He unfolded the signs and placed one six feet away from each corner of the air conditioning unit, facing the adjoining building. The signs read, CAUTION, CONSTRUCTION ZONE – HARD HATS REQUIRED!

After erecting the signs, Nikolai pulled off the heavy canvas tarpaulin he had used to conceal his guns and other equipment. A large clamp had been affixed to two of the corners. Nikolai unfolded the tarp and lifted one corner up to the edge of the air conditioning housing. He clamped it home and then repeated the process on the other side. He pulled the remaining two edges as far away from the unit as he could manage, and then anchored them to the roof with the belt sander on one side and a heavy portable jigsaw on the other.

The work took only a few minutes, but by the time he had finished, Nikolai had transformed the east side of the air conditioning unit into a portable work area. Stamped on the side of the tarp, in bright red letters, were the words DC HVAC INC – INSTALLATION AND SERVICE – AVAILABLE 24 HRS A DAY.

The KGB's theory was that hiding in plain sight would be the most effective way to avoid detection on the roof of a Washington building. Residents of large cities were so accustomed to construction sites and repair work on infrastructure that eventually the workers became almost invisible. It was simple human nature. People saw what they wanted to see.

Once he had placed his signs and set up the tarp, Nikolai finalized his preparations and then ducked his head and disappeared out of sight under the canvas lean-to. He had stayed there ever since, munching on his candy bars and sipping on his water, not even leaving the protection of the tarp to take a leak. When nature called, he simply unzipped and pissed into one of his empty water bottles.

To pass the time once day had broken, he disassembled and reassembled the Dragunov, working methodically, then checked the magazine on his Makarov pistol and sharpened his combat knife. None of it needed to be done but he did it anyway.

He checked his watch and discovered it was barely past nine. So he started over, did everything again.

Out on Columbia Road, eight stories below in front of the Minuteman Mutual Insurance building, Nikolai could hear the city as it groaned and creaked through another late spring morning, the nonstop rumble of cars and trucks, horns and voices floating through the air, and the occasional far-off scream of a siren.

Early in the morning the sounds of the police cars and fire trucks had caused Nikolai to tense up and become instantly wary, but he concluded in short order that there must be no shortage of crime in America's capitol city because the sirens seemed often to come almost nonstop.

The time passed slowly, but Nikolai was well acquainted with the prospect of lying in wait for his prey. He had hunkered down much longer than this plenty of times, spending one memorable mission shivering for three days inside the hollowed-out trunk of a massive downed oak tree on the outskirts of Moscow waiting for a local party commissar who had become a little too fond of the wife of a Red Army general.

The general had commissioned Nikolai privately, paying him out of his own pocket, not that Nikolai cared where the money came from. Somehow the guilty party had been tipped off that the general was gunning for him. The man had holed up inside his house like a scared rabbit, refusing to move.

Eventually he had, though, peeking out the back door—who

knew why?—and Nikolai had put a bullet through the center of his forehead.

After three days,

In the bitter chill of a Moscow winter.

So in many ways, to Nikolai this was a walk in the park. The only thing complicating the mission was the stature of the target, but Nikolai had eliminated high-profile men before and had always been as cold as the Siberian wind when the time came to pull the trigger.

Today would be no different.

*　*　*

June 2, 1987
9:56 a.m.
Minuteman Mutual Insurance building

At last it was time to assassinate the president of the United States.

Nikolai wished he could have napped at some point, but hadn't felt comfortable enough in his surroundings to do so. If someone discovered the taped latch on the roof access door and came to investigate, Nikolai knew he would have only seconds to eliminate the intruder and do it quietly enough to avoid jeopardizing the entire mission.

He stretched.

Yawned.

Checked the time.

Nine-fifty-six.

President Reagan's remarks were to take place at ten o'clock exactly. The KGB hadn't been able to access text of the president's speech so there was no way to be sure how long it would last, but the consensus had been that it would likely be short and to the point. The U.S. president was not a young man and the speech was to take place outdoors in the sun and heat of June in Washington.

This meant Nikolai needed to be in position and ready to go the moment Reagan stepped to the podium.

He shook out his arms and then did a quick set of deep knee bends to get his blood flowing. Then he crawled to the edge of his shelter and poked his head out the side, like a turtle gazing out of its shell.

He looked first at the much higher structure next to the Minuteman Building and saw nothing. Banks of windows soared overhead, but no faces looked down on him, at least none that he could see.

He shrugged. It didn't matter anyway. It was time to get to work.

He stepped out from under the shelter of the tarpaulin and carried his sandbags to the two-foot-high retaining wall at the edge of the roof, facing Columbia Road. He duck-walked as he approached, to better avoid detection by the crowd assembled eight stories below in the event anyone happened to look up.

After stacking the sandbags and creating a nice V-shaped notch, Nikolai retrieved his sniper rifle. Fully assembled, scope attached, full magazine. He combat-crawled to the edge of the roof. Reached the retaining wall and eased his rifle onto the sandbags. Peered over the edge.

The top of his head would be visible from street level but there was no way to avoid that. The Secret Service would be scanning the buildings, but from a distance of over one hundred feet and eight stories up, he would be as good as invisible.

The temporary platform from which Reagan would deliver his remarks—the few he would live to deliver—was filled with dignitaries. There was not one empty chair behind the podium. Nikolai didn't recognize any of the people, but why would he? They were undoubtedly all local politicians and businessmen.

The sun was shining brightly and everyone was squinting against the glare and fanning themselves.

Nikolai eased his Dragunov onto the sandbags, taking his time and seating it carefully.

Behind the podium a pair of shiny black armored limousines idled at the curb. As Nikolai watched, the rear door of the first one in line opened and out stepped the target. Ronald Reagan rose to his full height—he was taller than Nikolai would have expected— and strode briskly along the sidewalk. A group of people moved with him, like moons orbiting a planet. Nikolai assumed the moons probably represented roughly an even split between political aides and Secret Service agents.

When he reached the platform, Reagan climbed the stairs, moving well for a man in his seventies. He stopped short of the podium, waiting to be introduced. In his hand he held a sheaf of papers, undoubtedly the notes for his remarks.

At the podium, a youngish man, hair slicked back, glasses perched on his nose, was speaking into a microphone. The air was clear and Nikolai could hear every word. "And now, please join me in welcoming the man responsible for the resurgence of our economy, and of the United States in general, President Ronald Reagan!"

The people behind the podium stood and clapped, the crowd cheered, and Reagan stepped to the podium, pausing to shake the hand of the man who had introduced him. He smiled easily and waited for the applause to die down so he could begin.

Nikolai leaned onto the top of the retaining wall, bracing himself with his elbows, holding the Dragunov loosely in his hands. He peered through the scope and after a quick adjustment Reagan's face filled the viewfinder, his teeth white and straight and his smile perfect. It was as if he was standing directly in front of Nikolai, no more than a few feet away.

Nikolai centered the crosshairs on Reagan's forehead and prepared to change history.

48

June 2, 1987
9:57 a.m.
Minuteman Mutual Insurance building

Tracie raced to the roof access door and checked her watch as she did.

Nearly ten. She was out of time.

She reached the door and skidded to a stop, hyper-aware of the need for speed but knowing her only chance for success was in not alerting the assassin to her presence. She knelt and examined the space at doorknob height between the door and the metal jamb. The KGB operative had forced the latch back with duct tape.

Tracie opened the door slowly and stepped through, then eased the door closed. Turned and started up the concrete steps and then pulled up suddenly, squinting as she bent to look at the steps. A trail of fresh-looking blood meandered up them.

She hurried up the steps and in seconds arrived on the roof. The front of the building and Columbia Road were to her right, obscured by the rusting metal bulkhead. That was where the assassin would be, since President Reagan was scheduled to begin speaking any second now. For all she knew, the president was at the podium already.

She glanced left and saw a pair of shoes, black and heavy, attached to legs in uniform pants. They weren't moving. The murdered security guard.

She took a deep breath and turned her attention away from the body. She eased around the bulkhead, using the metal structure for cover, and her pulse quickened. At the far end of the roof, sighting through a sniper scope, rifle angled down and toward the platform where the president would soon speak, was the KGB assassin.

She prayed Reagan had not yet reached the podium.

The man was dressed in what looked like a janitor's uniform. A dark ball cap covered his head and he appeared calm and collected, the rifle held steady.

Tracie drew her weapon and stepped clear of the bulkhead. The assassin's attention was focused completely on Reagan as he peered through his scope. He would never know what hit him.

But there was a problem. She didn't have a clear shot.

She sighted down the barrel, holding her Beretta in a two-handed shooter's grip, and swore to herself, frustrated. She was trying to hit a target at least forty feet away with a handgun after running up eight flights of stairs, her hands shaking from exertion and adrenaline.

There was no way. If she fired now, she would almost certainly miss, and the advantage of surprise would be gone. The assassin would still have time to shoot Reagan before turning to defend his position against Tracie.

She stepped left and then forward, moving away from the bulkhead, hoping he wouldn't sense her in his peripheral vision.

Still too far. She needed to get closer.

Another step left. Two more forward.

Better, but not good enough.

She continued moving, knowing the president had to be on the platform now, maybe even behind the podium, so she likely had just seconds left. But her odds of hitting the Russian were still no better than fifty-fifty.

She had to get closer.

Through the warm air Tracie could hear President Reagan as he began to speak. "Good afternoon, Washington," he said. "Thank you for joining me as we celebrate the continued revitalization of a neighborhood that is quickly becoming a model for what can be achieved when government gets out of the way and allows its citizens to take charge."

The crowd cheered and Tracie tuned out the president's voice.

She took another step forward, her attention squarely on the assassin. Another step, and then she felt a tug of resistance above her ankle and lost her balance, toppling to the roof, crashing down in a spray of gravel.

She thrust her hands out reflexively and her weapon skittered away. She hit the surface and rolled, feeling pain in both palms as the gravel bit into her skin. She knew immediately what had happened, knew she had just condemned the president to death by her own stupidity and lack of awareness.

The assassin had strung fishing line across the roof, maybe a foot above its surface. A tripwire. In the sunshine, with her attention wrapped up in the shooter, Tracie had never seen it. She knew all this in the half-second it took to hit the roof.

She rolled once and rose to a crouch, scanning desperately for her gun. A slug struck the gravel no more than an inch from her left leg and she dived to the surface again, rolled again. The assassin had missed her once, probably due to surprise, but he would not likely miss a second time.

One desperate lunge, her feet scrabbling for purchase, and Tracie reached the cover of the air conditioning unit. She was safe, but only for a moment. Her weapon lay eight feet to her right, tantalizingly close, but directly in the shooter's line of fire.

She risked a quick look around the corner of the air conditioner and heard the *ping* of a shot ricocheting off the sheet metal. She drew back instinctively.

The shooter was walking slowly toward Tracie, firing with a silenced pistol, probably a Makarov PB, a favorite of the KGB. As soon as Tracie fell he'd dropped his sniper rifle and drawn the Makarov. That slight delay in changing weapons had probably saved her life—for a few seconds, at least—allowing her to reach the safety of the air conditioning unit.

But he was approaching fast, which meant two things:

One, no one on the ground eight stories below would hear a thing. The silenced weapon would allow the Russian to kill Tracie and then return to his previous position without missing a beat. No one below would even be aware of his presence. He would still be able to complete his mission.

Two, she was almost out of time. He would round the corner of the air conditioning unit in seconds and put a bullet in her head. He would not miss again.

Her brain processed all of this information in an instant and she knew she was out of options. Without any further conscious thought she dived for her gun, unable to see the assassin behind her, wondering if she would feel the impact of the bullet that would end her life or if consciousness would simply disappear, like a light bulb being switched off.

But there was no slug.

She slid across the gravel-covered rooftop like a baseball player diving into second base and was amazed when she reached her weapon still breathing. She wrapped both hands around the grip and rolled onto her back, looked up and saw the Russian approaching, eyes sharp, gun raised, taking his time.

She rolled instinctively as he fired and she felt a searing pain in her right shoulder, the impact of the bullet driving the right side of her body into the surface of the roof. She felt the gravel pellets digging into her back with a clarity unlike anything she had ever experienced.

She returned fire, squeezing off a shot even as the nerves in her arm went dead and she lost all feeling in her hand. The gun slipped out of her grip and clattered once again onto the roof. She knew immediately she had missed, the Russian's shot causing her shoulder to dip and her body to lurch to the right.

Should have compensated. Dammit!

The Russian continued moving forward.

Tracie stared into the gun barrel, the size of a cannon, and prepared to die.

49

June 2, 1987
10:00 a.m.
Minuteman Mutual Insurance building

Ronald Reagan's forehead was nestled squarely in the crosshairs of Nikolai's scope. The magnification was perfect, and so were the conditions: clear and calm. No wind. Nothing to disrupt the trajectory of the bullet he was about to fire, killing the U.S. president and accomplishing his mission.

He breathed in and out slowly, through his half-open mouth, perfectly calm. Focused. He took one last breath. Paused. Began to squeeze the trigger, a steady, constant increase in pressure—

And recoiled at the sound of gravel spraying as a body crashed to the rooftop. The noise came from behind him, to the left, in the direction of the bulkhead covering the access stairs from the seventh floor.

Nikolai understood instantly what had happened. Someone was here, and that someone had just fallen over the tripwire he'd strung across the rooftop as a last line of defense. A precaution he hadn't thought he would need.

Someone was stalking him.

Nikolai reacted with a skill born of training and years of experience. He placed the Dragunov carefully along the retaining wall while simultaneously pivoting to gauge the threat. Near the air conditioning unit his attacker sprawled face-first on the roof.

ALLAN LEVERONE

He lifted his silenced Makarov—he had placed it between his feet for easy access—and as the attacker rolled and began to rise, Nikolai turned in a crouch and squeezed off a shot.

Missed.

Nikolai hesitated. The attacker was a woman. He couldn't believe the United States government would send a woman to stop him if they had somehow learned of the assassination plot.

And where was everyone else? There should be dozens of agents, all armed to the teeth, wearing flak jackets and shouting through bullhorns. There should be attack helicopters and sirens and shouting and chaos.

But there was none of that, just one lone woman who had scrambled out of sight behind the safety of the big air conditioning unit.

He glanced around and saw her weapon lying on the roof where it had fallen when she stumbled over the tripwire. Probably she had a backup weapon, but Nikolai wasn't worried. Before she could shoot him she would have to aim, and to do that would require exposing herself to peer around the edge of the air conditioning unit. The moment she did that he would put a hole in her head.

He sighted down the barrel of the Makarov and began walking slowly toward the air conditioner. He believed in aggressive action, in taking the fight to his opponent.

As he approached, his attacker poked her head around the edge of the unit as he had known she would. But it was the wrong edge. He had been covering the right side of the unit, so when he spotted the face peering out at him, he had to pull the gun hard to the left before squeezing the trigger.

Again he missed. He cursed softly.

He kept moving, surprised the attacker had not yet returned fire. That lack of response could only mean one thing: she had no backup weapon. That meant she would have to make a move for the gun lying out in the open.

He adjusted course slightly, turning toward the attacker's weapon just as she appeared from behind the air conditioning unit. Her dive was perfect and as she landed on the gravel, her hands wrapped around the gun and she turned in one smooth motion and aimed it at him.

She's good, Nikolai thought with grudging professional respect. And he fired.

She dodged and he caught her in the right shoulder. She squeezed off a wild shot and then the gun fell from her hand onto the roof. She was helpless.

He took another step, centering the gun on her chest. He would put one slug center-mass, then finish with a double-tap to the head. Textbook.

The entire exchange had taken no more than a minute, and down on Columbia Road eight stories below, Ronald Reagan was still droning on about the American Dream. There was still time to accomplish the mission.

He began to squeeze the trigger and vaguely registered a blur of motion coming fast from his left.

Then he was hit by what felt like a guided missile and driven to the roof.

50

June 2, 1987
10:01 a.m.
Minuteman Mutual Insurance building

Shane reached the seventh-floor entrance just as Tracie was disappearing through the roof access door.

He staggered down the hallway, pain blasting through his head. His vision ebbed and waned, roiling black clouds forming at the edges of his sight. His mouth tasted dry and sour and he felt like he was going to puke. Maybe the tumor was going to take him right now. The doctors had said he had weeks left, maybe even a couple of months, but what the hell did they really know?

He reached the roof access door and pulled it open slowly. His hands were shaking and not from nerves. From above, a soft *phht* sound floated down the stairwell.

Sounded exactly like the noise he had heard back inside the base building at Bangor International Airport. Sounded like a silenced gunshot.

Tracie wasn't carrying a silenced weapon, which meant the Russian had fired the shot. Shane prayed he wasn't too late.

He willed the pain to the back of his mind, pushing through the darkness threatening to overtake him. Took the steps two at a time. Noticed bloodstains on the concrete. Didn't slow down. The blood was dry, meaning it wasn't Tracie's, meaning it didn't matter.

Shane reached the top and paused. In just the time it had taken

246

to climb the steps, three more shots had been fired, one of the from Tracie's gun. That gunshot had sounded loud and clear, a sharp *crack*, but from far below, Shane could still hear the president speaking. The gun battle raging on a rooftop just a couple of buildings away had not been heard, or had been heard but its significance not yet understood.

He eased his head around the frame of a rusted metal bulkhead, toward the sound of the gunfire, and his blood ran cold. Tracie lay on her back, blood leaking through her blouse from a shoulder wound. Her gun lay on the roof a few feet away and a man was walking slowly in her direction, pistol pointed at her. A long, black sound suppressor protruded from the barrel.

Tracie was helpless. She had seconds—or less—to live.

And Shane acted.

He forgot about the pain, forgot about the tumor eating his brain away from the inside, forgot about Ronald Reagan and about the CIA and Soviet assassination plots. Forgot about everything. Only one thing mattered, and that was saving the woman he had fallen so unexpectedly and completely in love with.

Shane rounded the corner of the bulkhead, at full speed by his second step. He had been an undersized linebacker on the Bangor High School football team, the guy on the defense who was considered too small and too slow to be successful, but who had been named to the All-Maine defensive team two years running.

Just as the Russian shooter looked up in surprise, Shane squared his shoulders and lowered his head and hit the assassin in the chest with everything he had. He hadn't laced on pads since the final game of his senior year a decade ago, but the muscle memory was still there, and he wrapped the shooter up with his arms and churned with his legs and knocked the man down like he was the unluckiest running back ever.

The shooter hit the deck and Shane's one hundred eighty pounds fell on top of him and Shane heard the "oof" of air being forced out of lungs, a sound he had heard hundreds of times during his football days, and he felt a surge of savage glee, an elation he'd never before experienced.

And then the man used Shane's momentum against him, rolling backward and kicking up with his legs, and Shane felt himself tumbling head first, feet flying into the air, and he landed on his back with a thud, and then the shooter was on top of him.

The man had dropped his gun when Shane hit him, and now Shane spotted it out of the corner of his eye on the roof right next to them.

Shane snatched at it and missed, scattering rooftop gravel. He grabbed for it again and watched as the shooter's hand reached it first, seeing the struggle almost in slow motion.

Shane gave up on the gun, instead wrapping his hands together and driving them upward. He was unable to get the force he wanted behind the blow, but connected solidly with the shooter's jaw and felt as much had heard the man's teeth clatter together.

The shooter's head was knocked backward and he slumped sideways, stunned, and Shane bulled his way onto his hands and knees and scrabbled to his feet.

And found himself staring directly into the barrel of the Russian's gun.

51

June 2, 1987
10:02 a.m.
Minuteman Mutual Insurance building

Tracie watched helplessly as Shane struggled with the assassin for control of his weapon. He had it for a split second and then lost it, and in that moment she knew with dread certainty that the KGB agent was about to put a bullet in Shane's skull.

Tracie turned and scrambled on her knees to her own gun, her right arm numb from shoulder to fingers. She ignored her useless right hand and picked up the weapon in her left and turned, amazed to see that somehow Shane had fought off the Russian and gotten to his feet.

But so had the assassin. And his weapon was still in his hands.

She raised the Beretta but was powerless to take a shot. Shane stood directly between her and the Russian. If she fired now, she'd put a slug in Shane's back. Even if he were to move suddenly, with the gun in her unfamiliar left hand she had no confidence she could hit the assassin.

The Russian raised his gun, angling it at Shane, but the Shane feinted left and surged straight forward, swatting the weapon upward, gaining himself a split-second reprieve. The assassin countered by kicking Shane in the shin and then pistol-whipping him, slashing the butt of the gun across the side of his face.

Shane went down in a heap and the moment he did Tracie fired, her weapon trained on the Russian's chest.

But her target was no longer there. The instant he hit Shane he leaped back, either in anticipation of Tracie's move or to get a better angle on the shot he would take to eliminate Shane once and for all.

Tracie didn't know which it was and didn't care. What mattered was that she had missed, and now the Russian fired.

Shane had hit the deck and rolled, anticipating the shot, but the Russian had expected exactly that and fired not at the spot where Shane fell but at the spot he would move to.

Shane took a slug in the chest and lay still.

The Russian wasted no time. He moved again and turned his weapon on Tracie.

She steeled herself against the pain and raised her gun again, but too late—the Russian fired. A stab of white-hot pain ripped through her left shoulder and she dropped to the roof one last time.

Her gun fell next to her but it was useless now.

She had no feeling in either arm.

She couldn't mover her fingers.

She squeezed her eyes closed and waited for the final shot, the one that would end everything.

From far below she could hear chaotic screaming and sirens, and the sound of panicked people running for cover. They had heard the gunshots. By now Reagan would be halfway to his armored limo. She would die knowing she had prevented the president's assassination, but it would be small consolation.

Shane Rowley was dead or would be soon.

Shane, whose only sin was to pull her from the wreckage of a burning airplane.

Shane, who had done more for her than she could ever repay.

Shane, the man she had fallen in love with.

A second that felt like a lifetime passed and when nothing happened, Tracie forced her eyes open. She lifted her head toward the KGB assassin and blinked, stunned. Shane had risen to his feet and was barreling across the rooftop at the Russian.

The man turned away from Tracie in surprise and squeezed

off a hurried shot. The slug struck Shane somewhere on the right side of his body but he kept coming, slowing only slightly. He had started out maybe fifteen feet away from the assassin and had now closed half the distance. He stumbled, placed a hand on the roof and pushed himself upright and kept coming.

The Russian fired again and this time the bullet hit Shane square in the chest, the second time he'd been shot there. He stopped and staggered and then, unbelievably, kept coming.

He hit the Russian before the man could shoot again, striking him like a freight train and driving him backward. The assassin windmilled his arms in a desperate attempt to maintain his balance and the gun flew out of his hand, arcing high into the air and then dropping to the roof with a metallic *clank*.

Shane kept driving with his legs, shoulder planted squarely in the Russian's chest, moving him backward but without the strength left to take him down. They were running out of room quickly and Tracie could see what was about to happen.

She shouted, *"Nooo!"* as the pair of grappling men struck the roof's two-foot-high retaining wall.

They were moving fast but to Tracie's horrified eyes the events played out in slow motion, like some awful sports clip being shown on the evening news. The Russian's legs struck the retaining wall just above the knees and he reached for the wall with both hands in an attempt to avoid tumbling over backward.

Shane pumped his legs one last time, churning relentlessly, and the Russian dropped over the edge.

And so did Shane.

He swiveled his head and locked eyes with Tracie and then disappeared.

A second later, the screaming intensified on Columbia Road far below.

52

The office of CIA Director Aaron Stallings was spacious and infused with an old money, country-club stuffiness.

Leather-bound volumes filled the oak bookshelves lining the walls from floor to ceiling. A small television set mounted in one corner of the office had been tuned to CNN, volume muted, and was broadcasting three-day-old footage of the events at the Minuteman Mutual Insurance building in a continuous silent loop. A massive walnut desk dominated the room. And the carpeting was plush and thick, serving to deaden sound so completely that voices seemed to struggle into the air and then vanish.

The overall theme of the office seemed to be one of stern intimidation, Stallings making the pecking order clear to visitor: he was important and they were not.

The effect was wasted on Tracie. Her future with the agency would be determined by this meeting, but she wasn't at all certain she wanted to continue, anyway.

She had been overcome with depression since watching Shane tumble over the roof of the Minuteman building three days ago, an ennui that seemed to have clamped onto her heart. She wondered if it would ever ease.

Shane had sacrificed his own life to save hers, somehow

struggling to his feet after being shot in the chest, then still managing to pack enough of a punch to overcome a trained and armed professional assassin despite being weaponless and suffering multiple bullet wounds.

He was being hailed as a hero, lauded on television and in the worldwide press as an ordinary man who had stumbled onto a plot to assassinate the president of the United States and then foiled that plot at the expense of his own life.

All of which was true, of course, as far as it went.

But the authorities were releasing few details of *how* this "ordinary citizen" had single-handedly taken down the lone gunman, or even how he had managed to uncover the plot while working as an air traffic controller and living his life far off the beaten path in Bangor, Maine.

His escape from the massacre at the Bangor Airport was receiving airtime as well, its link to the assassination attempt still unclear.

For now, the compelling human interest angle was dominating the news cycle, and Tracie knew that by the time it occurred to the networks and reporters to dig below the surface, a bland cover story would have been concocted, one that would satisfy the public while simultaneously avoiding any possibility that embarrassing details might be leaked involving potentially treasonous activity by a long-time, high-ranking CIA employee.

No doubt a team of agency psychologists and spin-doctors was hard at work right now, doing exactly that. Just another day at the company.

Of the assassin Shane had thwarted little was known, officially or otherwise. His broken body had been found on the sidewalk outside the Minuteman building bearing no identification, and Tracie knew the few details that would eventually emerge regarding the man would bear little more than a passing resemblance to the truth. They certainly would not include the fact that the gunman was working for the KGB with the tacit approval of at least one CIA official—information that would be buried so deep it would never see the light of day.

She pictured Winston Andrews smiling in approval.

Tracie sat up as straight as she could, no easy feat with both shoulders wrapped heavily in gauze and surgical bandages. Her arms were immobilized in slings, crossed over her chest, giving her the appearance of an angry housewife confronting an errant husband. The wounds throbbed incessantly, and doctors had told her to expect more of the same for the foreseeable future, although a full recovery was expected.

Stallings gazed at her, saying nothing. He had been silent since summoning her into his office and gruffly instructing her to take a seat in a chair placed directly in front of his desk. Tracie knew he was using silence as a weapon, an obvious attempt to draw her out, to encourage her to try and fill the emptiness with words.

She wasn't having any of it. She was very familiar with the tactic—had used it herself many times in interrogations. She knew she could outwait him and assumed he would reach the same conclusion eventually.

Besides, she was used to silence, comfortable with solitude.

She sat quietly.

Finally Stallings gave up and cleared his throat officiously. "So," he said. "Regarding the Gorbachev communiqué…" and waited.

She said nothing. No question had been asked so there was no reason to speak.

She'd been rescued from the Minuteman Building by a Secret Service agent, who rushed to the roof just seconds after the bodies of Shane and the assassin crashed to the sidewalk below it.

Upon her arrival at the hospital, a young CIA operative she didn't recognize took possession of the wrinkled envelope containing Gorbachev's letter shortly before Tracie was rolled into surgery to repair the damage done by the two 9mm slugs. The document had disappeared into the chasm that was CIA officialdom, and she knew she would never see it again.

She didn't care.

Stallings continued, a hint of annoyance creeping into his voice. "Some in positions of authority in the administration— myself included, if you must know—believe you should be placed under arrest and charged with treason for opening that envelope. Its contents were classified Top Secret, for the president's eyes only. Opening that letter is antithetical to every single operating principle here at Central Intelligence."

Tracie had told herself she was not going to give Stallings the satisfaction of a response, no matter how vicious or unreasonable the attack, but she couldn't help herself.

She shot back, "Really? And what about the *real* treason: the activity of Winston Andrews? What about that?"

"That is all hearsay, unprovable charges made by an unreliable witness against a dead man who served his country honorably for more than four decades and is not here to defend himself."

Tracie barked a bitter laugh and Stallings said, "But in any event, let's not get off track here. The subject is *your* malfeasance."

"Malfeasance? Is that what you're calling it? The president is alive right now *because* I opened that envelope."

"Yes, well, you could argue that, I sup—"

"It's not an 'argument.' It's a fact."

"Nevertheless," Stallings said. He was a large, jowly man, with fleshy pouches below his jaw that jiggled when he talked. "There's another factor to consider, one of the utmost importance: we cannot set the precedent of permitting operatives to handle classified intelligence in any manner they see fit during a mission. Were it up to me, and many others, you would become an object example to every agent, now and into the future, of that principle."

"This scenario was not typical, and you know it," she said angrily. "It was one in a million, not likely to be repeated in our lifetimes, if ever."

"However," he continued, talking over her as if she hadn't even spoken. "President Reagan refused to allow the issue to drop. He threatened to replace the entire management team at CIA if we took any punitive action against you.

"The upshot," he said, bitterness creeping into his voice, "is that your job is safe. For now. You're expected back into the operations branch as soon as you are physically able to return." He scowled, looking as though he'd just gotten a whiff of rancid meat.

"What about Andrews?" Tracie asked, refusing to allow Stallings the satisfaction of seeing relief on her face. She wasn't sure she felt any.

Stallings spread his hands in exasperation. "What about him?"

"Come on," Tracie snapped. "You know damned well he couldn't have been the only one inside the agency who was working with the Soviets. What is being done to flush out the rest of them, to ensure nothing like this fiasco ever happens again?"

"There's no evidence to indicate *anyone* besides Winston was involved, at CIA or elsewhere." Stallings smiled, his eyes cold and predatory. "In fact, as I already mentioned, there's not even any evidence to suggest Winston was involved. There is certainly no reason to pursue the matter further."

And just like that, Tracie realized the potential involvement of other high-level members of the United States government in the attempted assassination of a sitting president would be swept under the rug, just like the full story of the incident, just like the true identity of the Soviet assassin.

She flashed back to Winston Andrews' words as he sat in his home office just before committing suicide. *There aren't many KGB collaborators in positions of power above mine, but there are a few.* A wave of nausea washed over her that had nothing to do with her injuries.

"How are we using this fiasco?" Her voice had dropped nearly to a whisper.

"I don't know what you mean," Stallings said innocently.

"Come on, goddammit. I was almost killed, got accused of treason, saw my mentor take his own life, watched the man I lov…I mean, watched a close friend die to save me. I served up two Soviet agents on a silver platter in New Haven, operatives I'm sure you're grilling somewhere in this very complex as we speak."

Narrow-eyed stare from Stallings.

Tracie continued. "Stop beating around the bush. You know exactly what I mean, and I want an answer. You owe me that much. The United States is in possession of irrefutable proof that the KGB was behind an assassination attempt on President Reagan. How are we using that information to our benefit it we're not releasing it publically? There has to be a plan."

The CIA director's eyes darkened. He was unused to being questioned, especially by a lowly field operative who'd been called on the carpet, and he clearly didn't appreciate it now.

Tracie didn't care. She had had enough, and was about three seconds from quitting and walking out.

"First of all," Stallings thundered, "I owe you nothing. This agency owes you nothing. If the president hadn't learned the details of this disaster before we could contain them, you would be en route to Fort Leavenworth right now, Tanner. You would never again see the light of day if I had anything to say about it. It just so happens the right person is in your corner, so my hands are tied. For now," he added ominously. "But don't you dare get in my face with ridiculous demands because you feel we are in any was indebted to you. Is that clear?"

His face had bypassed bright crimson and continued straight on to purple, and Tracie wondered whom she would have to deal with when Stallings fell to the floor with the stroke that seemed suddenly inevitable.

"Are you going to answer the question or are we done here?" she asked evenly.

Stallings took a moment to compose himself and then surprised her. His thin lips curled into a tight smile that stopped well short of his eyes.

"You're right," he said. "Of course we're using Gorbachev's letter for leverage. We have already communicated our appreciation to Mr. Gorbachev for the extreme risk, both political and personal, he took in warning us about the KGB's highly irregular operation. We have agreed that during Mr. Reagan's upcoming trip to Europe, the president will call for the removal of the Berlin Wall and the reunification of Germany."

Stallings paused and Tracie whistled softly, impressed despite herself.

The CIA director's self-satisfied smile widened and he continued. "The Soviet Union is disintegrating. Gorbachev knows it and we know it. Even the KGB knows it. Their highest-ranking officials simply refuse to acknowledge it. Gorbachev does not possess the clout internally to risk the wrath of the KGB by stating the obvious: that the Soviet Union must be dissolved as the only way to save Russia from being destroyed from within.

"But with incontrovertible proof of a KGB-sanctioned assassination attempt of a sitting president to hold over the KGB's head, *we* now have the clout. Reagan calls publically for the destruction of the wall, the KGB is neutralized, and Gorbachev tightens his grip on the reins in Russia. Everybody wins, including the

Soviet satellites, which are able to slip out from under the heel of Communist oppression."

Tracie closed her eyes and saw Shane sailing over the edge of the roof, his head twisting in what she wanted desperately to believe was one last look at her. She saw the same scene whenever she closed her eyes and knew she would for a very long time.

"Everybody wins," she repeated, her stomach in knots.

Then "Are we finished here?"

Stallings stared at her for a long moment without speaking.

She opened her eyes and met his gaze straight on.

"Everything I've just told you is classified," he said. "If one word leaks out, I will make it my mission in life to see that you rot in prison, I don't care if that old fool Reagan *is* protecting you. Is that clear?"

"I'll take that as a yes," Tracie said. She rose and walked to the door.

"We'll expect you back on active duty as soon as the medical people give the go-ahead," Stallings said to her back.

"I'll let you know what I decide," Tracie answered without turning. She bent and opened the door awkwardly, turning the knob with her right arm inside the sling, and continued through without another word.

53

June 8, 1987
11:00 a.m.
Shady Oaks Cemetery, Bangor, Maine

The day was bright and hot, a brisk wind helping make the temperature almost bearable.

Tracie stood on a shallow hillside dressed in a conservative business suit not unlike the one she'd worn days ago atop the Minuteman Insurance building in D.C. She tried to fan herself and failed miserably, her hands still mostly immobilized inside the slings. Smoked-black sunglasses covered her eyes.

Far across a field, a crowd of mourners had gathered to bury Shane Rowley. He had been part of a small family, just himself and his mother. He had never spoken to Tracie of his father, and the one time she'd asked about him, passing the time on a long drive, Shane had answered bitterly that the man wasn't worth wasting his breath on.

Aside from Shane's mother, who was easy to pick out, bent and broken by grief, there were probably a couple of dozen other people. Co-workers, friends from high school.

The world had begun to move on following the initial firestorm of media fascination with Shane, the news cycle continuing its relentless, grinding pace even after just a few days. A small phalanx of television trucks and print reporters crowded the street just outside the gates of Shady Oak Cemetery, and the local police kept the media representatives a respectful distance from the proceedings.

Shane's mother had requested privacy and Tracie thought Shane would have appreciated that fact.

Tracie stood alone among small patches of overgrown grass in need of mowing, removed from the rest of the mourners despite having been invited to the service by Shane's mother.

Tracie had met with the grieving woman twice. The first time had been while still in the hospital following the surgery on her shoulders. All the media had been told was that Tracie was involved with the president's protective detail, but Shane's mother had insisted on seeing her.

The second time was earlier this morning.

Her name was Katherine, and she had been shattered by the events on the roof of the seven-story office building in Washington. Katherine Rowley was kind during both meetings, respectful of Tracie's silence on the subject of Tracie's relationship with her dead son, but nevertheless Tracie could feel a desperate desire for answers radiating off her, none of which Tracie was at liberty to provide.

So when it came time for the service, she made the decision not to add any more grief to a woman already overwhelmed by it.

She rotated her shoulders, shrugging to remove the stiffness brought on by the beginning of the healing process. Her range of motion would return to one hundred percent according to the agency doctors, and Tracie had no reason to doubt them. She was young and healthy and already beginning to feel stronger.

At least physically.

The doctors would clear her to return to work eventually, and she had already decided that when it happened she would go. She knew nothing else, possessed no skills other than espionage, and the prospect of walking away from the CIA and service to her country, moving to a menial job and a life filled with emptiness, held no appeal.

But she would never forget Shane Rowley. She uttered the words aloud, despite the fact that only the birds in the trees would hear. Speaking them instead of just thinking them served to make them real for her, to give them the permanence they deserved.

Shane had given his life willingly to save hers, and even though she knew nothing she could ever accomplish would make that sacrifice worthwhile, she vowed she would honor it—and Shane—by giving everything she had every day for the rest of her life in support of freedom.

It was all she had to offer.

Down the hillside and across the field, the figures dressed in black clustered around the lone coffin. Tracie watched, thankful for the dark sunglasses covering her eyes even though no one could see her, even though no one knew she was there. The service ended and a couple of mourners began to help Katherine Rowley to a waiting vehicle.

Tracie turned toward the wrought iron gates of the cemetery and walked away, shivering even in the heat.

Tracie Tanner returns in her second action-packed thriller, *All Enemies,* available now. When the U.S. secretary of state is kidnapped and held for ransom, all available evidence points toward the Soviet Union as the culprit. But Tracie Tanner is not so sure, and will risk her reputation, her career, and even her life to get to the bottom of the kidnapping...

To be the first to learn about new releases, and for the opportunity to win free ebooks, signed copies of print books, and other swag, please take a moment to sign up for Allan Leverone's email newsletter at AllanLeverone.com.

Reader reviews are hugely important to authors looking to set their work apart from the competition. If you have a moment to spare, please consider leaving a brief, honest review of *Parallax View* at your point of purchase, at Goodreads, or at your favorite review site, and thank you!

Also from Allan Leverone

Thrillers

All Enemies
The Omega Connection
The Hitler Deception
The Kremlyov Infection
The Bashkir Extraction
Final Vector
The Lonely Mile
The Organization: A Jack Sheridan Pulp Thriller
Trigger Warning: A Jack Sheridan Pulp Thriller
Death Perception: A Jack Sheridan Pulp Thriller

Horror/Dark Thrillers

The Lupin Project
Covenant
Mr. Midnight
After Midnight
Paskagankee
Revenant: A Paskagankee Novel Book Two
Wellspring: A Paskagankee Novel Book Three
Grimoire: A Paskagankee Novel Book Four
Linger: Mark of the Beast (Written with Edward Fallon)

Novellas

The Becoming
Flight 12: A Kristin Cunningham Thriller

Story Collections

Postcards from the Apocalypse
Uncle Brick and the Four Novelettes
Letters from the Asylum: Three Complete Novellas
The Tracie Tanner Collection: Three Complete Thriller Novels

Made in the USA
Middletown, DE
01 March 2022

61894222R00149